RC THOM

ANOTHER ANTHOLOGY the same BUT Different

Another Anthology: The Same But Different
Library of Congress registration number: 1-11759255981
Registration date: Sept 26, 2022

ISBN for Print ISBN: 979-8-9861808-2-3
ISBN for E-book ISBN: 979-8-9861808-3-0

Content Editor: Lisa Cross
Cover Photograph: Daniel Olah via unsplash.com
Book Design: Gayle F. Hendricks
Line editing and proof reading:
Angel Ackerman, Parisian Phoenix Publishing,
angel@parisianphoenix.com

R.C. Thom
Email: humanrights4all@aol.com
Web: RCThom.com

Suggested retail E-book price is $4.99 US
Suggested retail print book is $12.95 US

This anthology of 21 short stories, and three bonus nonfiction essays,
features sci-fi with fantasy element twists. Some are idea stories
while others focus on character examination expressed
via sci-fi concepts and-or mainstream fiction settings.

Disclaimer

The characters you will meet here are not real people and they do not
directly mimic any people I know living or dead. None of the scenes they
appear in were actual. Some places and events are close to historically accurate. The details of events, real or not, in this book were entirely invented by
me. This work of fiction is not meant to be factual. Some of my fictional people are shown within a historical context but don't rely on that being accurate. What these characters say and do is fictional unless stated otherwise.
When I mix science with fantasy that is where I especially make stuff up but
I do employ actual sciences and the scientific methods thereof as well.

CONTENTS

INTRODUCTION

This collection of short stories is the same but different. Book publishers and movie makers are always looking for that mystical piece of work called the-same-but-different which they can't define, but they know it when they see it. That is not the way I mean it.

This anthology is the same but different for me. What is the same, from me, are stories that twist things out of shape. I used a good helping of satire here and there as I have done in the past.

What is different? I backed off the quirky stuff a bit to make room for conventional storytelling themes and ideas. I tried things I hadn't done before. I jumped into topics, ideas and styles I've brushed up against plenty but were outside of my usual wheelhouse.

Here I did more with classical short story forms and concepts. I have been expanding my horizons which is the same for me but not different at all. If this collection has a theme, it is exploration. It's me looking at the same old world but with a slightly different light.

Ok, maybe it's a very different light. My goal is to entertain with ideas of a unique flavor which is not in your usual short story meal. I hope you enjoy it. I had fun writing this for you.

THE JESUS PROBE

Author's note: This story first appeared in my anthology, *Stalking Kilgore Trout*, 2017. I used these two characters, Gabe and Mike, and their career problems, as a subplot in my science fantasy novel *Book of Answers*. This story as seen below is the original barring minor corrections. When you meet Mike and Gabe again in *Book of Answers*, you will find they are in over their heads, as usual.

We were in hot isotopes, me and Mike. I expected the announcement when it came over the intercom.

"Angels First Class Gabriel and Michel report to Control immediately."

I knew it was coming but I jumped anyway, not smart in low-G orbit. The last time I heard Control demand our immediate appearance, they were really unhappy. Instead of preventing a religion, we started one.

But it wasn't my fault.

We wore our ship whites, all cleaned up. Even our wings were groomed, white on white, on white. The corridors, floors, and walls—even us—all gleamed white, company policy. We bolted from our cabins at the same time and I almost crashed into Mike. If Mike's wings weren't fluttering, I'd have run him over. Mike was as nervous as a sacrificial dove.

On our way to the meeting, we hardly said a word to each other. With all the spyware onboard, it wasn't smart to talk off the top of our heads. All sentry ships were the same. With so many races working together, only factual honesty was permitted. The ship's computers saw to it that everyone knew what everyone said—just ask the computer. No holds barred.

Thankfully, our thoughts were our own. At least we had that union rule to rely upon—No mind reading permitted.

We walked in silence. The corridor walls, floors, ceilings, and every part of this ship were stark white, but I wasn't feeling too bright.

Speaking of dull bulbs, Mike voiced one thought aloud.

"You know, Gabe, this isn't our fault. We can't help what a stupid probe thinks, especially the AI-7."

I answered him as anyone on this ship would. I gave him the standard answer. "That may be so, but, we're still responsible."

Mike's face went glum gray.

"We shouldn't have used an AI-7. We screwed up. We trusted Control," Mike said. "Artificial intelligence is fine for gathering intel, but you never know for sure what they're thinking, or how they decide on what action. They're not much different from Control in that."

Mike laughed. I couldn't help it, I laughed too, but it was going to cost us. No need to give the computer any more ideas so I didn't share what I was thinking. But, to cover our asses and rub a little salt…

"Hey, we didn't want any probes on this job, remember," I said. "They ordered it and they got what they paid for."

Mike rolled his eyes as we entered the conference room. He did it in the blind spot. Ship management's eye-scan system missed it. We were a small gathering, just the ship's captain, two project controllers, and a rep from the Record Keepers' Union.

The Keepers were a throwback to the old days, but they did have value. Keepers recorded what the computers could not, they sensed emotions. You never knew what they were feeling themselves because of their environment suits. I could ask the Keeper, union rules after all, but it's hard to hold a conversation with an eight-foot bubble and maintain a straight face.

Me and Mike were the only bipeds on this mission, actually the only beings on board that looked Earth-human at all. Take away the wings and white skin and we look remarkably like them. Resonance-shift cloaking changed our skin and hair and hid the wings easily enough. We and our union brothers walked with humans undetected for thousands of years.

Infiltration was easy; the rest, not so much.

That's how we got these great jobs in the Planet Molders Union as field operatives. We got hired in the primitive planet Economic Development Department of this sector's Galactic Operations Detachment. In one way or the other, everyone onboard worked for the G.O.D. But God, as me and Mike liked to call them, was never happy. Is it our fault God makes unreasonable demands?

Our ship's contract was based on progressive results and this planet kept going backward. Only mature, rational beings can join the trade conglomerate. Our job was to help Earth's people evolve mentally by feeding them tiny bits of technology, like metallurgy, and dissuading logic-killing social trends like mythologies and religions.

It wasn't going well. If things didn't turn around soon, me and Mike will become the ship's next sacrificial lambs. Unless, of course, Control screws up and takes the hit instead of us for a change. That may qualify as a miracle.

We took the only two white plastic chairs at the white metal table. My wings buzzed like hummingbirds sucking plutonium. The ship only had two chairs. The other crewmen didn't have asses to sit on.

The Control guys were both Salmelions—hairy five-hundred-pound Earth-like slug creatures sporting a spiny mane. The top and bottom were exactly alike and interchangeable. With the ass-chewing we were about to get, I thought, these two chairs were about to become obsolete.

The captain, who passed for a giant four-legged tree frog, popped up his eye stalks. The Controller's spines bristled. These gestures meant both men were serious. The Recorder, well, inside his environment suit, it was impossible to say what he was thinking. Damn tinted windows!

"Mr. Mikilow, Mr. Gaberilow, so glad you could break away from your busy schedule to join us," Control One said.

I hate when Control is sarcastic.

"What is the status of the probe?" He asked.

Control Two added his voice which twinkled like Earthling wind chimes.

"We don't have to tell you two how important this project is. You know the Empire needs the resources this planet has to offer. With this recent turn of events, it may be another thousand years, if ever, before the G.O.D can invite them to join the trade conglomerate."

His spines were blue with malcontent. He needed another six hundred years before he could retire. Of course, he figured it was our fault. Management always blames the peons. I think that's a job requirement.

"I hope you two can salvage this mess," Control Two said. "The contract is due for renewal in one hundred years and that will not happen unless we show the PPED progress. What is your report?"

I swallowed hard. I felt like an asteroid without an orbit. I reminded myself this wasn't our fault, not really. We only do what management tells us. I wanted to ask why we were always in the hot seat when their directives don't work, but I had to report.

"As you know, this probe is an AI-7," I began. "It's a device well known for having bugs. I know that's no excuse for letting it get out of hand, but there were difficult circumstances."

"What kind of circumstances?" Control One asked.

His bristles rippled which could be a sign of displeasure or maybe he farted.

Mike jumped in. "We didn't pick this probe, you know. I didn't want an AI-7. We needed a twelve to override the damage Moses did. This one wasn't designed to reverse the effects of religion. You guys should know that."

Control didn't like Mike's contribution. Union rule number two: cover your ass, if you have one.

"If you had extracted Moses quietly, as instructed," Control One said, "we would not have this problem."

"Sending a boat was too visible," Control Two added.

Mike was about to blow a portal seal. Job sent that boat down, not us. Junior management did that one. So, I kicked Mike under the table. Management is always right, right? I needed my job.

"Stick to the current facts," Control One and Two said in unison.

"Yes, sir," I said and began my report again.

"Things were going well. The subject seemed perfect for the probe. He was a Hebrew, right bloodline, and the woman was never pregnant. We couldn't have asked for a better receptor. The probe went in nice, not a hitch."

"Not a hitch," Mike repeated. "She wasn't even married yet."

I kicked Mike under the table.

"But," I continued, "by the time the subject was thirteen-Earth-years-old, we started having problems. The human was tentatively accessing the probe, apparently, but the probe did not report it. The probe and the subject wanted the same things—"

"I should have known something was up when the probe named itself 'the Holy Spirit,'" Mike interrupted.

I kicked Mike again. Thankfully, he shut up. The Controllers were not at all well informed about Earth's social structures and how that works within religions. We didn't need to open up that can of antimatter.

"You did not detect this anomaly?" Control One said.

"No," I said, "when a subject and probe are on the same cerebral bandwidth it's impossible to read their interactions. This was a real fluke. Who would've thunk it?"

"Go figure," Mike said with a half-smile. "I bet the probe liked it."

"You should have been looking out for that," Control Two said. "We had this sort of problem with the Moses probe. We had to pull the Enoch probe."

I didn't need that reminder of past failings, and Enoch was a low blow. That thing should have been scrapped eons ago. Both probes had different technical issues due to rushing in with equipment that wasn't tuned properly for humans. It was management's bad call. Never use the wrong tools. I let them push me. I got blamed for that one. I should have called my union rep.

My wings fluttered uncontrollably. It took a minute to relax them. I had a moment to think. Were these guys trying to sell me down the river? I needed this job. The unemployment rate back in Heaven was ridiculous. What'd they expect from an experimental probe anyway? This AI-7 probe wasn't tuned right; it wasn't tested. I had to be careful.

I continued once my feathers stopped vibrating.

"So, the probe and the subject melded, but, we're not sure when. The last three years of the host's life showed us something weird was happening. We stayed back, tried to figure it out…but, although it was going off script, the probe was working correctly."

I took a big breath. I didn't know if it ran right or not. I kept talking.

"The subject said all the right things to counteract the earlier bad social conscience implants. You know stuff like, 'forget Moses, here is a new way.' People were following. Social molding was in full swing. Things looked good. But soon after…the probe clearly lost control. The subject took over the probe."

Everyone in the room knew the implications, and how unlikely that was—a new binary life force with so many complex variables just didn't spring up like that. There was either something special or something spooky going on with Earthlings.

"Why did you not immediately kill the subject and extract the probe?" The captain said.

"We tried," Mike said. "We even sent in our S.A.T.A.N. kill-bot. The robot tried everything. No help. Satan eventually tossed the guy off the Temple roof. The subject must've learned to access the energy stream, he just floated away. Then, he turned around and killed the kill-bot!"

My foot interrupted my partner again. Mike tended to say too much.

"They were working together," I said. "The probe and subject were going in the same direction. Rather than us using an ionizer nuke, and scrapping the whole project again—that'd set us back—we tried a direct intervention. We became part of the subject's inner circle. We steered him. We thought it was working. Things were good."

Control Two sneered with green spines, "but things did not stay good, did they?"

My stomach tried to crawl into my mouth. I almost spit up a feather ball. Never preen before a big meeting.

"No, sir," I said. "When things got hairy, pardon the term, we tried to isolate them and nuke them, small scale, without major impact on the population. But it was too late. They just wouldn't leave the populated areas. Too many damn disciples. We didn't want another Sodom on our hands. The salt fallout alone cost us millions to clean up. We made a perfectly good sea into a dead sea. We switched to plan B. We'd try and get the probe as the guy died."

"We got lucky on that," Mike added.

I kicked Mike.

"The guy believed he was a real deity," I continued, "but a few nudges at the Sanhedrin, a few dreams planted in the governor's mind and he was a marked man."

"We set it up real nice," Mike interjected, "all we had to do was tail him and wait."

Control One and Two looked confused. Their bristles stood straight up.

"What is tail?" They said together.

I ignored the question. My gullet started grinding. We almost lost the game. As I searched for my next words, Mike jumped in.

"We couldn't predict how hard following this guy would be. The entire city turned out for him. They were in the streets. We couldn't get within a hundred yards of him. The government had him, sure, execution was a done deal, but we couldn't get close enough to do a probe rescue."

Mike and I were both gritting our teeth at that memory; there were throngs of people pushing and crushing us. My wings are still a mess. We almost didn't save ourselves, much less the project.

"We got lucky," I said. "The guy, the probe, and the people were going nuts. The city was on fire with emotional turmoil. We were desperate. We had to get out. Raw emotions screwed with our holographs. We jumped over a city wall and landed in a refuse dump. We decided to hold up there and rethink it. That's where we got our opportunity. We saw the guy hanging from a tree up on a hill overlooking the dump. He wasn't even dead yet."

"It may not have been luck," the bubble said.

Everyone made sounds of agreement. Maybe the AI had regained control. Mike went on.

"So, we saw our chance, see. The guards were keeping people back. Gabe and I became guards. We got in on a dice game to get in close, we needed to extract at just the right moment. I talked to the probe in mind speak. I let it know we were ready. I told it to give me a signal, give me a sign when it was ready to evacuate."

I cut Mike off.

"After a while, the probe took over. The guy was nearly dead. This human was way ahead of his time, fully integrated. When he said, 'into your hands, I commend my spirit,' Mike stuck the extractor into the guy's side and sucked the probe out. Just in time. The guy dropped dead and started glowing."

Control One was not happy. A glowing dead guy was not a good thing. I braced for the hit.

"It is good that you removed the probe," Control One said, "but a host body will not decay normally. You must remove the body. We must not leave evidence on the planet. If we break regulations, we don't get paid."

He was right, of course. But not many Earthlings saw it. Mostly Romans and nobody local believed them. The Jews and everybody else, not Roman, hate the Romans.

"They're a primitive people," I said. "We all know it will be a long, long time before they become rational."

"Nonetheless," Control One said, his bristles showing annoyance. "We can't leave a host body behind. What are you going to do about it?"

Mike beamed.

"We already took care of that," he said. "After the riots, three days later, we went and got the guy. He's in the sick bay now. The probe programming department wants to see what makes him tick so we don't make this mistake again."

Control's bristles went pink with approval. No real damage was done. So, I took the opportunity and offered an idea.

"Once he gets through re-education we could use him on the team," I suggested.

"We really can use a local adviser," Mike said.

"That is good," Control One said, "I am sure he will make a fine crew member."

"Did you get away clean?" Control Two asked.

"Pretty much," I said.

"Please clarify," the captain directed.

"No big deal," Mike said. "When we were collecting the body, a couple of women walked into the tomb. His wife and mother, I think. We weren't in holograms so they freaked and ran."

"It won't be a problem," I added. "Females have no status in this primitive society."

"Make sure. Send him back to explain this to his relatives," Control One said.

"Are you sure that's wise, sir?" I asked. "I mean, remember what happened with—"

This time, Mike kicked me under the table. I shut up.

"Don't question my authority," Number One said, bristling in irritation. "Had I been more involved, this would not have happened. Do what I ask."

I was thinking to myself *what an ass*. He doesn't know squat about Earth. Mike and I have been on the ground for a thousand years. I was getting ruffled, my feathers, too. I knew this was a huge mistake, but I needed this job. I had to bite my forked tongue.

It was then I noticed Mike's sidelong smile. He'd be happy to let Control One fall flat on his face, or whatever passed for a face, which may have been his ass as well. Mike had something up his robe's sleeve.

"Yes, sir," I said. "I will go and brief Jesus."

Number One looked perplexed. "Who is Jesus?"

"The new guy. Christ, this going to be interesting," Mike said fighting to keep a straight face. "I can't wait to see how Jesus works out."

Mike loved to mess with Control. Control didn't know sarcasm from sacred prayer. I smiled widely, hoping the bubble saw it as approval regarding Control's newest bad call of a decision, and not the way I really felt. I knew in my soul that the next ass-chewing to come down from the G.O.D. won't be chopping on me and Mike's asses. I'd bet my union halo on it.

CRAZY EYES

Author's note: This story and the next came to me out of critique group discussions on the topics of tone, voice, and setting. I wrote this and the next to illustrate and practice certain craft ideas. *Crazy Eyes* was written with a limited word count of 900 words.

Everybody turned out for the shoot-down. Even Doc Blake came to take bets. Word gets around a small town right quick. Robert "Clubfoot" Adams was fixing to shoot the legs out from under Crazy Eyes O' Neil—the half-breed. Crazy Eyes didn't have a chance.

I'm town clerk and it is and was my duty to tell it true. There was no contest betwixt them, but this contest was legal just the same. Clubfoot was in business with Crazy, Crazy runs the herds, and Clubfoot brokers the meat. Last auction, only a little of that money got paid to Crazy…so Crazy called Clubfoot out, fair enough. That shiny, new gun of Clubfoot's was evidence enough of where that money done went.

It wasn't high noon yet, so we all amble into the saloon to place our bets. I put ten, truth be told, on Clubfoot gainsaying his advantages. Doc took all comers two-to-one favoring Crazy Eyes, foolish for Doc. I handed my ten-dollar piece over directly.

Set aside Clubfoot's got that new pistol, center-fire…45 Long Colt, cartages holding 40 grains, best gun of 1873, or so they tell it. Meanwhiles, Crazy shoots an old war-time Le Matt percussion. It only shoots round balls. Thirty-six calibers' too weak at fifty paces—even me, a clerk, knows that.

Better than his pistols, Clubfoot's got himself a trick.

Club's skinny and he turns sideways to shoot and that ain't the half of it. He's got one leg shorter than the other and he wears a block under his left boot. He kicks the heel off when he draws and lops way over to shoot, you'd think he's going down but he ain't.

That boy's hard to hit.

Crazy can't hit the side of a barn. One eye goes one way and the other eye goes the other way. One's blue and one's brown. His ma was Cree, his pa Irish—God rest them souls—which accounts for two eye colors. None of them O'Neil's can shoot worth a damn and everybody knows it.

We piled outside and there they came from opposite sides of town. Folks spread up and down the boardwalk for watching. The shooters stopped when the distance was about right—each agreeing to take three steps, draw, and shoot—that was the arrangement. I watched closely. The call goes out. Clubfoot kicked off his heel before they start. Crazy can't see it. Club's walking in on his toes.

Three steps on the judge yelled, "draw."

Like a twisting snake, Club falls left pulling that new Colt. Crazy stands like a barn door and gets off the first shot—Crazy hit Club's gun barrel— blew the pistol right out of Club's hand. That's the darnedest thing I've seen since that trick-shooter passed through town last fall.

Club produced his old Colt Navy and commenced to shooting. Crazy was firing all the while. Crazy's La Matt got eight chambers. That's a lot of black powder. Crazy can't see no-how. Still, he hit Club's other gun. All of Club's chambers fired together. That blow-up made a fog the Devil himself couldn't see in. It stunk to high heaven to boot. Nobody can draw a bead in that mess. We all strained for the result whilst praying for wind.

Was Crazy hit or not? Turns out, no, he wasn't.

Be-in' nobody got kilt, they called a truce. Them two shooters and we all filed back into the saloon to lament our losing bets. Doc, the good old soul he is, bought for the house and we all drank plenty. After a few, I mosey up to Doc and I ask, I had to know his advantage.

"Doc," I say, "how'd you know Crazy would hit him, and twice. Them other rounds weren't far off, neither no how."

"The Harvard School of Optometry," Doc says. "It's science, science, my boy."

Doc said a lot I didn't understand about optics but it amounted to Crazy only got one eye and that makes him shoot leading right. Clubfoot always falls in that direction from Crazy's point of view. Doc speaks true being a doctor. Doc's the one who gave Crazy that blue eye to begin with. T'was the only glass-eye Doc had at the time that fit. Crazy's first shot always goes right says Doc. But after that, he's dead-eye Dick.

"Don't forget, Benny," Doc says on my way out. "You come Tuesday for your spectacles, you hear. I'm about finished grinding your new lenses."

"Naw, can't, I done gambled my ten-dollars spectacle's money."

"Tell you what," Doc says, "If-in you had them eye-glasses, you might have seen the resolution of this here shoot-out a-coming, as I did. You come over anyway, pay me when you can."

"I'll do that, Doc," I say.

I wouldn't have seen it coming, but I might-a heard something to hedge my bet. Doc likes to talk. I don't mind listening…when I can understand him.

I went back to work and dutifully recorded the events of the day for the town's record. Seeing my calendar, I dipped my pen once more and drew a circle around Tuesday next week. I'm fix-in to go and hear more about science. Seems science gives an edge on any bet, true enough, as far as I can see.

DEEP POOP

ob Holloway stopped dead in the middle of the gold mine's staging lot. Something was wrong. The big compressor outside his office trailer wasn't humping. That one ran pressure to a hard-rock-eating rotating shovel in Shaft Ten. That pump sat idle when it should be going mad.

Home Office geology had predicted a gold vein in Ten's direction, but Bob didn't think so. It didn't smell right to him. He was the super on-site and had a better direction in mind, to begin with. But the bosses had other ideas. Bob entered his office trailer with deep worry.

It didn't take long for the dig super down in the hole to call on the radio. Eddie ran the main hub and he had made the right call to shut production down. Ten seconds after Bob finished with Eddie on the radio, the direct line phone to Home Office blasted off. Bob put the call on speaker and took a step back.

"Holloway, you better have a good reason. Why did you stop Tunnel Ten? You're costing me money."

Bob felt the VP's psychopathy seeping through the wires. The boss's voice projected a dead cold that could burn steel. The man didn't tolerate excuses.

"Sir, we have a situation. I ah, I mean…a coal pocket, or something, I think, I'm not sure but, but, we ain't set up for venting methane and—"

"You think! You think! I don't pay for guesses! You go down there and find out! I want that mole running in one hour, you hear me?"

"Sir, it takes more than an hour…"

The Home Office's phone slamming on the other end shook his desk.

"Son of bitch hung up."

He wished it was the compressor but it was only his knees knocking. *Damn computers.* HO's Production Department rang his bell before he had time to get into the ring. He called the staging yard super on his walkie-talky.

"Tony, get over here. Cover me. I'm going down in the hole."

Bob didn't wait for Tony. He ran from the trailer with his headgear and water bottle in hand. He didn't use the mask. There wasn't much dust in the yard, meaning ore wasn't moving fast enough. Getting gold out of hard rock and making money at it was a game of tonnage. The last thing he saw before entering the main tunnel was a dump driver sitting on the roof of his truck smoking a cigarette— and it wasn't break time.

What Eddie said on the radio didn't make sense. Bob's unease mounted thinking about it. He went straight for the express elevator and commandeered the special-use cage reserved for emergencies. It took only an hour and fifty-nine minutes to hit bottom. His site-super position had its privileges. The best perk was he didn't have to work in the hole…*until now.*

What Eddie described sounded like a coal hit, but not exactly. The team's horizontal wheel had been scaling rock face when it hit something like a gas pocket, but it didn't act right. The blowout had a lot of pressure behind it. It pushed the digger back five inches and flung oily reside and carbon dust all over the tunnel. Nobody got hurt but as Eddie said, "the place stinks to high heaven."

How is that possible this far down? It's not. Can't be coal, something odd is going on.

Bob knew his geology well enough to know coal pockets aren't supposed to be there. *Whatever that deposit is, it ain't good.* They weren't able to deal with coal. Coal generates combustible gasses and fine dust which requires special containment and ventilation equipment, equipment they didn't have. Sealing it shut was the usual way of dealing with a rotten branch tunnel.

"No point digging where the gold ain't at," he said reciting the unofficial company motto.

Bob avoided the hole but the ride down wasn't bad, it gave him time to think. This cage was the only place he had, there or at home, where he had nothing to do. The radio was no good. The elevator's com was useless against the cables' squealing. This lift was more a coffin conveyor than an emergency medical exit. If they told him he had to use mine elevators during the interview, he wouldn't have taken the job.

Bob enjoyed digging for interesting things but this was not that. The job didn't satisfy his curiosity itch or anything else. A question gurgled in the depths of his guts until he had to spit it out.

"How the hell did I get here," he said.

Bob's rattling cage didn't answer.

The ghost of every dead miner would have shouted, "the money!" if ghosts were real. And, Bob would have joined the chorus if it were possible to shout and be heard above the din.

He wanted to be an archeologist. That was the dream but Dad pushed him to, "do something practical. Go where the jobs are." Dad paid for school. Bob honored his dying father's request and took up artifact hunting as a hobby to placate his need while applying for university jobs without hope.

Straight out of college, he got hired for landfill monitoring. That practical job smelled terrible. Core sampling compressed garbage wasn't as bad as the corruption-stink sweltering off the people who owned and operated city dumps. Big corporations weren't any different. Life at Mine Core was just as odious.

The monotony also stunk. He spent his days in the trailer watching computer screens in between getting berated by HO over the phone. Every time a car derailed his phone bellowed.

But still, he was lucky to find any geology-related job. Mining was better than nothing. But he felt his geology degree wasting away. The idea rasped his ass like petrified toilet paper.

All of my student loans for this?

"If only I could break into archeology…"

He rejected the notion. Archeology needs geologists but geologists were stacked a hundred deep waiting for that kind of cherry work.

He turned back to the problem at hand as his ride neared the bottom. Unit Ten, the new tunnel, just started producing. Backing the equipment out into the hub won't be too bad. HO hated setup delays. Removing equipment goes faster.

Production numbers won't fall far.

Eddie was waiting at the lift. He was white but it didn't show. Bob only ever saw him after cleanup. If not for the voice, Bob wouldn't have known the man. It was oddly quiet when Bob exited the cage.

"You're in hot water if they sent you down here." Nothing was running but Eddie spoke loudly anyway.

"More like cold water," Bob said. "Home Office wants us digging in an hour. Had I sent your gang to Seven as I wanted…This one didn't smell right."

Eddie's hollow face was covered in soot, but that didn't hide the man's worry. Eddie took Bob's elbow and walked Bob down Branch Ten. Ten's crew followed. Eddie waved his men back. His gang trusted him. Eddie's safety record was top-shelf.

Arriving, Eddie's hand-lamp lit a spot. He put a hand on the oily wall above where the scaler had broken through. The smell about knocked Bob over. It stunk worse than when his garage freezer got unplugged and he didn't know it for months. Wasted that meat.

"Get a load of this," Eddie said. He wiped goop away with a gloved hand.

Bob held his nose and moved closer adjusting his headlamp. The matrix oozed black oily water from small cracks but otherwise was somewhat solid. It mimicked that frozen mud-flow he had read about in an archeology periodical.

"Appears loaded with debris, hmmmm," Bob muttered.

Shapes like compressed paper and cans were pressed into the mix. *No, that can't be.* Bob's landfill surveying experience tripped an alarm. He had seen this sort of thing before. *Garbage lasts hundreds of years buried, not millions. Can't be garbage.*

"This deposit's 500 million years old," gushed out of Bob's mouth. "What am I looking at?"

He stepped back breathing hard inhaling the stench.

"It's an outhouse, I'll be dogged," Eddie said. "When we were kids, we used to dig them up for bottles and coins. Just dirt, you understand, nothing filthy. Turds were gone."

"Can't be an outhouse, it's too big and sideways, if it were dug as a garbage pit, it'd be vertical, not horizontal…it'd be…geologically old. Eddie, give me your rock hammer."

Bob tapped the surface. Softer material fell away first and exposed fossils which weren't unusual in certain mines but bones didn't belong here. He had never seen the like. Garbage dumps don't concrete this way but given enough time…Dumps don't produce crude oil, or do they? Landfills aren't this deep, not in hard rock. Confusion gave way to adrenalin and he swung the hammer a little harder.

"There…shouldn't be any of this…here."

Bob didn't know what else to say. He extracted another bone, a big one, an animal bone… striations…tool marks! *Somebody's steak dinner.*

"This can't be."

Bob rubbed the bone and sniffed his fingers. "Methane."

Bob's fuse lit. He chipped away like a power hammer until running out of steam which didn't take long. What looked like a book and some other objects of petrified garbage had fallen out.

Bob took the book-shaped shale sample and it split open in his hands. The image of a being with two mouths and four eyes holding a plate of food and a weird fork stared back at him. Text overwrote part of the image.

"Hieroglyphic writing," Bob slurred, dizzy from shock and fumes.

"If Betty Crocker came from space, that'd be her," Eddie said.

The picture was clear and not just another Jesus-on-toast figure. Ten fingers, six joints on each one. Bob counted the fingers again and dropped the rock. It bounced off his steel-toed boot but didn't break.

Eddie, shinning his headlamp over Bob's shoulder, nudged Bob to turn around. He did. Eddie held out an object and put his hand-lamp's beam on it, the same item as in the picture, the same two handles. It was bent but recognizable. Gold doesn't tarnish.

It hit Bob.

"Fork, fork…Magazine ad. It's a…an ad."

The twist in Bob's gut didn't want water, but his parched mouth overruled. Bob sucked down his entire bottle in two gulps. It took some of the oily air taste out of his mouth.

"This is big, really big! We gotta shut off production," Eddie said, shaking all over. "Call the Big Cheese. We'll be media stars. We got, we got…I need a drink."

Eddie produced a flask and they both took a deep swing.

"Who're we gonna call first," Eddie said. "I say the news before them office dicks take all the credit."

"And lose our jobs, are you nuts, let me think," Bob said. "I got a wife and kids. They'll take credit anyway."

Bob was screwed no matter what he did. Stop production and Home Office will cut his head off and stuff his neck with lawsuits. Report this and hell comes home to roost. No matter how he sliced it, Bob was in deep poop.

The honchos only care about profit. Idle mines don't make money. They won't risk a stop-work order by exposing this discovery. The Federal Mining Commission will close it down. If not them, the CIA will. There's too much on the line. If the archaeologists come in, it's the same result: A hundred miners out of work…*myself included.*

"Home Office won't shut down. They'll cover this up," Bob said.

"Sounds about right," Eddie said. He hit his flask again.

"Archaeology won't move them. They don't care. The risk of paying out claims on dead miners, say…caught in a toxic gas leak, that they will care about."

"That'll cost them."

"Eddie, give me your radio."

Bob took it but hesitated.

Radio repeaters and communication lines were what HO wanted to be maintained at any cost. The Bigs ran operations from Wall Street. Computers tell them when machines stop but not why. They only understood the results. *Smellivision hasn't been invented yet.* The home office can't smell gas. HO didn't spend the money to computer-wire the gas detectors. HO's bean counters were too cheap.

Bob's responsibilities included maintaining air safety. He squeezed the radio's trigger.

"Tony, it's Bob. Get the bulkhead crew down here, fast, I mean now. We gotta seal a gas-generating vein. Ten's gang is moving over to Seven. Bring the slurry gun. Big pocket, Ten's gotta close. Suit up, oxygen tanks, hazmat, the works. I'm clearing this hub."

"You'll get hell," Eddie said. "We're in good ore."

"They won't see," Bob said, thinking of the work crew in their protective gear. "When the cement cannon comes in, Eddie, make sure they shoot from way back. Have them put it on thick. Seal it tight."

"What about the stuff? It's gotta be worth big money, right? We're walking away from a fortune here."

"It's not ours to walk away from," Bob said. "Not yet. Nine is closed, nobody's digging in there. Runs parallel to Ten, doesn't it? I'll need to monitor the situation. I'll set up my safety office in Nine."

Bob's headlamp reflected Eddie's ear-to-ear reaction. He got the picture. *That garbage vein wasn't gone. There's always a back door.*

The ride up felt as if the lift ran on his excitement. Possibilities churned Bob's discovery butter. He arrived topside before he knew it. He didn't need the time to rethink. His solution had to work, but he rehashed it anyway.

"It's for the best, for everyone."

There were many possible explanations. It might not be what he thought. The Company regularly refilled played-out holes with compressed garbage. Mine Core's empty mines still paid dividends. Some locations grew mushrooms, others stored nuclear waste. *Maybe that book wasn't from Earth. Maybe aliens shipped garbage here half a billion years ago like America ships its waste to whoever will take it.*

An answer could be had. Whatever the facts were, they weren't going to pay Bob's bills.

Somehow trilobites and arrowheads weren't that interesting anymore.

The big compressor had fired before he reached the top. He felt the emergency shaft's air pressure pulsate. Eddie's scaler was relocated and back at work in Seven. Bob exited the staging area and stepped out into the sunlight with possibilities glowing inside. He stopped to recover his sight before proceeding across the staging lot.

He still had Eddie's rock hammer. Bob checked to see if Eddie had marked his tool. It was too dirty to tell.

"I'll hold onto this for him."

Trucks were lining up and others loading. Manpower doubled in Tunnel Seven and it showed. Production rolled again. He began crossing the busy yard. Tony, up at the trailer, waved his bandana like a signalman standing on hot coals. The phone beacon atop the office trailer's roof flashed red-hot. *Home Office on the horn.*

Bob didn't hurry. *Once HO hears how much money a hundred dead minors might cost, they will accept closing Ten. Couched with the language of lost money, setting up a safety office in the hole is cheap insurance. Nine's the best place to keep tabs on a combustible situation.*

"When gas leaks, things go bad fast. The whole place will have to shut down," Bob said to test the sound of it.

It sounded like solid fiscal logic to him.

Eddie's rock hammer felt good in Bob's hand. Bob crossed the yard thinking he had better bring his hobby hammer in from home. He finally had a good reason to use it.

GOD BY DEFAULT: SANTA AT THE END OF TIME

My day started like any other day in dystopia. Lacy and I lived in my old Victorian townhouse upon a hill in ruined San Francisco. Everyone, in what was left of the city, lived on a hill. The tsunami wiped everything away 60 feet above the high tide line. My place was higher. That disaster three years ago was just one blip in the new world disorder. Death was spreading. I sensed it marching up the coast.

We never did get electricity back so this became a city of refugee squatters. That was fine with me. The College of Alameda, where I had worked, got wiped out. On 'wave-day,' my student Lacy Bishop came home with me. I hired students to clean my house and care for my sizable courtyard's vegetable garden. That garden came in handy.

Lacy stayed after the event with no place to go. Twenty years her senior, I didn't mind the company or the sex.

It was 5:30 a.m., my guess, no one kept time anymore. Sunlight crept through open windows and into the dirty room where we slept. A sunbeam hit my face like a cold rag. The tarp had torn again.

A plastic sheet covering the transom remained and glowed with the promise of another warm rain-free October day. I got up and dressed in ragged running shorts, dirty sweatpants, and a torn sweatshirt. I slipped my feet sock-less into a pair of old Nike running shoes that didn't match.

Lacy stirred.

"Where're you going? It's too early," she said half asleep.

"Running," I said curtly. I was in no mood for her old argument.

Lacy pulled upright, rubbing her eyes.

"Running, what the F is wrong with you? Why do you persist? Burning your body's energy. Food is hard to find and you go burning calories all to hell…you can't run from…from…"

She trailed off, dropping her protest early. She felt Earth's death coming, too.

"I eat no more than you," I said without ire. "Less than most. If I want to run, I'll run. I must."

"You're crazy," she said falling back onto the pile of rags we called bed. "You can't outrun getting old. That's what you're doing."

Running was crazy, she was right. Running wasn't a health guarantee for long life, more the opposite. I could not explain my addiction. My compulsion was not logical. Running, for me, fed me better than food. I had to run. I had to crack my pressure valve. That morning's compulsion was greater than ever before.

"You can't outrun it."

"I'll give it the old college try," I said. She was wrong. "It's not aging I run against, not that, and I'm winning."

"What?"

"Death. I'm outrunning death."

I said aloud what gnawed at me, deep inside, for the first time.

Running had made me mentally strong, but too thin. I claimed the trade-off was worth it. Storing fat for the cold season was what any sane survivalist would do. Lacy was right. Yet, I had no need for my body. I didn't think or feel like any other person I knew. I was certainly unlike the other survivors and saner from my point of view. Lacey's pet phrase for me was, 'justifying-junky.' There were times when I agreed.

I began my usual run within the crisscrossing deer paths between rubble piles and thus I let my mind wander.

I had sensed from my childhood that these were humanity's last days. I felt the end of time coming which I could not explain. I did not need to rely on feel; the evidence provided. I cared, and there was nothing I could do about it although I tried. Nobody would listen. The stupidity in politics had never been worse. Oddly, the closer we came to extinction, the faster the waterwheel turned. Yet, I relaxed and waited. I accepted it.

The world was busy blindly rearranging deckchairs on Earth's floundering ship at an ever-faster pace. I had done the same, filling my time with what didn't matter until I couldn't.

I stopped my run on the cliffs for a breath of sea air, the sun just breaking. Not a single ship at sea and that was good. What ships still sailed were inhabited by men with bad intentions.

The deck chair designers didn't see the end coming although it was plainly visible. It was as clear to me as my grandmother's prized crystal Christmas tree ornament. I saw the forest and every tree's connective roots. The forest burned while human life's bucket brigade poured on gasoline.

Such were my thoughts that morning, the same thoughts as in my previous day's run and the run before that. On that last morning, I woke knowing it was time to leave.

I had to go. Lacey knew it, too.

"You can't outrun death, Tomas. You can't. Stay with me," she had said.

"Let death catch me if it can," I said.

I began running with Lacey's ironclad plea pulling at my back. I was sad to leave her. But soon I felt the other pull, a stronger force. Magnetic north called.

We, runners, are all of a like mind, which is a mind non-runner cannot understand. People say we are different, loco. I have forever been different. People have called me loco since my youth and long before I spoke of premonitions.

They said I was crazy before the governments collapsed, which I had predicted in my books. The establishment hated me. My books burned away layers of corporatism. I wrote to expose corruption and government ineptitude. What was to the establishment unspeakable, I wrote. The system had lost control and I said so. I wrote what the powerful were known to kill journalists for writing. I was loco. But the timing worked. Governments were too busy plugging dykes. They didn't stop my publications.

I turned from the sea and ran on. There was Old Bob down ahead in the distant Golden Gate Park. He cooked his rat in the dark over low coals to keep beggars from stealing it. Good old resourceful Bob.

What I had published was at the core of human discord, the causes and results of human nature's failings. We, humans, had hit our evolutionary wall. I, as an anthropologist, wasn't highly trusted in academia. Truth-tellers never are. Historians and social psychologists didn't accept my evidence. They didn't like me sharing such ideas. Disjointed pieces of reality are how I assembled an intolerable picture puzzle. The media attacked my books. My findings were alarming. Thus, my dire warnings were ignored.

The Ivy League and I had a falling out. I wound up at Alameda. No other school would take me. I was untouchable just as my locomotive feet didn't touch the ground.

The spires of the old Golden Gate Bridge caught bright sun rays. I changed direction and ran toward Golden Gate Park. Mists bellowing up from the bay enveloped the bridge's undercarriage making it a bridge in Heaven. Such fog rose quickly. It threatened to engulf the damaged bridge's rotting deck, thus making the crossing a blind man's dance.

I stopped a moment, considering the bridge and how it rested on that pillowed coffin bed of wet clouds.

The last book I published wasn't referenced as well as it should have been. It wasn't necessary. I published my uncanny insights and not how I came by them. I wrote what my colleagues refused to know. By then I was soundly the village crack-pot, or a Russian spy, or a CIA insider, or a radical from the left. Or was I a right-wing radical? Tinfoil hat readers embraced the book which set their minds ablaze. I wished that blaze would spread but it didn't.

Another fire flared to life on my left as I ran down the hill. It was nothing, not people. Old fires came and went from deep inside the lower ruins from time to time.

The CIA had come to see me on campus once—no doubt to light a fire under me ahead of burning down my career. The agent had said, "'Nobody likes a profit of doom, least of all the U.S. government. Stop setting fires."

He had made his demands. I shut my mouth and put down the pen. Rather, I settled in for a quiet teacher's life. That was the deal he had offered, and I took it. A tidal wave cut that deal short.

I did not stop foreseeing changes. The wars between states came as I anticipated. Food and water wars and all the rest, as well. I wrote that the E.U. would attack their former master, the U.S., years before they did it. The Russian/Chinese invasion of the Middle East came as expected. Everyone lost the wars. The fractured United States couldn't stop what it started a hundred years prior.

Up a big pile of skyscraper rubble I went, and I lost sight of the park. It felt like a shadow in my heart. Going over a fallen leviathan is faster than going around it. Compelled to press north, topping the heap, the park came again in sight and relief with it. Lacey faded from my mind as the fog below began dispersing.

"Good," I said, "My way is clear."

But it wasn't.

San Francisco ended ahead of the wars giving us a measure of safety. We, survivors, had no information about the larger world other than the propaganda on the radio. I rightly guessed what had happened and what would happen, but not what would happen to me. I reached with my mind as I ran then as now. My visions were not wrong. Death was indeed racing up the coast.

Lacy never accepted my visions or understood why I run. That morning was different. There was light in her eyes. I was too hard on her. Nothing seemed right. My compulsion overwhelmed me. I had turned my back on her and my sense of reason.

I knew, deep down, that I wasn't coming back. I had laid sleepless every night for weeks until that day. I flew and I did not know why, but I had to run, run long and far. Run to make ready, make ready, for what? I did not know.

I stopped at the foyer mirror many mornings and, on that day, as well. There was no door to stop sunrise from lighting in. A ropy thirty-something-bodied man was I, but new youth had been laid over this old man's soul. That was me but not me. Long hair and beard confused my age, but it was me under the dirt and hair. I was too young. I hadn't aged in thirty years of running. Not a day. That should have told me something.

I asked myself, why don't you age? I had asked that question a million times, and on the morning, I set out, I asked yet again. My reflection answered.

"Because you are called. Run...you must."

My answer was not me. It came from the looking glass. My reflection spoke, not I.

"Run north. Go, you must go now. Run."

Those words were not mine, and yet I repeated them nearing the old bridge. Something other than me had spoken from me.

I stopped on the crumbling entrance ramp of the Golden Gate and there I struggled within. I should die with Lacey, I thought. I turned. The uphill ruins stood starkly bathed in red dawn. I felt as if I had not seen such fallen spires before. Nothing but death was there. I turned again.

The Golden Gate Bridge loomed before me drifting in and out of sight by way of cotton-thick mists. The crossing was dangerous and barely passable on a clear day. It was crazy, loco, and too risky to cross. Impossible in that fog soup. It was the only direct way out of town going north.

The far shore called. It sang, just a whisper, but I heard it. Dangling cables lucky enough to catch the dawn glinted red warning high above, but I could not resist the Siren's voice.

I began running, not away from anything, not away from Lacey, but toward something...something.

The bridge, badly damaged, was no longer an impediment. Green grass dressed the entrance ramp and went on a little way onto the bridge's deck. I ran fast flying over the slippery-green threshold. I raced over flora without leaving a mark. Running was loco. I leaped across the first crumbled section of the roadway and landed on another. I sprinted ten yards for the next great leap. I sailed through the wafting fog and onto another patch of road, and then onto the next, and the next. The sharks below were disappointed.

For years I struggled against that voice. Letting go of my resistance allowed my legs to follow. I had ignored the call until intellect gave way to wild abandon. Impressed inside me was this message—do not stop. Desire crushed intellect. Need drove my passage.

Without asking why, I ran. I lost all sense of time and place by achieving the runners-high. That place where we runners go to escape the miles, that was my refuge. There the world and its troubles melted into dreams and dreams become real. I ran on, and on, and on. I ran clothed in dreams.

It is known that exhaustion will generate altered states of mind but this was more. It controlled me and I became a patron of hell's movie house. From above, I watched myself run with clarity. I passed by ruins, fires, and bodies, and the many devices of war. I dreamt of myself being a runner inside a story, a story set in the future, present and past. Run, run, run. I had had dreams and visions before but I was never able to step outside of my reality. I hadn't known a runner's high of this degree.

Seventy-five miles north of San Francisco, the sun was low. I felt the need for rest and I fell onto a rocky beach and slept where I lay.

I woke in the morning to the sound of dawn's voice. Still, she was calling. Fishermen were climbing down a bluff toward the sea while chatting. They didn't see me although they came close enough to smell my sweat.

I felt no hunger, no desire for the fish or crabs they might catch. They vanished into a fog. I got up and ran.

Again, I entered an altered state. Yesterday's run changed me. I lived outside of time, caught between dimensions. In my time, no time passes. In the world, time continued funneling down, always down.

I ran for a week. I felt no weather, no cold, no hunger only the need of the north. The further I traveled the less real I and the world became.

I ran the cost until reaching Alaska. There, where I rested, great military ships were at sea and landing crafts were deploying Russian troops. I looked at the future and they were all dead in the snow. I walked between bloody ghost faces. I searched desperate pleading eyes in battle and found them soulless. All will die, all doomed. No longer was there a future or a past for them. For them death was real. All in a dream. My dream.

I did not want to see anymore. My heart felt crushed and broken. I turned away from the coast. Blindly I ran east over rocks, snow, and permafrost, always toward the magnetic pole. Unknown forces guided me though I did not know it. I became an invisible force. Seven days without rest—when the desire to run ceased—I stopped. Magnetic north. No need to go on and nowhere to go.

Stopping was a mistake.

I materialized in a white-out landscape. There was no line between earth and sky. Standing alone no longer outside of reality wrought pain. I collapsed to my knees. Biting cold tore at me. Hungry white tigers attacked. My tattered coverings lent no protection.

I needed help, but only more whiteness answered my cry. My fingertips turned black before my solidifying eyes. Pain raced through my feet and hands. Death marched. Icy soldiers pressed upstream into my extremities seeking the fortress of my heart to destroy.

I fell face down into the promise of inviting snow, falling, falling as onto a pillow, but what a stony pillow landing. I was nearly knocked unconscious but I managed to roll onto my back.

"I'm dying," I hissed through hardening lips.

I had never prayed before, but I then uttered my first comment to God despite my lifelong non-belief. God would not save one such as me. I addressed Him but not to beg favors, or cast aspersions, but rather to offer an observation.

"You…failed…Merry…Christmas."

I surrendered to death. My eyes froze open and a swelling whiteness engulfed me. My vision narrowed to black slits. The world was ending, all of it, and why shouldn't I end, too? They were blind, I was not. I had a sight, but what good did it do? Nobody got saved. Mankind is extinct. White turned black. Frozen eyes can never see again.

I was wrong.

Researchers had long ago revealed that freezing is a comforting way to die. There comes a sense of well-being, sleepiness, and warm rushes. Freezing, in the end, is pleasant. I did not expect the cooing of an angel.

"Now, now, my sweet Tomas," I dreamed. "You are well, we have regenerated you. Fingers and toes, all fine dear Tomas, sweet Tomas…"

I felt warm hands in mine. A deep comfort. I thought to open my eyes just to make sure. But I am dying, I thought. If I could see at all, all there could be was blinding, white pain. My eyes were left open and ice cannot see. I opened them. A woman…beautiful…smiling, white, long face. White dangling hair. Soft down framed her face. A golden halo ringed her head.

"This is a good dream," I said inside my dream.

"This is not a dream," she said.

I startled up, tearing myself from the soft warmth. I cried out.

"This is impossible! I'm dead. You're an…angel…"

"No, Dear One, I am not. Not exactly. And you are not dead. I am more than possible. I am here. We were expecting you. We called you. Welcome to the North Pole."

I rubbed my eyes. She was still there.

"How can this be?"

"Rest now," she said.

She handed me a cup of hot cocoa, the first cup of the stuff I'd had in my hands in forty years.

"This will help you sleep. When you wake, the human girl, Bobbie, will guild you."

I took a sip, then a deep drink. It was just right. Cocoa perfection. I drank the rest in gulps.

"Implies you aren't human," I said, cup in hand, eyeing the last sip.

She tried to take it, but I did not let go. A thick ceramic mug is better than a knotted fist. If this is real, I thought, I may be in trouble. Logic dictates caution. First thought: I wanted a weapon and then shame pierced me with icy heart-shots. I shivered.

She didn't answer. My heart staggered. Rather than accuse, she smiled impishly and gently pushed me back into softness. I felt no fear. My grip loosened. She reached again and took the cup out of my hands. I was a repentant little boy. She placed the tip of her index finger on my trembling lips.

"Hush, rest now Profit of Doom, rest. You are forgiven. There will be answers later."

I closed my eyes thinking, "death isn't so bad." What they say is true. Freezing is a good way to die.

I woke alone, not a person or sound in evidence. I felt alive and refreshed and felt no threats. I took stock.

I noted the walls and ceiling resembled poured concrete. The lighting, something I had not seen in years, was by way of vintage commercial fluorescent fixtures. This room reminded me of the 1950s cold-war shelters. This place felt older than war. The government and everyone else used LED lighting. But, of course, I told myself, "This must be an old secret government base." That was my first assessment.

I must have been rescued. Why did the doctors send a nurse dressed as an angel? They did not do such a thing. I imagined it. A person was here but she was not an angel.

I tested my faculties.

The bed was feather-soft, real enough, and not a hospital bed. The military doesn't provide patchwork quilts made of holiday-themed panels. The blanket and sheets were pine-scented, decorated with tiny evergreens, and not tagged government issue. The bedding must have come from a department store before the New Dark Age. The embroidery on my bedding should have told me this wasn't a government installation. This place, to my mind, could be nothing other than a well-organized military facility.

The antique wooden nightstand next to the bed held a glass of milk and a plate of cookies which appeared while I slept. Wall-to-wall deep-green carpet covered the floor. Framed art of good quality depicting winter scenes adorned the walls. The exit door was made of cherry wood and left ajar.

"The government doesn't spare any expense for its comfort," I said to hear myself. My voice was real, too.

The medical people had dressed me in red wool pajamas with matching slippers. There was a flap where one should be. I felt fine and rosy. The carpet? Soft and warm. Heat radiated from below it. I slipped through the door like an elf on Christmas Eve.

The hall appeared made from rough concrete. I examined the walls and ran my hand over the surface. Not cement, I thought. Perhaps they were giant blocks of cut stone?

"Megalithic structure," I said.

I tested it with a rap. It rang from my knuckle like stone but the surface wasn't right. Blocks cut from rock don't leave a deep sandpaper finish. What process made this strange texture? Was it permafrost, but not wet or cold?

Closed doors lined either side of the passage. An open arch lit the far end of this long, long hall. The other direction was cave-black. I moved forward, slow, carefully, not sure if I was dreaming or dead. I arrived at the arch and the light beyond blinded me at first as I stepped onto a stair landing. I could do nothing but peer into the dazzle of green, red, and white lights below me. Slow in coming but my sight adjusted. Impossibilities lay below this balcony. Stunned, I uttered a complaint.

"The angel lied. She lied. I am dreaming."

A vast underground cavern, many miles long and as wide, lay under me. I stood atop a stairway made of glass. The ceiling was a hundred feet above me. I swooned at the spectacle.

In the distance, there were spaceships—giant metal globes, and castles of stone between them, and a conifer forest, stone bridges, and rolling hills with a village and workshops in the foreground. The landscape was a fairyland. A science fiction movie set had never been built so large or so far north. I ruled that out.

I pulled my attention back to the foreground directly under me. I could not comprehend it. I swooned again seeking a rail to lean on, but finding none, I lowered myself down upon the top stair riser and sat on the glass.

Workshops and cubicles dotted the floor and were occupied by very small men and women with pointed ears wearing green or red suits and black boots. Among the small beings, there walked winged angels twice their height dressed in flowing white robes. The angel of my dreams had multiplied.

I rubbed my eyes before thumping the side of my head with an open palm. It didn't help. They were still there.

Reindeer and unicorns walked freely throughout the grounds. The stairway projected forward and down in a graceful arch and, it being clear, did not obstruct my view. A minotaur passed directly underneath me. I watched it, hang-jawed, from thirty feet above. I wasn't cold, but I froze in place. My immobility came from fascination or fear. I could not tell.

"It's huge, yeah," a girl's voice came from behind me.

I twisted half around.

"I see you're up." She giggled. "Pretty cool, don't you think?"

I stood, spun, and gasped. The woman, pretty, tall, and blonde offered me a milky hand. Her age appeared in the teen years. But great age rang behind her voice. In further juxtaposition, her red jogging suit was embossed with childish holiday logos. A red cape with a white fur collar draped her shoulders.

"Pajamas?" I must still be sleeping is what I thought.

Her hand moved a little closer. She smiled with radiant teeth. I took her hand and it was rock-strong.

"I'm Bobbie. Gabriel told you I'd come, remember? It's cool to meet you. Tomas Vazquez, right?"

I held her hand too long. I did not know what else to do. Her touch was warm and powerful. She smelled of Christmas cookies and pine needles. I could not answer.

"You're new." Her voice projected lyrically. "Welcome, Prophet Tomas. You'll get used to it."

"Prophet?" I let go of her hand.

"They'll explain at the meeting. You're just in time. Follow me, please."

She glided down those crystal stairs with her cape fluttering. She flowed like angel hair on the wind. She reminded me of milk pouring over a waterfall. Everything in this dying dream mesmerized me. I was content to stay and watch from the stair.

She stopped ten feet down, turned, and looked up at me. I caught my breath. The bluest eyes I had ever seen or imagined snared my focus.

"You coming or not, Mister Blue-Eyes?" she asked, giggling again like a schoolgirl.

"Blue eyes, I'm Latino. My eyes are brown," I said.

"Not anymore. Santa's waiting."

I followed her downstairs and a hundred yards into the cavern. Mythical creatures of every description moved about on their own business and none paid us any mind. Strange that I feared not, but then again, this was happening inside my dying mind, I thought. Strange near-death experiences were known to psychologists.

She brought us to a large office-type conference room replete with a long table and chairs. A few odd persons were already there. It struck me as the same furniture we used at Alameda College. Bobbie and I took seats. I felt silly in my borrowed pajamas but I shouldn't have, given the room's company.

"Everyone isn't here yet," Bobbie said. "Chill. Have a cookie."

There were a few normal people seated, but not normal. Everyone wore Bobbie's impossible blue eyes and golden-white hair. I checked. My now long, but recently brown, hair had changed to stark white. I felt my face. The beard was gone.

How long was I exposed to the elements, and how long since I left San Fran? Was there time enough and sun enough to bleach my hair? When did I last shave? This wasn't a dream. I don't dream in color. One cannot dream with the sense of touch or taste.

I took a cookie off the sideboard which stood behind our table. I bit it. "It's real?"

"For sure," she said, "best I ever had."

The others came in a few minutes apart and most of them were not human. Elfish beings, angelic beings, a dark-skinned bearded man clad in first-century Jewish attire, a dozen small people—not midgets or dwarfs—miniature people with pointed ears wearing outlandish clothes. The small ones filled the room with laughter. But I felt an undertone of urgency. Last, a small buck deer with a bright red nose entered and took station at the head of this long table.

My table-mates communed peacefully while others stood and milled around sampling the treats which were set upon sideboards all around the room in easy reach. I was told we were waiting for a missing person to arrive. I sat quietly nibbling cookies until I fished the plate. I went on to chew my fingernails.

"If this is real…hell isn't such a bad place," I whispered to Bobbie, wondering if the other blue-eyed profits had similar thoughts.

Bobbie leaned close, "I know, pretty strange, right? It's OK. I've been here a while, you'll see."

Her speaking brought me out of my stupor. I gathered my wits. I thought it was the right time to ask questions but I didn't get the chance. The main attraction arrived with a horn blast. A short, fat man in red overalls and a festive-green shirt burst in billowing, "Ho, Ho, Ho!"

His long white hair and bread reminded me of the fish tank filter material I used in my home aquarium before the war. A material called angel hair. Loose strands floated around his head as if on water. His cheeks were flushed pink but his bulbous nose was drunkard-red. He went direct to the head of the table.

"Santa," I muttered.

"Yeah, isn't he cool?" Bobbie said.

"Sit down one and all. Ho, Ho, Ho! How's about refreshments?" The jolly man said. He pointed at the sideboards. "The oatmeal cookies are all but gone! Jesus, would you, please?"

The first-century man stood, waved his hand, and, in the twinkling of an eye, a silver pitcher of hot apple cider and plates of oatmeal cookies appeared.

"That's it!" I yelled. I stood clenching my fists. "I've had it!"

The room hushed. Bobbie grabbed my hand.

"I'm done here. This is crazy!" I cried. "This is my dream! I can do what I want. I'm leaving. Can't a man die in peace?"

I wanted to bolt for the exit but Bobbie's hand in mine had a calming effect. She drained my sudden resolve.

"Tomas, you aren't dead, really," she said. "It's cool, come on. Please sit."

She let go and patted my seat. Her touch comforted me and I obliged. The jolly man stood his place at the head of the table. His two hands were spread on the surface. He leaned forward before he spoke.

"Bobbie, you didn't debrief Tomas, did you?" He said with humor.

"No Santa. He just woke up."

"Ho, ho, ho...I see," Santa looked at me over his reading glasses. "Let me do the background before we get started. We need Tomas up to speed."

The deer spoke. "Not everyone's been fully debriefed. Yes, please go on."

"Rudolph is correct," Jesus said. "I'm out of the loop."

How can he be out of the loop? I tried to sit gracefully, but rather I fell back into my chair like a sack of rocks and a chair leg broke. Two or three helped me up and into another seat. The commotion settled quickly. Santa had to explain what was happening for the benefit of the uninformed, such as myself. I had overheard the table talk in which folks mentioned that a recently thawed spaceship crews were also present.

"What you see around you is all real. Your perception of this," Santa waved his hand majestically, "is wrong. You, folks, are not dreaming, ho, ho, ho. Your ability to dream is important, to be sure. That's why you're here, if you understand me."

Santa fluffed his beard out of his farmer's coveralls, pulled the high-backed chair at the head of the table, and plopped into it with unexpected grace.

"Ho, ho, ho...Let me first say we are not mythical beings. We are alien beings."

Santa paused to bite a cookie.

"Your myths are based on us." He spoke around a mouthful. "We used to mix with the population, you know...once upon a time, for research purposes, you see."

"And to affect positive changes," Jesus said.

"Quite right," Santa said taking another cookie.

He stuffed it into his mouth and slugged a deep draught of hot chocolate before going on.

"Mankind advanced so we weren't able to live among you anymore, you see. We, er...lost control. That's why one of you Earth folks here are needed." He waved his hand at us. "We haven't interacted with Earthling in centuries, you see. That's all done. We've been holing up here waiting for the extinction horizon to trip."

"Things got hot for our representatives," Rudolph said. "We had probes. You know them as UFOs. That the governments chased us was inevitable. That forced us underground. Your species' doom could no longer be held back."

"High destructive technology gained by low intelligence beings is the precursor for an extinction event," Santa said.

Santa picked up a cookie and marveled at it before taking a nibble, crumbs fell into his beard. The raisins were huge. He began again.

"We have always been active in our mission, as it were, but our mission is now drawing to a close. Only one more thing remains."

Santa nodded at the angel on his right.

"What is our mission, you may ask? We are shepherds," Gabriel said. "We don't cull the population, but we do collect specimens…and you, a chosen handful of survivors are they. We have our samples and just in time. The planetary matrix has failed."

"Wait," I blurted. "What do you mean, who are you…people?"

A girl sitting three chairs down piped in. Her voice was that of a flute.

"Please, I have a question. What about God and all that? How does that fit? I don't get it."

"Jesus, will you take this one?" Santa asked.

Jesus stood. He wasn't much taller standing.

"Sure thing. We here are inhabitants of the multi-universe. We are human variations. Our kind exists above your time and space. You might say we are God-like but we aren't gods. How? That's too technical to explain in a short time."

Jesus took a long drink from a mug of cider.

"But why?" The three of us doubters asked.

"Your societies didn't develop in time." Jesus said as a matter of fact. "Your inability to evolve psychologically killed you. Point is, we higher beings help the lesser types if we can…but we can't work miracles. I'm sorry, Earth didn't make it."

"That doesn't tell me who you are," I cried. "What about God!'"

Santa looked over his spectacles and his eyes twinkled. I've never seen eyes do that. His brow rose in a scholarly fashion. "That, Tomas, depends on your perspective."

"We come from higher planes," the elf said. "There are layers of reality. You may call it heavens. We transcend the layers. We watched over you for a time. We collect and preserve life when it fails, as it has here."

"The universe is a ball, inside a ball, inside a ball," Jesus said. "From the higher places we observe. Living realms collapse and restart over and over through time. Your mystics correctly called such events the end of an age."

"This can't be real," I said.

"Your reality bubble burst, get on the stick," Santa said. "We'll be moving on to the next reality shortly. You, Tomas, are the last to arrive before evacuation begins."

"Can't we stop it? Is there no hope?" I said, fearing the answer. "Must you leave? What will happen?"

"We'll go on and help the intelligent ones of another sphere," the deer said. "There is no one left here to save. Dead people cannot progress. We were only able to save a worthy few."

"That's you, folks," Santa said. "You can enter the multi-universe. That is, remove your foot in this world. When we take flight, you'll step out of this time and into another time-sphere with us. Unless you decide not to go. You can stay, of course." Santa flicked his nose with a finger. "This planet's sentient race would have built dimensional ships by now had they evolved which they didn't. They could have avoided destruction, alas, only a few of you developed."

"What's next?" I asked.

I felt dismal and excited at the same time. Sad to see our kind end, sad to see Earth empty of people, but excited at my possibilities. I accepted this new reality but I didn't know what to do with it. The implications hadn't yet flowered.

"What we have here, is the end of time, so to speak, in this version of reality anyway." Santa stopped and took a cookie, looked it over, and put it back on the dish. "Burnt Raisin. We called and the advanced ones came. Now, we must get the hell out of here and fast."

"The people," I stammered.

I fully realized it—all of Earth's people are gone, all dead. I shivered and mopped my brow with a fancy lace napkin. "What about the people?"

"We tried," Jesus said with force. "We worked our influences so that people may have evolved…and…the effort did not pan out."

A penguin said, "Did the best we could, these people blew it."

Jesus went on. "They missed the window and we're out of time, only a few hours left here."

Some of the other Earthlings sobbed. I wiped tears away but did not weep openly.

"Oh, Earth isn't over," Santa said. "It will be recycled. Everything exists in cycles. We were hoping to push Earth along in the right direction. Guidance will work better next time if only…"

There was that twinkle in his eyes again.

"We salvaged examples of the original, such are you, the dozen rescued souls sitting here, and we have our archives," Santa picked up a cookie.

A deep hush fell upon the room. I had the feeling he was getting to it, what this meeting was about. So far nothing was asked of me or the others.

Santa put down his cookie.

"I need your help, one of you needs to stay," he said. "You have come here by your fortitude and free will, under hardships and pain. Dare I ask this? I must. I cannot force you, but it is the only way to ensure that Earth will live again and thrive."

Santa paused and took a deep draught from his mug. He set it down with a wide smile outlined in cocoa-laden whiskers. Fat Santa huffed and puffed climbing up on his chair.

"I won't trick anyone. It's a long, hard, lonely job and only at the end will you have others like you." Santa held his mug aloft with a wink and a nod. "I will toast in advance. Hail the Care Taker. Should one come forward, of course?"

Every mug rose, mugs clashed, and long draughts followed.

"It is a leap of faith," an angel said. "The outcome is unknown. The new beings will not be sentient for millions of years. They will need attention long before it."

"They will never know that," Santa said.

"Someone must provide myths and legends," Jesus said.

"How do we fit?" I said, thinking of the fact that a human being, such as myself, cannot live for millions of years. And here they speak of people who will not exist for millions of years yet to come. But the prospect intrigued me. I cannot explain why.

"Why would you consider any of us?" I said not expecting a reasonable answer.

"You know the territory," Santa said. "You're evolved. You'll tap what primitives call magic— some will call it the 'power of God' if you will, but it is only physics. Work miracles when you must. You will learn how to manipulate matter. You'll get the hang of it. It takes practice. People respond to magic. Christmas magic wasn't enough…sadly."

"That's right," Jesus said.

"What we need," Santa said, "is someone on the job here. Earth implodes in a few hours and you Profits of Doom, are capable of surviving it. I'm not, I don't come from here. There's usually not much left. Almost all life will end. Then, it starts over. That's what mass extinctions are for. Look in your geological records, big resets, so to speak. Quantum re-setting is the Universe's way of cleansing itself. Happens all the time."

Santa stopped to take a long pull from his hot cocoa. He cleared the whipped cream from his beard with a fancy napkin and searched the long table, passing his gaze from one of us to the other. We who had been recused were those who were scrutinized. He stopped at me. That odd twinkle in his eyes captured. I swear I saw the cosmos within. If one could access the eye of God, it would be that. But I never believed in God.

"You in," he said, looking right at me as if he knew.

One by one, a dozen human sages, male and female alike raised a hand and said yes. Everyone was 'in' all except me.

An elf spoke in a sing-song voice, "One only one may participate. There is a risk. The one who remains here is here until time ends again. You can survive but you may well die before we return. Free will, stay or leave, only one."

Some of the raised hands went down.

"What about God?" I said, standing. "You didn't answer that question."

"You already know the answer," Santa said.

I had long ago thought if there was a God it must be the mass consciousness of life connected by an as yet undetectable aspect of energy. That, or God, might be a self-aware energy. God could be anything but a deity to me, and I was right. I had wondered about the term 'God energy' some used to describe dark energy. I borrowed and employed such concepts in my thought experiments. I was sure there was such a force, but the idea of controlling it never occurred to me. What God was, to my mind then, was an energy source beyond current access. Funny ideas. To an ant, I am God. To me, these multi-universe beings were not gods but only one hidden aspect of existence. This ending was only natural.

"Nature isn't good or evil or god. It just is. Energy has no morality," I said, "but you control spooky energy with a moral position. That makes you God. I don't want to be a god."

"God is not a person. It is a life force ever-growing," Bobbie said. "Life makes energy and that energy makes life, and it is accessible to us."

I had tapped into that power as I ran. I had brushed against it often before. It was how I wrote my doom books. Warnings emerged from that river of dying energy. I had never fit within the stream of life for reasons that I did not see before. I felt and thought differently and put myself forever outside of life to interrupt life from afar. Safe, alone. I saw what others could not see. All so clear. I dropped my cookie.

"You in," Santa asked.

"I'm in," I said. "I think."

During the closing hours, we prophets and wizards loaded ships. We moved cargo quickly as jolly elves. While I labored, I spun ideas. I, the Care Taker, will do things my way. I carried bags for them at the launch-pad, but that was as far as I went. The facility would remain after they departed. I still wasn't sure if I would remain on Earth. Nothing made by the hand of man on Earth will remain. That emptiness chilled me.

If I were Care Taker, I imagined, I would bring my charges to the gates of paradise. A better life for all who have faith! Faith in the power of love. No more fearful temples. I would make the unknown knowable. No one that enters my temple will leave ignorant. I, the baggage man, entertained such thoughts.

I will be a people herder. I told myself. *Wars, chaos, and starvation won't rage between city-states in my world. Desperate, lost people will flock to each other. Change is the fabric of existence. I would make it a better world.*

I worked dreaming behind my uncanny blue eyes. My long white robes and hair fluttered on cold winds when the roof opened letting natural light into the cavern. The end was near. One after the other, great fields of ceiling rock retracted and dimensional ships launched one after the other in a long line. They lifted, cleared the cavern, and winked out of this existence. The ceiling closed again after every departure. Santa stood on the gangway of the last ship. He beckoned to me. It was the last ship to leave.

I was the only one left in this massive underground world, standing on hard rock. With increased wind, a power came upon me. A precursor to what was to come, but that life was in the future.

Santa called with that damned twinkle in his eye. I felt the pull of universes begetting universes behind him as if he was God, but he was not.

"Tomas, are you coming?"

"NO."

After Santa lifted off, I closed the roof with a wave of my hand.

I am here alone in an unfamiliar world. The facilities didn't last but a short million years. I nudge things along as I may. Sometimes I watch evolution. Sometimes I cause it. On some distant day, intelligent life will emerge and I will be here. I can't die on Earth. I am outside of time. I will wait until the collection team returns. Then time will end again here and a new time will start for me.

I will do what good I can. I will do what Jesus did: serve the people. I intend to make the best effort I can during my tenure. I will become many gods as the others had done, but nothing like the gods they were. In my way, I will guide the people. My gods will be different.

The next people will build ziggurats to free thinking. The God of Science will be king and kill the God of Money. No offense to Jesus, who played Buddha, Zeus, and all the rest, but he could have done better. Mysticism was a failed strategy. I will not be God, though I am God by default. Humans will evolve, that is my plan.

Santa used to say, "Miracles can happen."

I will make miracles happen. I look forward to working with Santa again. He will return before time ends in the future. I know it.

He will return.

I know all things.

I am God.

PYRAMID SCAM

Author's note: This first appeared in the Greater Lehigh Valley Writers Group (GLVWG.org) anthology, *Rewriting the Past*, 2019. I wrote this specifically for that publication using their required theme and limited word count. This version is lightly edited from the original.

It was the last gathering of the ruling men. Long the elites knew that the comet would return and cause massive harm.

The Group, as they called themselves, were the rulers and they didn't tell the populace of the coming danger. Rather, they contrived a way to have the people build their refuges as public monuments—artworks for the people's enjoyment—the Group did not reveal the true purpose. In the end, Zeb's trickery was exposed.

Could his workers blame him? They would do the same. How else could he have justified such enormous undertakings at the public's expense? Zebedee thought it was genius of him to fool the public in this way. Moreover, hiding the Group's true purpose while appearing as heroes were honey on dried fruit. People needed work. Swaying them was easy. The rest of The Group had deferred to Zebedee's wisdom.

Each of them supplied the funds. Each family had built for themselves a massive shelter. The size of each hold was according to family status. Of course, Zebedee's pyramid was the biggest of them all, save the few across the great waters south of the ice packs. Only Zeb knew, as the head of astrophysics, people across the ocean cannot survive. The comet will impact the northern ice sheet.

Zeb stood at his chair as did the rest. They were all plain dressed in common clothing. It wasn't safe to go about as the wealthy educated ones. The people had only recently learned of the coming impact and they were roused. The night sky was lit with a new, growing sun and such light opened the rabble's eyes. The jig was up.

"We must now descend into our bunkers. The event is upon us," Zeb pronounced upon sitting.

"But my casing stones have not yet been installed," Trotman said. "I cannot get the workers back. No amount of money will they accept. You see how ungainly it looks?"

"They are leaving in masses, traveling to Anatolia," Trot's wife said.

"Do you not understand?" Jeb blew out a long, exasperated puff of sweat tropical air. "Tonight, the jungle will burn."

Zeb was amazed at how shallow they were with their petty concerns in the face of this disaster. Their gold, their money, their slaves, none of it mattered. Saving their kind did.

"Trot, old boy, get into your bunker and have the slaves seal you in before it's too late. As for me, I will go this afternoon."

No one had casing stones, they would have to take their chances. And, oh did Zebedee fight for the stones. He made political war on the Free Mason's union but to no avail. He was lucky they finished the structure in twenty years. The Free Masons had their fill of it a year before impact. So, the union defected and left for Anatolia, starting a trend, and the rest soon followed. The Group disbursed and each ruler went about their preparations. The population remaining knew not that this would be their last day living safely above ground.

Over the next forty years, while the sky turned black and the sun failed, Zeb and his kind expanded their network of tunnels and made the best of underground life. Only one of their sub-equator shelters failed and only because its nuclear pile exploded for lack of cooling water. The great river had radically shifted its course. That one was far from Zeb's complex and its demise caused him no harm.

Although the sky had cleared, the weather improved year-to-year, and farming became possible, Zebedee and his kin preferred the safety of their bunkers as the survivors above were seeking revenge. Underground, come what may be above, they could live well and long until their memories of the surface faded.

The hope was, in time, the Group will emerge and resume rule. But, why rule from above when ruling from their underworld was safest? Jeb decided to bring that idea to the next Gathering.

*****

Harim was a hero of the people. He was the one who motivated the people and convinced them to depart in time. Before the comet was close enough to see with the naked eye, he began excavations and many other miners and masons did likewise after his example.

Harim designed the largest of the underground cities. Such places were how people took shelter. He was a young man then but old now. Harim no longer hammered and chiseled setting the example of manual labor as he once did. This he did to preserve the laser cutters. He reserved his rock knives for one purpose.

The people made him union president and he wasn't required to hammer although he had done his share. The people trusted him but never again would they trust leaders unquestioned. He proposed a venture. Everyone voted. It was decided. Scouts were sent to see what they could. The pyramids and much else still stood. A new effort was decided. A force of masons ventured into the ruined world seeking justice.

Harim eyed Zebedee's monument the morning of the mason's arrival. Smoke came out of this pyramid along with the others. There was no sign of the residents. But they were there. Smoke vents spewed everywhere in the landscape.

Zackery, the new foreman, asked, "How to pay them what they deserve? This place is a honeycomb. We cannot fight them in the tunnels, it's suicide." He pointed at a laser cutter. "We can't waste equipment."

Saving the equipment was drilled deep into Zac's mind. But tradition must not overrule need. Harim scratched his beard choosing his words.

"If we used every powerpack in existence, we could not cut away enough stone to get them out—true enough," Harim said. "These structures, as I recall, are riddled with hidden vents, false passages, and voids. Never will you find all the escape tunnels and I don't mind."

"How will we have our justice?"

Zackery rightly spoke with a flummoxed tone and face. The Group abandoned them to die. All the people wanted justice. So many more would have lived if the priest-scientist had given advanced warning.

"How, how do we repay them?" Zac repeated.

"We fulfill our contract. We are honorable men, are we not? We were paid in advance for the casing stones, let us encase the pyramids. We thereby remake their refuges into tombs."

"Yes, we have cutters enough, and should we use softer stones such as limestone, yes, our power will last the job, and infilling with a lime slurry will plug any gap. We will canvas the land and pug every airshaft."

"That is why you were elected foremen; a Free Mason must think logically," Harim said.

He did not hide the pride in his voice.

"Do you think they all will perish? They are devious," the new foremen asked.

"Sealed in, some may wiggle out, but they will come out like worms on their bellies, their power crushed."

Hiram paused and looked up at the great monument he worked on so long ago.

"We must be forever vigilant. I have hope that this will end them for good."

And it happened that the pyramids were encased with gleaming white stone and every tunnel they found was cleverly filled. Every shaft was covered and the job was done well. Free Masons do not produce poor work. Their work was meant to outlast the ages.

Twelve Thousand Years Later:

Ned and Mark were arguing as usual at their regular tourist bar in Cairo. Ned was fed up with it. Both Americans were on the German dig team, but Ned was old school. Young Mark's recent doctorate itched under his skin. Unrealistic career possibilities were just spilling from Mark's know-it-all pie-hole. The young man didn't understand the reality or nature of archeology's situation. Ned took a long pull off his drink.

"It doesn't add up," Mark said, opening up a new rabbit hole at the end of another. "Why build a pyramid tomb at all? Ok fine, the King's Chamber has a box, but how can you say it's a coffin without supporting evidence? There's nothing on the walls, all the tombs of Egypt we've seen, were decorated. Even the robbed ones had traces of grave goods. But nothing in the King's Chamber, and Queens Chamber, nothing close."

"Occam's razor," Ned replied before taking a sip. The boy was revved up again.

"Why is it that the oldest structures are more sophisticated?" Mark went on. "I'm telling you the evidence points to an older, more advanced civilization. What about the precision, the perfectly drilled holes, how'd that happen? The Egyptians didn't even have the wheel. Christ, Ned, why can't you see it?"

Ned took the last pull off his drink nice and slow, making it last before crushing out his cigarette. He needed to wind down before addressing the kid.

"Look kid, I've seen all kinds of anomalies in twenty years of fieldwork, some of it was way out there. I'll grant strange things exist we can't explain. But here's the thing, if you want research money, a university job, grants, and book deals, you don't put that stuff on your shingle. You don't want to be the next tinfoil hat buffoon."

Ned lifted his glass, signaling the barman. "You heard what they did to Lester."

"But why? What's wrong with the truth?"

"I'll tell you what's true. You play along to get along," Ned put a finger against his hat like a gun barrel and dropped his thumb like a gun's hammer. "The money men don't want us to know. That's all you gotta know."

"What is it then? What don't they want us to know? Damn it, Ned, why do you talk in riddles all the time?"

The barman arrived. Ned tapped his glass twice indicating a double.

A flash of memory came to Ned while the barkeep poured. A thing he would never share with anyone off-hand, if at all. He said it anyway. The new guy was okay.

"I was your age in Nazca, Peru. I located a tunnel. A goddamn career-making discovery." Ned took a sip and pushed back his fedora. "I was standing there at the entrance ready to make history when I saw a light coming from the deep end. A man with a torch. Somebody beat me to it."

Ned turned more to the bar, hunched his shoulders, and put his hands on his glass for security.

"The man was seven-foot-tall, with six fingers on each hand and a cone-shaped head that wasn't from cradle-boarding. His massive jaws uttered one, cold whisper. 'If you value your daughter's life, you will never return.' It went back in. I ran like hell."

"Come on, Ned, what gives? That's a load of crap."

The barman appeared holding another drink. Ned signaled no thanks. Somebody bought him a round which he didn't expect. He had a feeling who it was, but resisted tipping his fedora in that direction. He had earlier noticed a dark suite-wearing western man sitting near the main door watching the room. Ned turned. The man was still there, and he swiped his nose with an index finger but there wasn't any fly on it.

Ned got up but he didn't pull his money. Let the kid pay. Education ain't cheap. Ned planted a hand on his colleague's shoulder.

"In this world, there are men in the shadows pulling strings, call them the deep state if you like, but the fact is if you cross them…Lester is lucky to be alive."

Lester had been on local radio talking about Giza's tunnel system. The next day he was found, by pure luck, in the desert buried up to his neck. He wouldn't say who did it.

Ned slid his bar stool in and slugged down his remaining whisky. He pulled his hat down lower than usual and walked toward the door, eyes forward. He caught the man in black moving toward Mark in the corner of his eye.

"Fine, bury your head in the sand," Mark called as Ned exited.

Ned didn't look back. He didn't stop, and he didn't hold his head high either, but at least it was still attached to his neck. Ned preferred his head six feet above the sand rather than six feet under it.

GO OUTSIDE

By Rachel Thompson with Lisa Cross

Gus felt like Mr. Underfoot. He didn't know what to do with himself. He stood in the garage before his barrel of scrap metal casting eyes at the door which led inside the house.

His grown kids' old bicycles, which he had saved for "projects," continued gathering dust, leaning against an old drill press. He had a vintage rototiller parked there, too, and some other small engine doo-dads to play with. Before retiring, he had all kinds of plans but old age's better sense told him that his proposed "money-making projects" were nothing but pipe dreams.

He liked to tinker. Gus wasn't a trained mechanic. He had been a machinist by trade before retirement. That new wire-feed welder he bought himself last Christmas, with his last Christmas bonus, still sat unused. What could he do? He felt guilty messing around in the garage while Mildred worked her tail off around the house.

That woman never stops.

He eyeballed the mud-room door again and figured he better go in and see what she needs. Millie was busy dashing around the house getting ready for her tea party. Gus followed as best he could. He did manage to get the vacuum out of her hands. He started on the rug but didn't use Millie's pattern. She vacuumed in strike lines, nice and orderly. Gus's way made the carpet's pile look like a cowlick convention.

The main pattern he came up with reminded him of brushed aluminum jeweling. He played with patterns for a while, made up his mind, and soon got lost in the process—lost the same way he used to drift into it when he ran the milling machine at work. He arranged an interesting fish-scale pattern and figured it was the best that carpet ever looked. Satisfied, he left it alone and rolled up the power cord. He was having fun until the boss caught up with him.

"For crying out loud, Gus, what will the ladies think?" Millie snatched the sweeper out of his hand before he had time to let go. "Walk away, I'll take care of it."

Every time he thought he was helping she'd chase him saying the same thing. 'I'll take care of it.' He left the parlor, wandered a bit, and wound up in the kitchen. Seeing dishes scattered about he thought he had better help clean up. Most of them weren't dirty, so he put them up. She left some food out, so he stowed the plates in the Frigidaire. He did not expect the reception he got when she skidded to a halt in the kitchen.

"What are you doing? I gotta mix the crumpets…"

She was off and running. There was no stopping her when she got this mad. She yapped a good five minutes before she came to a solution.

"They'll be here any minute. I got a lot to do. Please find something else to do outside."

How he handled her tirades was a secret. Gus had 50 years of practice. He'd kept his mouth shut, lips turned down, and played the beaten dog. He'd occasionally flinch so she thought he was listening. His trick was to drift off into his thoughts while the tempest blew the same as he did while running the machines at work.

Mom was always saying that sort of thing when Gus was a kid, 'Will you please go outside?' 'Can't you find something better to do?' 'Why don't you go outside and play?' When Mom was really mad there were no questions, just orders. 'Go out and play!' That was a demand, not a suggestion. Gus stood by remembering better days until she noticed he had tuned her out. She shook his arm.

"Please, Gus, find something to do outside. Where are my eggs, I swear I left them out to warm…Oh, for crying out loud…"

Gus flinched. She wasn't done yet.

Gus looked right at her, but his mother's voice rang inside him. Mom yelling at him to go outside is what registered. He drifted to that time he left the house very sad. But before long, he was out in the woods exploring. He found a cannonball from the Civil War. Another time Mom kicked him out, he and his buddies got together and played street hockey. The next thing he knew, they founded the first local street hockey league and it's still there now.

'Go outside,' had paid off.

"I swear, Gus! Your Momma didn't raise you right. Don't you know anything? Every time you come in the house…"

'Go outside.' There was that time when Gus was 13 and heartbroken over a girl. All Christmas week he had moped around. Even on Christmas eve, even after decorating the tree, he couldn't cool his slag-heap heart. Dad got into the act. Mom was behind it. Dad handed Gus the car keys, saying, 'Son, go outside and get that box out of the truck. Don't give me any lip.'

Going out was the last thing he wanted. It had been cold and snowing but Gus was so heart-cracked, he didn't even bother with a coat. He sprung the old Ford's trunk lid with ice flying and got shocked out of galoshes. It was a brand-new Sears mini bike with a three-horsepower Tecumseh motor, the best gift he ever got to this day.

Millie punched his arm. "I swear, Gus, since you retired, if you ain't underfoot, you ain't nothing…"

"Whatcha want from me? I'm trying to help—"

"Help? Help, if you want to help me, Gus, stay out of my hair…"

Gus had long hair back in the late 60s. All the kids did. There was that time Mom made him go out to play and Bill Hicks flew past Gus riding a Wizard motorized bike. Bill's long hair fluttering behind him was an inspiration. That day's excitement stuck to Gus right down to his sinews. Bill had gotten a famous motor kit that converts any peddle bike into a gas-engine motorcycle. That kid was king of the mini bikes. That Wizard was the envy of every kid on the block.

A soft touch on his arm brought him back to the present.

"I love you, Gus, but sometimes you drive me to distraction…"

She love-smiled at him like she did that day Gus got his first car when he was age 16. He didn't lose interest in the Wizard bikes though. He'll never forget Bill zipping by with bug-encrusted teeth, hair whipping like a torn flag. That day was something. Days that started with 'Go outside' often ended well even if Mom was only getting rid of him.

That old rototiller motor runs, I got lots of scraps.

"Gus. You aren't listening. Gone silly again." Her spring had unwound letting her usual love face come out. "What are you smiling about…What's funny?"

"Go outside and play," Gus said.

"What?"

"I got some stuff to do in the garage. I better get to work."

Millie gave him a hug and peck on the lips. She talked the whole time while backing him out of the kitchen and through the mud-room door. Outside in the garage, he took out a note pad and worked out how to mount that oversized rototiller motor on a peddle bike frame.

That big motor would have rattled Bill's teeth right out of his head.

The same sort of motor kit was still available. He could just bolt one on. That would be practical. *Too easy. Takes no imagining at all.*

Gus figured his design was better. He had been thinking about it for 50 years. He wasn't much of a wizard when it came to it, but making a Wizard fly had been on his mind for a long time. He had a fresh idea for the mounting plate.

"Sometimes it's time to go outside and play."

He blew the dust off his wired-feed welder and plugged it into the 220-volt outlet. He tried the feeder on a piece of scrap iron first. The bandsaw and bench grinder kick on when he tested them. Everything working, he selected materials and began.

AUTISTIC TIME

Author's note: This was originally to appear in my anthology, *Stalking Kilgore Trout*, but I held it back. I needed time to run it through my writer/editor friend who raised an autistic child into a fine young adult. I received her seal of approval in depicting the character. I held this back because I thought there was more to this story, and I was right. Kenny appears in my upcoming novel, *The Adventures of Tom Conley*. Below is the original, barring light editing. I incorporated much of this into my Tom Conley novel.

Pete "The Blaster" Brenner and his main bro hung out at Pete's hall-locker eyeing Kenny Parks. That retard was standing by the cafeteria door talking to a stupid dinosaur toy. *That's Mr. Webber's favorite idiot for you,* Pete thought.

"Look at that," Pete said to his wingman, Randy Pike. Randy closed his locker.

"Ten minutes 'til lunch and he lines up," Randy said.

"Special-Ed lets the 'tards go too early. They could get hurt." Pete winked at Randy. "Cover me."

Randy got the message and flashed his yellow-green teeth. Pete caught a whiff of tooth-rot. *I wish he'd brush once in a while.* Pete headed toward his favorite opportunity for a little fun. His point-man hung back by the hall's intersection just in case some teachers came along. Randy whipped out his cell phone to record. With Randy in place, Pete started the party.

"Hey Webber-tard, what ya doing, got any money?"

"What? What's that mean? Mr. Webber?"

"No stupid," Pete said laying his backpack on the ground. "A Web-ber-tard is a retard that goes to Webber's class, see?"

"I'm not. I'm smart, really smart. You're too dumb for Mr. Webber's class."

Kenny said it like it was a matter of fact.

"Ass-wipe." Pete felt his rage flair, but he couldn't do like Dad and haul off and clock the a-hole on impulse, he was too smart for that. *Screw him. I'm smarter, stupid retards.*

Pete grabbed Kenny's wrist and twisted his hand back around, something learned from karate classes. Kenny bent like a wet twig, but Pete still forced Kenny to let go of that little plastic toy that fell into Pete's free hand. Pete dropped the toy into his backpack's outer pocket. *That 'tard's never gonna see this again.*

"If you're so smart why you got a dinosaur toy? Man, like a three-year-old."

Pete put more pressure on Kenny's wrist. He expected Kenny to freeze but Kenny went so limp Pete almost lost grip.

"Not a dinosaur, it's Dimetrodon, a reptile from before them, like way before in the Permian, like not even—"

"Shut up, give me your money."

Pete put his foot out, twisted Kenny's arm the other way, and spun Kenny toward a locker. Kenny tripped but didn't face-plant into the wall or go down. That was a first. Pete thought he'd have to work on that move. Kenny was taller, no problem, and skinny like Grandma's tomato-sticks but a lot more flexible. The 'tard's ugly nerd-goggles flew off. That was cool.

"Pete! Trouble! Cool it!" Randy called in a high-pitched rasp.

"Got off easy this time, Webber-tard. You still owe me money."

Pete let go of Kenny and quickly moved to Randy.

*****

Mr. Webber rounded the corner. Kenny was hands and knees on the floor but he had his glasses in one hand. He looked up at Webber but remained on the ground looking for something. Webber pulled his pair of spectacles down and shot Pete a hard look.

He turned away and faced his student, "Kenny, are you okay?"

"Lost Dimetrodon. He was right here. Maybe he went to the…the…the before time…the Permian, maybe he went home. Oh, yes, he was the big shot, the biggest back then. Biggest bully ever."

"That's okay, Kenny. We'll get you another dinosaur," Webber said eye-balling Pete.

"Not a dino. He's a reptile. Reptiles…reptiles were more…always more, but everyone thinks they're not so great. Dimetrodon was the top predator 230 to 297 million years ago. He was a non-mammalian synapsid and—"

"I'm sure you're right, Kenny, when it comes to that, you are regularly spot-on."

Mr. Webber said it halfheartedly with an angry tone and instantly regretted it. Kenny was sensitive to voice tonalities. As a teacher, Webber had said similar things to Kenny a million times before but with enthusiasm. Paul Webber felt his day going off track.

Carefully, Mr. Webber helped Kenny up and they proceeded into the lunchroom together.

*****

"He's way stupid," Pete said. "How much you want to bet he gives me his lunch money twice tomorrow," Pete said it loud as more kids pulled up. Randy's yellow teeth agreed. Pete backed away from the smell.

"That 'tard is gonna pay," Pete said.

They lined up in the hall for Lunch Period One every day along the west corridor. Pete was already at the head of the line. He could be the first or last one to show up but it didn't matter. Nobody ever stopped "The Blaster" from cutting ahead.

*****

Mr. Webber and Mrs. Frances were on lunch duty, each one stationed at the common exits. Paul had been informed that a new teachers' aid would be joining them this period and Paul didn't mind showing a new teacher the lunch ropes, what little there was to know.

It was always nice to have another cow-poke to help corral all these wild colts. The new man was late, not a problem. It was his first day, plenty to learn. Regional high schools were large. He might have gotten lost. Lunch Room Period One hosted 180, like the other seating times. There were three periods of mixed-grade seating and this one had a bad mix. Lunch time was the Wild West.

Paul Webber often lobbied the administration to place his special-needs students with the freshmen, rather than the seniors, but then again, the freshmen were rough this year as well.

Standing at the open door, Paul Webber saw Mr. Black coming and made some guesses about the new man. He was a tall, a sandy-haired young fellow, wiry in a robust way. *Mr. T must be just out of college.* Maybe the new man had played sports. He looked fit. The man also had a nerd feel about him as well. Paul thought of himself as a good observer. It was part of his job, but he should have been observing in the other direction.

A crash rang out. The Special Education table had been flipped over just as Mr. Black stuck his hand out in greeting. Both men rushed to the scene. Webber's kids were in a panic. Food had flown everywhere. The likely bullies who did the dirt had already blended into a laughing mob. They dissipated before Paul could cross the room. He and Mr. Black righted the table, but there was no time for investigations.

Sally was crying. Suzy leaned over and tossed her cookies, her real cookies, the ones she had just eaten. Timmy was on the floor, licking soup off the next table's bench seat. The other five were in various states of shock or hysterics.

"Mr. Black," instructed Paul, "Get Timmy off the floor, then the others, one at a time, safety first. Don't worry about liabilities. Handle each one as I say."

Webber had seen it before. New teachers were usually scared of touching the kids. However, certain of his Special Ed kids required personal contact, and the ones that needed it got it. Some, like Kenny Parks, were limited that way.

"Right, right. Okay. Got it," Black said.

Black jumped right in to help get things in order. He first pushed the jeering students back without losing his cool. Black checked everyone on the floor for injures like a pro. Paul went directly to the students that needed the most specialized care. He was very glad Sally wasn't screaming. That tiny girl had inordinately large vocal cords.

No one was hurt. He did a quick head count, and no one was missing. By the time Paul Webber spotted his star student, it was too late. Kenny had become a standing stone leaning against the back wall like a half-buried, off-kilter Easter Island Moai. Mr. Black stood by, going pale. He had just picked Kenny off the floor.

Paul put up his hand. "It's okay. Don't touch him. It'll make him worse."

"What should I do? Is he having a seizure? Should we call—"

"No, no, he's fine, Mr. Black. He—"

"He was shaking violently. I thought he swallowed his tongue. I grabbed him and..."

"It's okay, really," Mr. Webber said using his professionally soothing voice. Mr. Black seemed to be somewhat reassured. "Kenny has episodes. He'll freeze like that when he panics. He calls it 'going away.' He'll be fine. Help me guide him into a seat so he can't fall."

"What'd I do wrong? It's my first day! Jeez, I don't want to get fired."

Mr. Black's youthful vigor deflated before Paul Webber's eyes. The young man flashed middle-aged. *Teaching will age you before your time.* Webber felt bad and patted Black on the shoulder.

"It wasn't your fault," Webber said. "You did well. You didn't know about Kenny's oddities. Each of my students has special needs. How could you know? Kenny will come out of it soon. But here's the thing with Ken, he doesn't like being embraced. He'll tolerate being touched lightly, or in small ways. He's improving. I'm teaching him to shake hands."

"I gathered him up like a sack of grain. I terrified him…I messed up."

"Only natural, Mr. Black. You did fine."

Mrs. Frances was busy getting the regular kids seated without much success. Webber needed to go and help her.

"Mr. Black, stay here. Keep Kenny company. Talk to him. He may come out of it. I'll help Pat, ah, Mrs. Frances."

Paul Webber joined the effort to restore order. Lunch was only forty minutes which came and went in a blur. Kenny did not move. Mrs. Frances offered to call the office for cover when the warning bell rang, because Kenny showed no sign of budging.

Paul rejoined Mr. Black at the Special Ed table. There the dismissal bell rang. Special Ed kids got released last—first in, last out—which helped prevent trouble. As mainstreamed students filed out, Paul chatted with Mr. Black. They talked of careers and graduate schools and Paul learned Mr. Black achieved a dual major at State University. First and foremost, Mr. Black was a paleontologist but one with a second major in education.

"And why aren't you digging fossils?" Paul asked.

Kenny stirred a little.

"I hope to and soon. I'm waiting to hear. I can't sit at home with student-debt accruing. The teacher's aide job popped up and I pounced. But I'm a shovel-bum through and through. I can't wait to taste dirt again."

"Fossil hunting sounds exciting," Paul said. He had a real interest in the topic because it's all Kenny talked about. "Find anything good in your field study days?"

Kenny's leg started. He often tapped his foot when he was interested in something, but not always. Paul wasn't yet sure why—excitement, frustration? The school's files didn't say.

The bell rang once more and Paul had his students rise. Vice Principal Evens came in to check on the situation and recognized Kenny's condition. Mr. Evens had Mr. Black stay to watch Kenny until Kenny recovered.

Paul said before going, "Mr. Black, when he comes—"

"It's John. Call me John."

"John, then. Call me Paul, unless the kids are about, of course. When he comes around, please walk him down to me. You may have a long wait. Hold his hand, but don't touch him over much. You saw what happens. You'll love Kenny. He's an encyclopedia of dinosaurs. Ask him, and he'll surprise you."

*****

Black sat with Kenny until halfway through Lunch Period Two, all the while he talked paleontology and the kid responded in increments, a faith smile here, a lifted finger there. The more Mr. Black talked shovel-bumming, the more the kid came to life. John Black did a lot of volunteer field work with kids while a student at Old U. He loved field work and the kids made it better still. After Black was sure Kenny could manage, they set out together for Special Ed.

The five-minute walk took ten minutes plus because John didn't know where he was going. This school was a dang-gone maze. Kenny never stopped talking paleontology. Nothing he said was wrong and a few things he said were cutting edge and beyond.

To satisfy his curiosity, John followed up that night and read Kenny's dinosaur blog. The kid's ideas were surprisingly insightful. How and where did a kid that could barely write a complete sentence get all this stuff? How did he know about Mesalands Community College's rare finds? Nobody outside of John's clique heard of the place, too many paleontologists included. That bone-shop sure as hell wasn't on TV's history shows, too cutting edge.

Working on his education degree required some special education stuff. The autistic kids in the case studies he had read amazed him. Meeting the real deal, Kenny Parks, was far more interesting than case studies.

Mister Parks knew things nobody outside the field knew like that hadrosaurs were the largest Ornithischians. That's fine, but how'd he knows the latest evidence confirms they had feathers? The kid wrote that blog entry before such findings were published. Kenny's essay reasoned it out from known evidence—he figured it out. Nobody extrapolates data like that.

Over the following weeks, Webber requested John's help and got it, but John was a roving aide and he didn't get to know all of Webber's kids well. Halfway into the spring season, John was called for a big dig in Montana's Badlands National Park.

Word got around that he was leaving. With many congratulations, his fellow educators wished him well. Many said they were sad to see him go. It wasn't like Old U after his master's degree, and current doctorate work. Everyone in academia, when it came to funding, were back-biting bastards who celebrated you leaving.

I should stay here at Central.

The teachers gave him a little party in the staff lunchroom at the end of his last day. There, when Kenny should have been on his bus returning home, Kenny burst into the teacher's room and ran up to John. Kenny took John's hand, gripped it hard, and locked his eyes on John's mouth. It was as close to eye contact as Kenny could manage. Kenny never looked anyone in the face. John felt so moved he didn't know what to say. He fluffed Kenny's hair instead.

"Got to tell you goodbye. Goodbye. Nobody listens. You listen. You know I know, so I have to tell you." Kenny lowered his voice and looked at his shoes. "When you find the baby T-rex, BA-hill...Look under him. He's protecting the eggs. That's new...T-rexes lived like lion prides... you'll see."

"Keep digging, kid," John said. "You'll do all right." John ruffled Kenny's hair again like John's dad used to do to him. The kid's face lit up. "You dig it, kid?"

"I'm digging, Mr. Black. I dig it. I dig it all up. Don't forget the eggs. T-rex eggs."

The hall monitor caught up and ushered Kenny to the office. His mom would come later. This had happened before. John had met Kenny's mom while punching out at the office once at day's end. Funny about his mom, she didn't seem much like anyone's mom. She had the bearing of an on-duty cop.

Kenny never missed the bus while conscience. He missed it only a few times before because he was 'away' inside his mind. John wondered about that place only Kenny knew, a place where the other kids could not hurt him. It seemed to John that Kenny had more quality time away than in reality. But John also saw that he had a positive effect on this mentally-challenged student. John was glad to have done well for the young man.

John stopped in the parking lot and looked back at the school's front door. It was the first time he left a job feeling good about what he had accomplished. He almost stayed on. But John's future lay ahead in the deep past.

"To be discovered," John said repeating Kenny's favorite expression. It felt right. "I'm all about discovery."

John got into his truck, feeling as though he had missed something, and drove off uneasy.

*****

Skinny John was what the students called Assistant Professor John Black on this dig. That's how they distinguished him from the other Johns.

He had been on this dig for two seasons as an adjunct, and the site was still a puzzle. Dig leader, Dr. Jonathan Mede, called for an early meeting by individual word-of-mouth to discuss the dig. No one told Big John Callahan. Nobody trusted Big John, especially Dr. Mede. Big John treated students like slave labor.

Six-foot-five Callahan, just short of overweight, had a wild coiffe of hair on top of his head which had a mind of its own. He tended to sleep late, drink more than his share of the hard-to-get beer at night, and did very little else but watch over everyone's shoulder. Callahan was as much a mystery as this site. It wasn't that Callahan was intimidating like other ego-driven academics were, something else about him bothered John. The troll was subtle at times, but also critical of small things, and he had a lightning flash mean streak. One never knew when or why Big John would strike.

Callahan's only interest was in what others found. The meeting was called without Callahan so students could have a shot at claiming their own discovery credits. Everyone thought Callahan was looking for something special that he didn't have to dig for himself. John thought he was seeking a missing piece of a publication puzzle. Big John was working on something he wasn't sharing but he was also happy to take credit for anything good the students found. Mede's face posted disdain whenever Big John stuck his nose into things. Nobody knew what Callahan's actual qualifications were. The University had sent him without explanation.

Dawn in the badlands was beautiful but no one paid attention this morning. Gathered in the mess tent that doubled as a field lab, the show was on. It wasn't the fantastic sunrise on display. It was chunky Dr. Mede nervously scratching his salt-and-pepper beard.

The stove was behind the dig leader's usual seat. Getting coffee, Prof. Black noticed Mede's laptop was open and on the Shovel Bum blogger site, Mede's morning habit. *I should read that blog. Mede sure finds it interesting.*

"All here, good. So, what have we?" Mede said.

Sara spoke, her specialty being foot prints.

"It's got to be different animals at slightly different times, maybe offspring returning to their birth ground generation to generation to mate, maybe to lay eggs. This many T-rexes can't be grouped. They're solitary hunters…right?"

Tom, as always, had to disagree. "No reason they can't be here together. They were scavengers, after all. Any big dead thing brings them in. Why should they not get along? They had plenty of food—"

"Where's the sauropod remains then?" A student asked.

"Hadrosaurs. This was their migration route," another student countered. "One of them makes a good meal for a mating pair. There'd be nothing left of Haddy but splitters."

"They did have a fantastic sense of smell," the team biologist said, scratching her chin. "They'd come in from 50 miles around for a big carcass. Maybe they got along like vultures do."

This set off the usual debate, predator vs. scavenger. But something else was going on. This place was like no other yet discovered and there had to be a reason for so many T-rex tracks in one place. Everyone talked at once until their hushed tones rose loud.

"No, no, no. Stifle it," said Mede. "Let us not revisit that again. Geology, what have you got?"

Dick didn't like the spotlight and flinched when called upon.

"My data suggests they are of the same layer. I don't see enough differential in soil layer content. What's curious is I'm detecting heavy sulfur with cyanide in this stratum, especially on T-tot's hill, and not below it, because the wash removed that soil. Same thing in later levels as well. I think it was volcanic gas. Must have killed them all at the same time."

"How can that be?" Eva demanded. She was a recent graduate brimming over with new knowledge and some of it obsolete. "We have two adult females," she went on, "different ages, a big male and a smaller one, the small ones might be contemporaries of the same clutch, but I don't see how they could have remained together in this small valley with limited resources and..."

Yeah, and what about that yearling we flew out last week?

T-tot was a lucky find, an entire animal still articulated eroding out of the crest of a hilltop. That never happens. Another few years and it would have crumbed away if it wasn't spotted.

The team named it T-tot. Strange that its body wasn't scavenged. John heard the arguments before. T-rex was a lone hunter and would kill and eat any other Rex it encountered, like a bad B-movie. T-tot should have been lunch and not preserved so well. The standard T-rex lone-hunter theory didn't make sense to him. If one big Sauropod keeled over, a hundred Rexes could eat for a year. There was no work or risk involved. But what explained disarticulated herbivore bones this far from the herds? John didn't accept the competition-for-food angle. Slow-moving stupid food on the hoof was as thick as mosquitoes on the nearby plains and many must have died along the way as migrating animals do. If T-rex hunted at all, pack hunting was the best strategy. They needed more data to prove it.

John got up and poured himself another cup of coffee. Mede still had the Shovel Bum blog opened. John read Mede's screen from behind. The lead-in was "T-rex cared for its young, but it was a family effort..."

"Who wrote that tripe?" John asked looking past Mede's scraggly mop of hair. Mede didn't answer being too busy as the debate moderator.

John read on. Someone named Kenny Parks wrote the essay.

"I know that name."

John almost dropped his coffee. His knees felt weak. He held onto a stainless-steel field sink next to the stove. The camp cook came in then, an old Mexican guy named Jorge Rodriguez. Jorge was also the hired lead digger. Jorge gave Mede the cut-neck hand signal. Callahan was coming.

Mede brought his man Jorge on all his digs. The cook got to work while Mede directed each one to his day's work. Some of the interns got busy helping with food. Soon, everyone was occupied.

John tried to be causal while eyeballing the chair next to Mede. Mede was busy attacking his pile of eggs and potatoes. John didn't have an appetite. He slid in next to Mede uninvited.

"Dr. Mede, have you read this Kenny Parks blogger before?"

"Kenny Parks, every post. He's a high school student—brilliant. Fantastic insights, he's right more than wrong. He's better than any freshmen at Old U." Mede cast his eyes toward the freshmen's table. "He answers questions on the forum page. I try to stump him, but he's good. Still, he goes way out on a limb."

A plate of bacon passed down the long table and Mede took a large helping. He stuffed a strip into his mouth before continuing.

"If you care about your career, you won't take theoretical leaps based on thin evidence," Mede said. He shoved more food into his mouth. "Like that kid, Parks."

Mede was a good observer, nobody read the ground as well, save Jorge. Mede also read people and he read them between their lines quite well. Odd talent for a shovel-bum, John thought.

"What's up, John, you look like you saw an anomaly." Mede asked.

"I had Kenny as a student. He told me something to look out for…It's nothing. That reminds me. I must have left my good brush up there when we setup T-tot for the helicopter lift. What hill was that again?"

"Number six. What a bad ass hill that was, steep approach," Mede said. "Not a lot of room to work."

"Bad ass, BA…I better go and see if my brush is up there before work starts."

John got up with his head reeling. Mede grabbed his arm and pulled him down, bending John close. Mede lowered his speaking volume.

"If you see Callahan," Mede paused to scratch his beard. He did that whenever disturbed. "See him or he sees you, go the other way. You get me?"

"I think so."

John turned to go. The cook stood close behind them. He must have heard. Jorge winked at John before turning back to the stove.

That's weird.

Old U had wired the dig for live internet cameras. Tech students ran the satellite link, the computers, and the camp's power system. When the generator ran, the world watched them dig.

It was a PR move. John thought the tech student program on-site wasted dig money. It occurred to John that Kenny must have been watching BA hill along with thousands of others. Web feeds around the site made it harder for Callahan to act like an ass but he found ways.

John stopped at his camper to grab his homemade excavation kit and a light mason's hammer. Equipped, he hurried to Hill Six. Kenny's BA Hill.

Callahan was nowhere in sight. John climbed the crumbling matrix of BA Hill with his chest pounding. The grid pins had been removed. He went straight to the divot where T-tot was plastered in place. They had mudded him for removal where he lay. John opened his kit, took a dull screwdriver, and scratched where the little dino had been. The camera was still there, but he didn't think it mattered. This hilltop was tapped out. The cameras shouldn't be running and he felt glad for that. He didn't want to look stupid in front of his colleges and lose this job.

Intent on his work, John didn't hear the generator firing. A few minutes into it, he found an egg, then another. His gut wrenched. *Just like Kenny said.* All around fern and twig impressions, this was a nest. The entire top of this hill was eighteen feet around and descended ten feet to the trackway—all the same color.

"This hilltop's a giant nest! Holy crap."

John rocked back on his heels thinking this place must have been used for generation after generation and thus got bigger and taller with each new layer of fresh lining. *Why didn't I see it before?*

"Looks like she had an appetite for eggs, of course."

John twisted. Callahan leered at him. The giant extended a hand and pulled John up like a bundle of dried sticks. Big John's grip was painful. Callahan pushed some dirt into the egg-bearing hole with his size 14 army boot.

"No need to play with Diplodocus eggs. They are as common as dirt. We have Tyrannosauruses to find."

Callahan's voice was cold and steady. Adjunct employee John Black felt a chill of academic menace behind it. *I know Rex eggs when I see them.*

"I'll cover them for another day," Callahan kicked in another clod. "Get going, Black. I'll take care of it."

John had never seen the man with a shovel in his hands before. Maybe the camera was on? John marched straight back to base camp. He was hot, tired, dirty, and disconcerted. The more he thought about Callahan the more John's usual good nature collapsed. When he got to the mess tent, he struggled but still resisted ripping the tent-flap open like a hungry velociraptor. Students should still be inside and that would be bad.

He entered with a stiff jaw but nobody was there except the cook. John thought it odd that the dig supervisor was still there and not at the dig where he belonged. John felt a new tinge of anger, that old man was too close to Mede. Jorge was an unqualified hanger-on wasting grant money. He wasn't even a good cook. The inequities of life were piling higher.

Mede is in charge. He should fire Big John and that cook, too.

"Where is he, Jorge?" John was aware his voice seethed and he let it.

Jorge put a finger to his lips and pointed to his ear. "Boss is scouting north gully on his way to Dig One, si, si. He will be there soon."

Jorge pointed to the back of the tent with his chin. There was a ravine back that way, out of camera range. It's where the students went to smoke pot, or make out, and everything else that the paid staff wasn't supposed to do. Every Old U dig had students and it was always the same. Digs always have the traditional no-teacher zone. Professors will politely look away. Jorge pointed his chin at the tent's back wall with more force.

"Sorry, señor. He has gone," Jorge tossed the side of his head at the back wall.

"That's fine. I'll catch up with him later. I'm going to Three anyway," John said.

Jorge turned around and cleaned the cast iron griddle with an oil stone, no oil. It screeched like a mating raptor. John ducked under the tarp and descended the narrow ravine which opened into a wide wash. Dr. Mede was down range scratching at the rock in his hand with a straight brass pick. John marched up pointing a finger.

"I have a bone to pick with you—"

"That's why I hired you, my boy. Can you dig it?" Mede said.

He laughed and slapped a pant leg. A joke? Mede never joked. It took John aback, which snuffed his wick but not his complaint. Mede's expression turned dark.

"What is it, son?"

"Callahan covered Rex eggs…told me to get lost." John took a breath. "T-tot was guarding a nest. That entire mound, generations built it…T-tot was sitting on eggs. You saw how it was positioned. It was a T-rex family, a pride…lions! It's important. It's—"

"It's off the table, son." Mede put the pick back into the pocket-protector inside his safari vest's breast pocket. "I know, I saw it. You'll find in this business—you are new, of course—that if you want a career…Certain things our donors are concerned with won't come to light, not if you value your neck."

John exhaled aghast.

"But this is a major discovery! This could be published. It's—"

"It's not worth your life, John." Mede patted John on the shoulder. "There'll be others. Things slip through. They can't man every dig. They show when they think there's something important. How they know, I don't know. Next season, there won't be a generational T-rex nest here to study. I had hoped to keep that cat in the bag awhile."

John fell to his knees. He had screwed Mede's plan to keep Callahan off the find. John wanted to ask who Callahan is but he didn't get the chance. The man came up from behind Mede out of another ravine. John heard his boots crunching gravel before he saw him. Mede had that same rock in his hand.

"See anymore?" Mede said. "I think you may be right. It could well be a baby rex coprolite. Good eye Black. Big John, what do you make of this?"

Callahan took the specimen. The man wore an antique Jeweler's glass on a silver chain around his neck. It was a pretty thing of flora-engraved silver and not effective. Nineteenth-century technology was useless here. Big John looked like Cyclops reading the bumps on Jason the Argonaut's head.

"Yes, I see. That could be," Callahan mumbled. "I don't think it warrants further research, but log it for future study."

"Of course. Good idea, Professor Callahan," Mede said with tight lips. "I'll make a note."

He took a little notebook and a sample bag out of a leg pocket and pretended to write. Callahan turned and headed upslope. John Black played along and pushed dirt around with his finger. Mede had a long history of good finds, some very uncanny. John wondered how many more he should have published.

Callahan proceeded toward camp. Mede helped John to his feet.

"This sample is junk," Mede said and handed the specimen to John.

John didn't need to look closely to know it wasn't a coprolite, wrong color and consistency for the location. It was a fossilized plant stem. Many such samples tumble down to lower elevations as they erode out. Such things were everywhere. John marched back up the ravine with a new appreciation of his position and confirmation that Kenny was right. But how did Kenny know?

That night in the mess tent, John pulled up Kenny's blog but the post about T-rex family pride was gone. He went to the chat room to ask around. The moderator's chat window popped in on his screen. He didn't instant message the moderator.

The message read, "Saw him cover the eggs. He'll pay. I'll tell you where something good is next time."

The window vanished.

John tried to respond but Callahan came into the tent. It was time to shut the generator down anyway. John got up and went to his camper and opened the pint of good whiskey he was saving to celebrate his first big find.

"Here's to you, Kenny Parks."

John intended to drink up, get blasted, and drown his disappointment. But rather, he set the bottle aside after a few sips on realizing no amount of drink could relieve the bitter taste that the name Callahan left in his mouth.

*****

Kenny didn't mind his travels. When he wanted, when things were not nice mostly, he could go and he did. The dinosaurs weren't glad to see him. Oh no. Not anything like Mr. Black happy, but they didn't mind Kenny either. Kenny wasn't stupid, oh no, he didn't go all the way in mostly. Mostly, he liked to watch.

He knew them all by name and he knew about many others that other smart people like him didn't know at all...yet—to be discovered! He always avoided the other smart people. And, oh yes, Kenny, you could go, too, if you wanted. He said that to himself a lot. He did, too, but never stayed long.

Die there and there you are forever. But it was safe unless you got stepped on. Even big predators had pea brains. They ran on instinct and if you didn't smell like something they ate, they'd leave you alone, long as you didn't do something dumb like run, or get too close to a nest, or hang around after you make poop. Poop is a magnet—if it poops, it's food.

That idea always made him laugh. Everyone at Assembly laughed, too, when he read his science paper at school.

Lately, Kenny didn't want to go away. Oh no. He has a blog spot! On a real dino blog and people ask him about things and he tells them. People on the airwaves need him a lot, a real lot. He saw Mr. Black and that dirty CIA man. *I'll fix him.* Computers are easy. He follows threads. He looks at people on their cameras and phones like the CIA. He watches Pete "The Blaster" a lot, and some of the other kids, too. When Kenny goes away, they leave. Easy breezy.

But that Pete, oh no, he won't let up, and it was Pete's fault anyway. In the future, the CIA man will ask, "How did you discover sending people back?"

Kenny wasn't stupid in the future. He played dumb. That was smart. He won't tell them years from now when they figure it out anyway.

In the future, he told the President. Kenny goes walking in the school's hallways really fast. That's what he does. Mr. Webber let him go one minute, just one minute, always one, just one, before the bell. Oh, he would fly. He walked so fast, not run, you're not allowed to run in the hall, oh no, 'don't you run in the hall.' Everyone says so.

Kenny was booking. Around the corner, Pete jumped out, and too late to stop. Kenny jumped away into the Jurassic because he was thinking about it for his blog. They crashed and Pete came along.

Kenny was there with a giant spider four feet across spinning in a dead tree. It caught a tree-glider, a reptile the size of a cat. The glider was getting spun into a ball. Fascinating, but something was distracting Kenny. Something was screaming. Was it the flying reptile? Nope, it was dumb, stupid Pete.

"This is my place, no Pete allowed," Kenny said and went back.

There were people there waiting at school. It was a real short trip. They both landed on the ground where they crashed. People wanted them to go to the nurse, but the mom the adoption agency gave to Kenny won't like, it, oh no.

Pete didn't want to go. Oh, no. He didn't like it, either. He messed in his pants. Pete ran to the restroom. People left Kenny alone. That was good.

The first time, last fall, the first time, that Kenny sent somebody else. It was the year after Mr. Black left. That's when Kenny learned the trick. He had found another door. Oh, yes. Easy Breezy.

*****

"Why'd you let that Webber-tard off, man, graduation is here," Ralph said. "Get it while you can."

Ralph was a junior and set to take over the crew next year. That kid was always rattling on full of crap. Randy lost his balls and bugged out. Ralph was getting too big for his britches. Pete was glad he was graduating.

"Don't you want-a mess over that Webber-tard?" Ralf said.

Pete didn't have an answer. *Say what? Yo man I'm scared. No way.*

Pete didn't know if his trip with Kenny was real or not, or if that moron doped him somehow. Every time he screwed with that Special-Ed kid, he'd fall into a bad nightmare and snap out of it screaming. It was way too real. Mom freaked out. The doctor said it was seizures. Dad slapped him around for it, too.

Yesterday it got worse. Dared to do it, he tripped Kenny at lunch. The kid smiled like a creepy idiot. Thank God he didn't do anything else. That face was the worst, it creeped Pete out. That a-hole plucked his nerves raw.

Kenny was the last thing he wanted to see this morning. Ralph started yapping but Pete didn't hear him.

At home, yesterday afternoon, Pete checked his email like always. There was an email from his account like he had mailed it to himself. *Weird.* He opened it. Kenny had to have done it. It said, "Are you ready for the Permian Extinction?"

Then it started, and he couldn't move. He was in a swamp full of insects the size of cows, and he was there for real, but just long enough to get wet. Boom, he was back in his chair covered in mud. He made the carpet a soaking mess. Mom was pissed.

That was last night. Pete drifted back to reality. Ralph was talking.

"Finals next week. Webber's crew won't be here. Make your move. You a pussy or what?"

Pete just couldn't back down. No way. "Watch what happens at lunch."

Next period came and went and Pete wasn't up on hitting the cafeteria. He planned to skip out, but he got swept up with the gang and they flooded into lunch together. They got food, ate, and did what they do, spitballs and insults flew but Ralph didn't forget.

"Go for it. You're the man," Ralf said. "Me and Bing will distract the Teach, lay that mo-fo down, bro."

Pete got up slow, took up his backpack in half-time, and dragged ass toward Webber's table. Bing and Ralf took their trays up. Bang! Crash! They knocked the pile over and started a fake fight. Kenny stood up and took a step forward.

"Don't touch me, look, Ken, old buddy. Let's talk. I—"

"Don't run when you get there," Kenny said.

"It's like this, Ken. The guys will think I'm a puss. Can you do me a favor and play like I'm messing with you? But I'm not. We're friends now see, and—"

"You can live there. Plenty to eat, but don't run. Nothing shiny is good. Shiny attracts them." Kenny pointed at Pete's cell phone.

"We good, you and me? Right, pal?" Pete said. He took half a step back.

"If you don't smell like the food they know, they won't eat you. Just remember about poop."

Kenny held out his arms, stepping closer quickly, and hugged Pete. Pete, surprised, didn't back up. He landed in the late Cretaceous. There was a volcano venting hot gas nearby and a lush little valley around him. He stood on a huge nest made of piles of sticks and ferns. At his feet lay huge eggs. A two-legged raptor jumped and landed right in front of him on the other side of the nest. It stood Dad's size—six feet tall.

"Don't run. Don't run. Don't move," spilled from his chattering teeth.

It's big lizard-head cocked. It's nose holes pulsated as it swayed back and forth. Pete heard its big nostrils sucking air. Droughts of air ramming down its snout-holes rushed like a wind tunnel. If a monster could look puzzled, it would look like that—a German Sheppard reacting to a dog whistle.

"Oh shit, oh shit! Nice doggy."

It jumped across the nest. Green cat-eyes hung at Pete's face-level, snot dripping, slime hanging off its teeth, rotting fish-breath worse than Randy's. Pete squeezed his butt cheeks but his bowels opened anyway. He remembered what Kenny said at Assembly. "T-rex won't eat what he doesn't know. Poop they know. If it poops, it is food."

"Oh, shit—"

It happened in one blinding motion. Young Rex came on hard, head first smashing Pete's face. Pete's front teeth flew out in several directions. T-tot took Pete by the shoulder and tossed him off the nest leaving the backpack behind.

Pete landed thirty yards away in a ditch full of mud and giant piles of shit. He hit head-first but survived for a little while. He felt himself passing out. He fought it. He thought if he closed his eyes, he'd never wake up again. It was the first and last well-reasoned thought he had.

*****

That strange bi-ped was a missed opportunity, Tot thought. It could have been a nice meal. Its weak bones were digestible. They broke easily. But he, the little one, was left at home for a purpose. He guarded the nest while the rest of his family were away hunting. He was told to stay in the nest and he wasn't going to argue. He obeyed orders, but he wanted food. He tore the backpack to shreds seeking edibles.

He swallowed that plastic diplodocus Pete forgot was in his pack along with Pete's meatloaf sandwich.

The toy didn't digest. Rex's gastro system had no fauna that could deal with plastics. T-tot didn't even know when or where he passed it out. But someone knew.

The next day the hunting party returned, dragging the hind quarter of a hadrosaur. The pride's top female indicated T-tot earned his meal and let him have it alone. The body in the ditch was already rotten. The Matriarch sniffed the thing, thought it was vaguely familiar, but decided it wasn't worth eating. When rain fell that night, that odd creature washed down into a deep catch with the other discarded undesirable parts of meals. Bone pit ten gained more fill.

*****

By late spring of season two, the dig was going well. Everyone settled into a routine. The only interruption was the disappearance of Big John Callahan.

Callahan's camper and all his effects were left in place. The National Park Service thought he had wondered too far from camp and got lost, which wasn't uncommon in the Badlands. Three days after Callahan went AWOL, a tow truck followed by a black SUV came. Men in black suits—federal investigators they said gathered everything belonging to Callahan and vanished. John didn't see any of their ID cards.

Hot weather came on hard the day after the feds left and Callahan was soon forgotten. John arrived for breakfast an hour before dawn a week after the Callahan affair. Because of the heat early starts and afternoon naps became the order of operations.

John had taken up following the Shovel Bum blog which hosted a lot of different people posting essays. Most of it was interesting, but Kenny's stuff was what John wanted. Kenny wrote poorly with too much repetition which made it hard to read. Even so, Kenny wrote important things. His insights and conclusions, based on the available evidence, were sharp and logical. John thought the kid must follow all the top digs and read the latest academic papers.

Mede and Jorge Rodriguez were in a corner deep in talk. The generator was running and John didn't hear them. Jorge was busy with Mede so food wasn't coming anytime soon.

John felt a tinge of jealousy. How could an old laborer and the good doctor have such an intimate relationship? John wanted to get closer to the headman and not just for career possibilities. Mede wasn't like most other academics who came and went. Mede wasn't an ego-meister, never nasty with younger people.

Food wasn't cooking, so John booted his laptop. An instant message popped onto his screen.

"Move camera six, ten degrees south and down two degrees. Big find today," appeared on John's screen.

Somebody's idea of a joke? Mede's computer was left open, so John got up, rounded the table, and checked Mede's screen. Mede didn't see it. It was the same crap. John scanned the few others in-house drinking coffee and reading computers, and none of them reacted. Turning back to the computer, the message was gone.

"Anyone else get hacked?" John called.

Nobody answered in the affirmative. He glanced back at his computer and the message was gone there as well. He was about to head for Mede anyway, to try and get on the old man's good side, but changed his mind and blew it off as unimportant.

Next season's team wasn't decided yet and John wanted in. Just as John relaxed back into his seat, Jorge took off like his hair was on fire. He almost knocked over the geologist as she entered. Mede, meantime, came and closed his laptop while looking around John as if John were blocking Mede's view.

"Janis, your turn to cook," Mede said so everyone heard. "Quick, now eat and clean up. It'll be a hot one today."

Janis the geologist and Bob the intern started by cracking eggs into a stainless-steel bowl. A student got the bacon going which watered John's mouth. He would like better food, but the bacon's salt was needed. More people filed in, and the place came alive with conversations, popping toasters, and hurried food consumption. John and Van, the new guy, went over the dig plan and John forgot about that odd instant message.

John and Mede lagged, as usual. They were supervising staff and not shovel labor. Students did the majority of the digging. John enjoyed getting personal with dirt and missed rooting around in rocks and soil. Things were organized, so he and Mede ambled toward the dig together in no hurry. The sun topped the horizon as they made their way.

Mede's face showed he was in thinking mode. John shouldn't broach the subject of next season, but such was the life of an adjunct—he had no choice but to go begging for the next gig. John interrupted Mede.

"Doctor, I wanted to ask you about—"

"Not now, Professor Black, I know, I know, dig's winding down, your time is coming. Now let me think."

They walked on in silence. The day's project was more of the same, exploring a wash below and south of where they found T-tot. They were in an old water run-off channel deposit that had captured and forced materials into a catch. Layered sediments of mud were evident meaning the water flowed seasonally. Over time, it became clay which in turn became shale, shale littered with T-rex footprints of all sizes and, apparently, contemporaneous. There must have been a water hole or spring near and John thought today was the day they'd find it. That dangerous idea, that T-rex was a pride keeper, lingered in his thoughts. "New evidence is best presented in baby steps," Mede had said and John agreed in principle.

They arrived at first light. Jorge was already busy. Students were scratching and brushing along the old creek bed and all working in the same general location. It wasn't the place John would have picked.

Jorge is on the wrong track.

"Hey, Pros Black's here," Sara from media studies said with too much enthusiasm.

She seldom used the word professor. All staff was Pros or Prof. to her. John didn't care for it. As the media student that ran the live feed, Sara often ran onsite live reports. That wasn't John's concern and he generally avoided her. Paleontology wasn't her major.

Sara marched up to him waving a computer tablet, "Pros, how about a few words for the blogosphere?" Sara asked with force, making it hard to ignore her.

"Sure, why not?" John said, thinking how over the top she is.

She motioned John to get in front of the camera, which was mounted on a tripod, but he had an idea. He had her adjust it to capture the freshly-placed dig grid made of ropes suspended between pins. Sara had a tablet-cam and monitored the picture as things were moved. Beyond the grid, a student in the background brushed a footprint where a patch of shale protruded out from under a sandstone layer. She showed him the shot on her tablet.

"Okay, Pros, move left…A little back…There you are! One, two, three… action! Take it away Professor John Black."

"Fine, thanks, Sara. Hello, shovel bums. Today we hope to find a water source or some other reason why so many T-rexes left their prints here. As you can see, check our website for detailed stills, T-rex crossed paths often in this area. Was it mating behavior? Why all ages? So far there are no indications of bird-like dance displays as others have noted regarding other species on other digs. Thanks to blogger Kenny Parks for posting that article. Check our blog at Old U. for more on the latest theories regarding raptor mating behaviors. Thanks, Sara."

John started to go back to work, but she wasn't done.

"Pros, can you show us your picking techniques? Demonstrate for us how you look at the ground. Can ya explain what you see? I'll bring the tab-cam in close. We're going split screen."

"Right-o, to use Doctor Mede's phrase," John said. "Let's move away from the active search grid for this demonstration."

He didn't want to disturb the work in progress and picked a spot to show her his techniques behind and off to one side of the work area. She adjusted the fixed camera's angle southward and further downrange.

He bent to the ground and unrolled his canvas tool organizer. John was proud of his homemade kit. He didn't mind showing it but Sara stopped him before he could extoll the virtues of his fine-excavation set.

"Pros, can you go back up a bit? More left."

"Sure thing."

Sara worked her hand-cam and switched the camera view back and forth between close shots and long shots from the mounted webcam. The whole time she talked to the live audience, if there was one. Who would get up this early to watch people dig holes? John asked himself. She moved in and showed him her tablet's view. She filmed and talked while he unpacked his field kit, for the second time.

John spread his tools around. The spot was adjacent to a likely piece of ground he was interested in. On Sara's cue, he talked about how he used what he had and why. His kit consisted of a clever combination of household items, wood carving tools, tiny demolition bars, dental picks, soft and hard bristle brushes, a pocket knife, and a light mason's hammer.

"Okay, Pros. Show us your stuff in action."

"The matrix is soft here, so I'll begin with a medium stiff brush like so."

"That's good, Pros."

Sara moved in closer with the handheld video camera.

"Look at that, a coprolite, and it could be a young T-rex." He brushed more and started with a small dental pick. "Yes, definitely raptor feces. See the bits of bone? This looks remarkably like a human tooth."

John picked at the base material around the tooth and dropped his tool. John reeled back onto his butt. He never saw a tooth like it. Could it be a new species? He got himself turned around feeling lucky. It struck him that this discovery was on a live webcam.

"Let's see the gatekeepers disappear this," John whispered.

"What's that, Pros?"

He didn't answer. Excited, he started excavating around the specimen by scratching away at the soil too hard and too fast with a hard pick. He wanted that coprolite out of the ground and on camera before somebody like Callahan showed up to kick dirt on it. Back in the field lab, they'll x-ray it. When he was ready to pull it, he motioned Sara to come in close with the camera.

"This is the big moment," John said.

John heard the lens' motor whirl. Sara zoomed in with both hands on her cam. John examined it in place a moment longer. It appeared to be a fine example, not smashed or broken, just as it was deposited seventy million years ago, a very lucky find, that tooth protruding out of the coprolite wasn't a known species. He felt sure of it.

"This can't miss. It's still in situ."

John had his fingers on it ready to lift the entire coprolite out of the matrix when Mede came up. Mede bent over John's shoulder and whispered, "I told you, your luck would change."

John lifted out the coprolite with care. It broke in half anyway. Within it, a tiny face stared back. It resembled diplodocus but it was thirty times smaller than any egg-bound sample of that creature can be. The lens' motor strained.

"What am I looking at?" John blurted out in his shock.

"Plastic toy," Mede said.

Mede walked away chuckling.

*****

Staff agreed it was a modern lost toy and nothing more. John didn't agree but he kept his mouth shut. Rather than argue the impossible, John left the site that night and drove his class-C camper all night going back to Woodberry, outside of Chicago.

Kenny would be at summer school. All of Webber's kids had summer school. But didn't Kenny graduate? He made it to the teacher's parking lot and slept in his camper all weekend. He was ready when the school opened Monday. John didn't sign in. He had a bad feeling about it. Mr. Webber drove in with that same old, faded Volvo. John intercepted him in the parking lot.

"Mr. Webber? It's me, John Black."

"Well good to see you, lad. What brings—"

"Kenny. Kenny Parks. Do you still have him?"

Webber's face looked puzzled before he backed up, wide-eyed. John took it down a notch. He had to come up with a story fast so he spits it out.

"Kenny wrote me, said he was in trouble, and—"

"I'll say, the FBI came and picked him up, right after graduation. I haven't seen him since. It seems his stepmother and Pete Brenner went missing. They think it's him."

"Guess I'll contact the FBI. You know, follow up," John muttered, not knowing what he should do.

"Don't do that, John," Webber searched the lot, as if he feared being watched. "I was warned. You should go. I never saw you."

Webber turned and rushed on toward the school. He had gone pale on the mention of the name Kenny Parks.

John, spooked, got back into his truck and went back to Badlands National Park. But he drove slowly, thoughtfully. When he got to camp late afternoon the next day, Mede was in the lab and didn't say a word about John's sudden departure.

"It is nice to have a special helper in your career corner, isn't that so?" Mede nodded at Jorge as he said it. "Good finds can slip through the cracks. The trick is knowing how to grease the cracks."

Mede splayed his hands.

"I don't understand. What are they afraid of?"

"I don't know," Mede said, "It could be they can't admit to past sins. That would upset their carefully controlled public perception of reality. They'll never admit T-rex evolved higher intelligence, for example. You didn't hear me say that."

"I see your point, Doctor Mede. Mind if I help you with that?"

Mede didn't answer. John didn't need one. John picked up a mini rotary tool that ran on batteries and started removing the matrix from a crocodilian jaw bone. Mindless jobs helped him relax.

*****

Five years passed and Kenny's blog had dried up. Mede had retired a few years ago but Jorge stayed with Old U a bit longer. Mede's recommendation was a career boost for John. He was still only an adjunct, but one working steadily. Old Man Mede's former dig master had an eye for finds which didn't hurt John's career.

By working with Jorge, John got to know the older man well. Five good years went by smoothly with important but small finds popping up every season until one day Jorge quit without explanation early in the dig season. John's expert digger left Old U's service never to return. John assumed the better finds had dried up and Jorge lost interest. A week after Jorge's departure emails started coming that gave suggestions. Was it Jorge? The sender didn't give a name. More good finds followed through the season. The mind-blowing finds John had uncovered weren't welcome. John only pursued what was acceptable.

John got back to the Badlands after a short break to find an email waiting for him at breakfast. John's site and surrounding area had been renamed Rex City. The email header said, "Big find in Rex City." John opened it and read out loud.

"I have a gift for you, under the juniper, sixteen inches."

Odd, John thought, there aren't any junipers here. It had to be Jorge, but the tone sounded like Kenny Parks.

John had to think hard. There was one juniper he recalled. A tiny bush. How it survived in this place would be an interesting question for a botanist but not for him. Even so, he decided to have a look.

He found the bush down-range a mile from BA-Hill. John dug out the plant, tossed it aside, and kept going. He felt compelled although he had no reason to feel that way. Before long he found himself excavating the upper gut of an adult T-rex. A rib bone led him in. He should have stopped, but he kept going. In the hole, at sixteen inches, he found a jeweler's loop. It was silver tarnished back. The glass was gone but he made out a faint flora engraving on its frame surface. John swallowed and took a breath.

"Kenny," he whispered.

Kenny's crack about Callahan rushed to mind. *I'll make him pay.* One of the students walked up and peered over John's shoulder.

"Holy Cow, it's metal, there can't be metal inside a dinosaur. I don't believe it. If this is real…Oh my god! Aliens, I bet."

"Relax, Danny, it's a geo-cache. Somebody buried it," John said, thinking fast.

"But I watched you dig it out, undisturbed soil, and…and…It's aliens. Gotta be."

The boy's red-face drained to pale. John Black laughed. "Ever read Kenny Park's blog? Someone goes around and does this. They use a portable microwave device to stitch the soil back into a passable brackera. It's a trick."

Danny Peterson looked dejected. "I'm so dumb."

John put on a better face. He hoped it was believable. He wanted to be kind to the young man. He wasn't one to embarrass students. The kid had to feel crushed.

"You're fine, Danny. I wasn't making fun of you. Somebody worked hard at this deception. Had you dug it yourself, you'd have felt the softness of the earth. You'll get the hang of it."

The kid looked relieved. John didn't see any light bulbs go off. Good.

Dr. John had a knack for making students welcome and it paid dividends. John thought some repayments were not yet realized and were "yet to be discovered," as Kenny liked to say. The important thing for John was to protect his students. The boy didn't seem convinced.

"Danny, you have a good eye. I'm sure you will do well."

Time was funny, John thought. It works both ways. Everything comes back around. Giving good gets good back at you, in time. Sometimes it takes a long while. The gifts one Special Ed student gave him proved it. Kenny's hints never failed. That email had to be from Kenny.

"Danny, go back up to the main dig. I'll fill in this hole and follow."

Watching the boy go, John wondered if that antique eyepiece was once a gift given to Big John Callahan. He had his doubts. People didn't give bullies nice things.

"Callahan probably pinched it," John said, rolling it in his hand.

John noticed a human finger bone in the spoils and kicked it into the hole. He covered it over with dirt. He shoved the rest of the dirt over the spot and replanted the bush, just in case.

"No point in fooling with it, but why not plant a seed?"

Professor Black decided to sit with Danny's class group at lunch. Nothing unusual about that. Funny how Danny found him so far from the main dig. Why was this second-year student, who knows better than to wander off into the wilderness alone, a mile down range when he should have been elsewhere? Danny didn't know. He said he was 'just drawn' there. John felt he and Danny were on the same path but the boy had no way of knowing. One must be careful. Kenny's words echoed in John's mind. *Yet to be discovered.* John decided to follow Mede's example and keep a protective eye on Danny.

SAME-DAY EYE SERVICE

Bob worked at home like most other computer people at RobotCore. A work place injury was the last thing he expected.

The Ghost Hunter's manager was on the news last night claiming his client, the scammer, had died by otherworldly means. The manager was to come on television's *Morning Live! Show* to explain his version of events. The show was due to come on soon and Bob didn't want to miss it. Bob thought the manager did the murder and Bob wanted to see the interview. Mysterious claims made him laugh. Bob enjoyed debunking spiritual idiots. Logical deduction was his passion.

Morning break, he put the TV on with seconds to spare and rushed into the kitchen to start the coffee-maker. He ran with his company-issued pen in hand. Everyone got a fancy pen at Christmas. Entering wearing only socks on his feet, he slipped and fell face-first, hands out, and speared an eye with his RobotCore pen.

The injury was caused by company property on company time. He had a solid work-injury claim. Luck was with Bob. Big Roy's Walk-In ER, newly opened, was only half a block away.

"They'll take anybody's employee insurance."

Bob wasted no time. He arrived moaning and holding a hanky over his eye within minutes. No doubt the pierced eye was dead. Even with one good but tearful eye, he could see the place was mobbed. He pulled his insurance card anyway.

A hostess nurse wearing a white ten-gallon cowboy hat saw him in the lobby foyer. Clipboard in hand, she made a beeline to him.

"I see your problem. Happens all the time around here," she said. "People shouldn't run with scissors."

Bob half expected her to spit tobacco juice.

"It was a pen," he said.

Pointing a thumb sideways, she said, "Next door. Same Day Eye Service is right next door. We'll send you there anyway. They ain't busy. Let me see that."

She snapped up the insurance card he held out. How the bill gets paid is always the first question medical processors ask. She handed it back right quick. Host nurses are insurance experts, after all.

"Yup, you're covered," she said, "I'll call Same Day for you."

The eye care joint took Bob in right away. The girl at the check-in desk took the usual information saving the medical options for last.

"Ya want a mechanical eye or a human eye? We used to do pig eyes but nobody wants them anymore, ya know."

"I never thought about it," Bob said. "I work in robotics. You'd think I'd go for the robotic... but, well...I think I want a human eye. Why not? Insurance covers it, right?"

"Yeah, sure. Let me show you what we got. It ain't much." The girl messed around on her computer. "Say, you're in luck. If ya want, we got a fresh human. A nice one came in this morning, just cleared inspection." She flipped a smaller screen over to him. "We got lots of mechanicals, too. Any mods ya like, we got. Today's your lucky day."

They didn't have many human eyes in stock, but that one eye, the newest arrival, matched his color. Just a half shade off his blue. They didn't have any other blues. He was indeed lucky to find one at all and the right color, too.

"How many donor eyes are out there floating around? There can't be many," Bob said.

"Got that right," the sales girl said.

He still needed to think about it. Bob wasn't fashionable. The kids go around in weird unmatched eye colors but that wasn't his style. The color was off somehow, but then again, it had to be better than a robotic eye. Nobody will notice. Bob could tell the difference between a fake eye and a real one any day, he thought. He had worked on eye programs before joining RobotCore.

He touched the screen making his selection. "That one looks right to me."

"Good choice, sir. You're in luck. That one's a perfect match."

The procedure went well. He got a week of paid medical leave but he felt fine. Bored, he did a little bit of light work that afternoon wearing the eyepatch. Same Day Eye Service provided an unconditional three-day return. No questions asked. After the satisfaction warrantee was up a replacement would have to come out of his pocket. He wore the patch overnight as directed but was eager to try out the new eye so he took the patch off sooner than prescribed.

More weird building sounds than usual had rattled the ducts last night. Bob didn't get much sleep and woke a little blurry. It took a minute for his new eye to adjust.

The man upstairs worked in the paranormal research department at RobotCore and was always fooling around at night with ghost calls and other strange things. What a riot. Bob pretty much slept through it most of the time but last night was rough.

Same Day Eye Service said he could use the computer a little with two eyes the day after installation so he did. He was told not to do anything visually intense. He put relaxing nature images on the screen with smooth-jazz music. The doctor said to take it easy. If the light bothered him, he was to wear the eyepatch. Bob tried watching deer prancing in a meadow but horrible imagines of dead WWI trench-soldiers kept bleeding into his peaceful video. The music sounded as if a live audience were there and horrified by it. This was very annoying.

He gave up and put on the TV. Same problem. Bloody people, zombies, and all kinds of B-movie representations kept bleeding in. It wasn't the TV or computer. He wasn't crazy. His annual psychology test had come back good. He slipped the patch back over his eye and the sideshow vanished.

"I'll be a prosimian's uncle."

It had to be the eye. He pondered it. Perhaps mechanical mods were added to the donor's eye—but they would have told him that. Maybe they didn't know, maybe it had enhancements when they got it. Maybe they didn't check it for add-on devices. There's no truth in advertising but giving away expensive hardware for promotions, without telling, didn't add up. Occam's razor. Somebody screwed up and gave away free mods without knowing it.

Free or not, Bob didn't like it. If he wanted mods, he would have asked for them. But what if it's not that? What if something other caused the eye's ghost visuals?

"Maybe it's quantum."

Bob currently designed robotic pneumatic systems and related practical applications, but he loved theoretical math. If ghosts did manifest it would have to be a multiverse phenomenon. Spirits weren't real, but maybe…Quantum mechanics buzzed around in his mind, that is, until he scratched his head and the eyepatch slipped off. A pirate with a hatchet buried in his skull came at Bob swinging a cutlass. Bob covered his eye. The apparition disappeared.

"This must have driven the guy who had this eye crazy."

Bob called Same Day Eye Service and made and appointment for the next day. He was told to leave the eyepatch on and he did.

The next morning Bob sat down with the eye care specialist at Same Day Eye Service and made his request.

"I don't like this eye," Bob said. "I want something else."

The girl looked offended. Bob wasn't the fussy kind, but that eye just wasn't right. Having no eye was better than that defective eye. He often rolled over for pretty sales girls, but not this time.

"Whatcha don't like about it?" She pouted her lips.

"Never mind that. The ad said money back guarantee—"

"Alright, alright. I'm only asking so we don't make that mistake again, alright? Whatcha gonna do with the eye?

"Eye? Oh, the old new eye. I never gave it any thought, I—"

"We gotta buy-back program ya know…pays 500."

Bob couldn't say no. Not only did Same Day Eye Service give him a free electronic eye, the latest thing, but they also paid him too. Checking post-op a few hours later, he didn't see any difference. The replacement unit matched perfectly. He didn't know why he wanted a human donor eye in the first place. The idea was creepy in hindsight. The new one looked great and felt better. The procedure went fast because the socket-adaptor was already in place from the other eye. After an hour under the knife and two hours in recovery, he felt fit and ready.

Bob left Same Day and saw Phil a little way down the block on the sidewalk heading his way. Phil, a company man, was the guy that lived above him on the second floor. Nice guy. Phil held a frozen porkchop over one eye with one hand and he had a bloody RobotCore pen in the other hand. He didn't look good.

"What happened?" Bob asked.

"Slipped in the kitchen, put this pen through my eye. Going to Big Roy's ER."

"Tough break. Don't bother with Roy's. They'll send you to Same Day Eye Service anyway. They aren't busy. I'll show you."

Bob walked Phil to the door and stood by while Phil got a seat with the check-in girl. Seeing Phil was in good hands, Bob went home. He liked the new eye very much. There weren't any ghost images that didn't belong. Nothing but empathy for Phil haunted him.

*****

The girl took Phil's information before they got to brass tacks. He was in a hurry to get treated. He was in pain and didn't want to hear it when the girl pushed the mechanical eye. He told her twice he wasn't interested. He knew what he wanted. Forget robotics. His company worked on that crap. He wanted a real eye but not just any eye. It had to be fresh.

"Alright, alright, let me see what we got." The sales girl dug into her computer. "Ya see that thing in the news about the Great Seer?"

He moaned his answer. He was in no mood for small talk. Phil had studied the Great Seer's career. There was something to it. Too bad the guy kicked off before Phil finished with him. Phil wouldn't accept that guy's three-days-dead eye even if he could get it. What if the dead mystic really did see ghosts?

"Dang, this system," she said. "I swear whenever they load stock…"

Week-old eyes worked just as well as any. But Phil had his superstitions like anyone. He scratched the older ones she mentioned off his list without looking. He refused to take the one from a murder victim. He'd never accept one from a child, either. But he wanted a real eye. Iron in the eye socket was creepy. Real always beat artificial in Phil's book.

The girl kept going on and on about the mechanical units they have in stock as she scrolled until Bob lost his cool. The pain got to him.

"You got human or not? Call a cab. Big Bob's Eye House is giving away free sunglasses—"

"Alright, alright, take it easy. I get ya. Say, look at that. Seems we just got one in, and just now it cleared inspection. Fresh this morning. Green like you. Today's your lucky day."

She pushed the screen around. Phil's one good eye was watering too much. He knew it was better to check the legalities himself but he couldn't read the small print. He liked the eye immediately, though, but he still felt like he had to ask.

"This eye ain't that ghost hunter fellow, is it? I don't want nothing from him."

"Naw, he kicked the bucket three days ago. This came in alive and fresh this morning. You'll have-ta wear a patch for seven days. Ya get paid time off. Is that alright?"

"This is my lucky day, where do I sign?"

Phil felt good after surgery. The company gave him the week off as expected. Phil would never cheat himself and so was determined to keep the patch on as prescribed. Same Day Eye Service even cleaned and returned his RobotCore pen. He felt as if his luck was indeed changing.

SANTA'S SPECIAL GIFT

Santa and Elf Bob surveyed a dingy, desperate home.

Santa froze, tinsel caught his eye, "Well, look at that Bob. Have you ever seen such beautiful ornaments?"

Bob turned from stuffing stockings. "Amazing what they do with beer cans."

"They truly have Christmas hearts despite that drunk who beats them," Santa spit on the carpet. "Disgusting man."

Bob's Nice Meter chimed. "He's on the walkway, you about done?"

"One more item," Santa unsacked a large bottle of strong spirits and set it down.

Bob wagged his finger. "They got it bad enough. He doesn't deserve it. He'll pawn half these gifts."

"My special gift to the family," Santa said. "He will drink it all and die before dawn. Ho, ho, ho, ho."

"They do deserve Christmas peace," Bob stuffed the last item. "The way he sleeps it off, they won't notice he's dead for days."

"Christmas miracles do happen, dear Bob, let us go. He is at the door."

The elves stood by the chimney as a rumpled, violent, drunk staggered in. Only pure hearts can see Christmas magic. The drunkard ignored Santa and the gifts layered under the tree. But he saw the bottle and nothing more...ever again.

OLD LADY BRUISES

Another's note: This nonfiction idea popped into my head as the injury took place so I wrote it after licking my wounds. This was first published by my friend, Angel Ackerman, at Parisian Phoenix Publishing (https://parisianphoenix.com). This is presented as she edited it for her blog—crackerjack editing work in my view.

You've seen them—the old man or old lady—they're everywhere. Molded from the common cast, their forearms look as if they've reached into the jaws of death. But, perhaps, they had only reached for a can of tuna.

You wonder if it's cancer or medication, or another sign of death's encroaching door: liver spots, blotches, pulsing veins, and forearms rasped. Nasty beat-up arm skin. Mechanics working overhead from a grease pit look better.

"What's wrong with these people?" You ask.

I assure you nothing but aging is wrong with these people. At a certain age, skin becomes sensitive. Grandma cooks like a machine at Thanksgiving, bruises and all, doesn't she? She is still fit and able. Our skin gets old before we do.

I have reached a milestone. I just received my first old-lady bruise. I saw it coming but now it's here. I have arrived. I am officially old.

Moving a portable oven, I bushed against a rail, nothing bad, didn't hurt, hardly noticed it. I said to myself, "I wonder if that will leave a bruise?" I went on to think much later, "No, it's fine."

It wasn't fine.

The next day I discovered a purple Rorschach ink blot tattooed on my forearm. The dreaded old-lady bruise had arrived by overnight delivery. I think the Tooth Fairy was involved.

Two quarter-sized blobs surfaced just under my skin. Lesser splotches danced in between. Over the years, the few freckles I had as a kid, reproduced and joined hands. I saw lichen-skin flying in from way off, but then it crash-landed. My spreading freckles—the kings and lords of my aging skin—have abdicated: a new destroyer of skin supplants them.

Paying attention to aging doesn't let it sneak up on you like a unique rabbit. One can feel and see the results of aging as it comes, but how many of us are willing to admit it's here?

Unanticipated realizations strike like a sprained back. Milestones make one face facts…willing or not.

Age happens. It sucks. What you get is old-lady arms, everywhere-hurts, and the hostile take-over of gravity ensues, but also, a deeper understanding of everything comes. The good and the bad are represented by my new, but temporary, tattoos.

I'll wear them badges. I should have used more sunscreen, but then again, some sunscreens have been reported to cause skin cancer.

Sigh.

I thought, "OK, I'll get a real tattoo to celebrate my old ladyhood."

This was, after all, my official coming-of-old-age event—I deserve a real tattoo. But then wisdom reared its logical head and said, "No, you'll get a bruise."

I don't want to get stuck in the bruise or not to bruise loop. I hope my logic chip doesn't age-out but then again…

I'm not ready to give up living. I'll take my lumps and the bruise-tattoos that go with it. That is why we see old, old people out and about with their splotchy wisdom written large. You might wonder how they stay alive. There's more blood under-skin than inside their bodies.

They ain't done yet. That's how.

I just stepped onto life's third rail. I should get a tattoo.

THE LETTER CARRIER

Author's note: This was written for the 2023 GLVWG's anthology ' Writing Across America' which is a themed publication. This will appear, post-editing by them, in a slightly different form than what appears below.

Life in the automation age was predictable even in New York City. Anything out of the ordinary was news. Real news, big news, news to do with important things in the world, wasn't reported, giving that it hurt public morale. Human interest stories were popular and one oddball came to the public's attention.

Working from home like most people, Chelsey Chase sent the juicy stuff in by messenger written on paper. She received job orders the same way. The internet wasn't trustworthy and competition keen. A new assignment came to her in the most usual way.

Chelsey Chase's phone rang.

It was a phone call. It rang three times before she remembered people used to actually talk on phones. The caller ID said it was the office. Editor White himself. She pushed the button. He didn't waste any time.

"Chase, get you over to Manhattan and find this character—this letter carrier—if he is real."

A picture of the man came up on her screen.

"But Perry," she said, "I got video, why can't I just do the job here and—"

"Not good enough, go and see. You know how they fake footage."

White hung up.

There was nothing for it but to do the job as directed. She needed to get out of the cube anyway. She thought a little fresh, dirty air might be nice for a change. She could bill for the out-of-office time, too. She didn't mind getting paid for a wild goose chase.

On her first lap, the letter carrier appeared to be a homeless man as she zipped by. That he looked too good to be homeless is what tipped her off. When reporter Chelsey Chase spotted him next, she almost crashed her Z-cycle into a messenger on a Razor Board in her hurry to pull over.

"The man does exist."

She looked at him carefully not wanting to believe it. *Yeah, that's him.*

The postal worker carried a huge leather satchel—made from a real animal's hide. The bag hung from a wide strap resting on his boney shoulder. His blue uniform had a thin black stripe running down each leg and sleeve like the released jailbirds who wore similar pants and carried big bags, as well, although jailbirds set free slung their bags more like Santa Claus.

She crossed the street in the middle of a block dodging Urban Parcel and Speedy Mail Delivery driverless trucks. There weren't any maned cars in sight so she felt safe enough to risk the crossing. She didn't worry about the messengers who were well-practiced pedestrian dodgers, the private drivers were the deadly ones.

She ran up behind him.

"Mr. Albert, are you Mr. Albert? Hi, Chelsey Chase, City Beat, *Zap News*," she said out of breath.

He moved fast for an old man. Each booted foot thrust out a bit sideways and back again in odd duck-walking locomotion. His long skinny legs took big, long strides. Chelsey had to pump her short legs in go-cycle fashion to catch him, although he didn't seem to be in a hurry.

"Why yes I am." He let her catch up. "New here in Turtle Bay?"

His wrinkled, long but kindly face stopped her advance. People that old were rare, and people doing physical work at his age were unheard of. His uniform was tidy but old-fashioned. Turtle Bay was the only historic section left in Manhattan and he fit in as if by design. The block had been preserved in an authentic decrepit condition although Mr. Albert appeared fit himself.

"I don't get it," she said. "Why do you walk?"

"These old brownstones ain't fitted for modern mail delivery," he said.

She scrolled through her prepared questions and that didn't answer any of them. The big one was, "why do this job at all, what are his real reasons?" She had her handy-cam ready and opened her mouth to ask the first set of questions, but a messenger on a hoverboard yelled, "Cut!" and zipped in between them.

"Oh, that's Phil," he said. "He delivers the U.S. mail for Speedy Mail, a subcontractor. I am a little late myself, come along if you like."

He walked away. She followed. His long legs propelled him at a good clip although he didn't struggle. He stopped at a four-story walk-up brownstone with a white marble façade and glided up the long stair-stoop with a dancer's grace. Chelsey stopped on the walkway, bent at the waist, hands on her knees. She sucked air. He rang the bell before she regained enough oxygen to spit out the next question.

"Hello, Miss Vonnegut," he said handing her a small bundle. "Looks like the usual. I'm sorry but there's another rejection letter."

"Gosh, Mr. Albert I could paper my walls with the damn things. I send them out and pray, but I'm not getting anywhere."

"It's like I like to say, Alice, God helps those who help themselves. Don't you dare give up. I have a guest with me today." He pointed a thumb behind him. "Next time I'm by, we'll talk. You can show me what you're working on then, if that's alright?"

"I don't know what I'd do without you, Mr. Albert. I guess we both better get back to work."

Mr. Albert skated down the stairs. Chelsey straightened up.

"You know them by name?" Chelsey asked still a little breathless.

"Of course. I do walk this route. Miss Vonnegut is a distant relative of a famous dead writer, Kurt Vonnegut."

He waited for a positive reaction but got none.

"I see you haven't heard of him, too bad."

Mr. Albert turned and proceeded on smartly. Up the next stoop he went. The door swung in and Mr. Albert was met by a trim and handsome young man, perhaps the building super. The letter carrier produced a thick, handwritten letter. He held it up between his thumb and index finger.

"It's fat. Grandfather has a lot to say." He rubbed the envelope between his fingers. "I told you he'd write back. Nobody ignores a personal handwritten letter."

"You're right, writing to him was the right move. Thanks, Mr. Albert. I owe you one. Come on in."

Mr. Albert disappeared into the building before she made the first landing. This deep four-story walk-up had four apartments on each floor and no elevator. Chelsey changed course and opted to wait on the sidewalk, fearing she would lose him in the maze.

Chelsey had a hard time keeping up with him all day, even though Mr. Albert slowed down for her. On occasion, as her rest and time allowed, she fired off questions as they went. She tried to get her basic questions out first: where, when, what, and so on. She would always build up to the hard questions by going through the easy ones first.

The letter carrier stopped to take mail off a robotic messenger. He sorted the new items there on the sidewalk before putting them into his sack. Having the air and opportunity, Chelsey spit a question.

"Mr. Albert, why does the government even allow you to do this job?"

"Seniority. I've been with the P.O. sixty years. They're stuck with me."

He turned and flew up the next stairway. He didn't seem stuck to her. This building was six stories with no elevator. The post boxes in the foyer were ignored. He pulled open the inner entry door instead.

She yelled, "Hey, wait!"

He stopped. She made it the rest of the way up the stair-stoop and into the foyer.

"Where are you going? What about the post boxes?"

"Crooks steal mail. These letters are important. I can't let that happen."

Off he went, bounding up that flight of stairs as if gravity took a vacation.

She didn't get to her big questions all day. In between stops, he told her the history of every little thing as they walked. Mr. Albert spoke fondly of the people who came and went over his years on the route. He knew all their stories and all the places they had been, and he shared a few zingers. He knew everyone on the block. He stopped to pet every dog on the street. He waved at every bike messenger, scooter jockey, and hoverboard pizza delivery person that zipped by.

"Mr. Albert, why…aren't…you—"

"See that hydrant? That's where Jimmy the Knife took a bullet in the 1930s. He tried to intimidate a newspaper reporter who was packing." The letter carrier chuckled. "'The pen is mightier than the sword,' but a .38 works pretty well, too."

Up the stoop, he went and disappeared.

"What's a hydrant? Packing?"

The next stops were much the same. Some residents would meet him at the door, even when he didn't ring the bell. She soon stopped trying to follow him up into the multi-story apartments. She got him on video engaged in pleasant conversations on the stoops. Front doors and the sidewalks were the only places where she got to video. He'd offer a little advice to the resident each time.

After leaving one building where no one answered the door, he seemed disappointed.

"Oh well," he said. "This is where E.B. White lived, a famous writer, a top man. He doesn't have any relatives living here, but Mr. Trout, who bought the place, is a writer as well."

"Sorry," she said. "I never heard of E.B. White."

"That's too bad. I wish Trout were home. Trout's an interesting man, he's been all over America. He's got stories. I'll tell you. With him, you can take a trip and never leave the farm."

"I already got enough bystander footage on my camera."

"In my day, people wrote things on paper and didn't need the AI to write it for them," he said. "People used to need to know how to write, even for video. People used to go places and see things in person. You should try it sometimes."

"What writing or travel?"

"Yes, do that. Do them together. You are doing it now."

She thought that was an odd idea. Why would anyone go anywhere when everything is on computers? The hologram theaters in town were so real who could tell the difference?

Mr. Albert continued and finished his route still full of good humor and vigor. Chelsey was dog-tired but glad they ended up where she had started. Her Z-bike was still where she had left it and she didn't lock it. She had lost track of her questions and didn't have time to go back over the recording to see what she had missed. As they parted, she remembered the big question.

"Mr. Albert, let me ask before I go—"

"Actually, it's Lovecraft. My first name is Albert. Ask away."

"Why do you do it? Walk like this. What do you gain?"

"Gain? I never thought about it that way. I'm here for the letters, if that's what you mean. I'm a letter carrier. I mean…I mean, gosh…It's important. By God…I…I…I…"

Mr. Albert's voice went up an octave as he spoke.

"Sorry, I didn't mean to upset you…"

He stopped her and himself by raising a hand. He tipped his cap to her and caught a breath. His all-day smile got replaced by a serious face.

"Young lady, letters are important. The written word passes through my hands every day. This block is full of writers, dead and living, and the living still write letters—living letter writers need living letter carriers. We belong together. We hold each other up. I am honored to serve them."

"I'm sure you are, but—"

"Don't you believe in letters, Miss Chase?"

A postal driverless electric car pulled up.

"I…I…I suppose I do…"

He winked at her. "I got to punch out, they'll load my letter bag overnight. Bye, for now."

He got into the back seat of a U.S. Postal Service self-driving passenger car with his old leather sack, now empty, in his lap. He took off his cap, dropped it into the sack, and let his white hair flutter in the car's air conditioning.

He was the picture of contentment, and she didn't film it. When he waved goodbye, she waved back instead of recording.

She had no idea what to say on video about the last known U.S. Postal Service letter carrier, but she decided she will write that script herself. But first, to warm up, she thought to write that letter to her parents she'd been putting off—and write it on paper. She used to draw all over her school papers as a child and her parents praised her art no matter how the teachers complained.

"Email has no heart, paper's better. I can do better."

The old bodega where Kurt Vonnegut used to get his stamps, envelopes, and smokes still stood. Albert had pointed out the historic marker plaque which she hadn't noticed before. The stationary store was within walking distance from where she had parked her Z-bike. She walked thinking about trying her hand at letter writing.

Chelsey Chase left the store with a big canvas book bag satchel stuffed to overflowing with writing and art supplies. Somehow, the burden made her feel lighter. She slung her bag over a shoulder feeling as fee as Santa's literary elf.

Chelsey skated right past her Z-bike and floated home on inspiration's wings.

THE ANTHROPOLOGIST

Note: This story was generated from a prompt in which I had a craft goal in mind. This flash fiction story could not exceed 600 words for submission.

The former anthropologist spied a Bubble City cop on the City's boarder as he emerged from the underbrush. None of his adopted tribe members ever got this close. The cop didn't see him because Ned wasn't wired—he carried no electronics at all. Of course, the cop couldn't see him. Ned tapped him on the helmet from behind to get his attention.

"Hello, anyone in there?"

No body-language reaction. Ned thought it was because the armor controlled the cop more than the other way around. The policeman's computer legs didn't seem to know what to do. Ned had to walk around to face him.

"Evac faceplate," the armor-plated man said.

Half the policemen's helmet retracted showing a skinny-faced kid behind the headgear. The kid was much too pale. It made his red zits stand out.

"Sir, you can't be here. This is off limits. What is your number? Please produce your ID insert," the kid said, reading a script off an air-screen.

The screen blinked off and the kid saw Ned in real-time reality.

"Hey, you're naked! I'm gonna have to run you in."

"Go ahead, knock yourself out," Ned spoke with an even, unthreatening tone.

Ned wore clothing, of course. The tribes aren't savages. The kid expected him to be hardwired. He and his anthropology group didn't carry electronics when they went into the field twenty years ago. It would have upset the primitive locals.

He and his associates eventually went native, but Ned never stopped practicing his trade. *People and their societies are fascinating.* Watching Bubble City from afar with his new perspective, rather than city politics, brought unexpected observations. One rabbit hole led to another. The city was deconstructing itself and the people inside didn't know. City Father was in the process of losing his mind.

"What's wrong? Aren't you going to arrest me?" Ned asked.

The kid did a double-take and face-crashed inside his headgear. He recovered and continued typing his arrest warrant midair on a virtual keyboard.

"I'm ready. What's your number?"

"I lost it. Look, kid…I came here to give City Father a message," Ned started slow. "You don't need to take me in. I'll confess right here. This is all recorded. Let me confess, then you can arrest me all you like."

"I suppose that's all right."

The kid started another screen in the air. It was a lie detector connected to City Father. Ned had no intention of lying.

"You may begin," the cop's machine said.

"It's like this, kid, the city's intelligence is sick and it's made your society sick," Ned paused for effect. The cop didn't blink. "You wouldn't know this, but long ago we had a code to shut City Father down, a deconstruct. That voice command, and I quote, 'Reset maximum 1, 2, 3.' That'll kill the AI. You'll have to think for yourselves afterward. Somebody needs to enter that voice command before the AI wrecks everything."

"City Father does function poorly," the kid said. "It needs help."

"Stop command active. Waiting," projected from the armor's speaker.

It wasn't the cop talking.

"Execute," Ned said. The cop's armor lights winked out. "I'm done here. Thanks, kid."

Ned pushed back into the brush. He wasn't concerned about pursuit, but like Lots' wife, he turned back worried about the cop's safety. The armor's emergency escape popped wrong upon City Father's shutdown. The kid got tangled. He didn't have a chance of doing a foot pursuit. Ned felt bad for the kid. The cop's guns were dead, of course. Everything was controlled from and by the central computer and it didn't trust humans with manually operated guns. Ned helped the harmless cop get un-shelled.

"Better come with me, kid."

Ned's village didn't have guns, they didn't need them. The Tribes were ready to accept refugees anticipating the city's collapse. The Tribes voted Ted their emissary. He didn't feel good about winning this war—a lot of New York City people will starve. But that's how bubbles go, they blow up until they are popped.

Ned was as nice as anyone, but in this case, he, the anthropologist, had to be a prick.

FIRE WOMEN

Author's note: This stand-alone story came to me while sitting by a camp-fire. I later folded this character and her unique talents into my upcoming novel, *The Adventures of Tom Conley.*

Elk Horn Ranch was a commercial campground just south of Yosemite. Dan decided it was the place to take his young family. It wasn't far from a fair-sized town. He wanted to be near civilization just in case something happened.

The campground was located directly off a busy state road and that was handy for a fast exit…should anything go wrong. The kids hadn't gone camping yet. Dan wanted them to see the real outdoors. This camp spot featured an untamed setting. Wildlife abounded. There was a creek, kid-friendly trails, and approachable wild deer. The kids, two boys, age seven and nine, and a girl, five, were excited. Dan worried in the back of his mind. Was this a good idea? What if one of them gets hurt? *Got it covered. This place is safe.* Everything added up but Dan had an odd feeling.

He and Allison had stopped camping after the first baby. The first was a shock to his system but the next baby was second nature. After number three, his confidence grew and he deemed them old enough to enjoy his love of the outdoors. Nature called and the Wong family answered.

He convinced himself it would be fine. Sally was finally old enough.

"About time we got back to the forests," Dan said poking a stick at the coals on the second night. His boys were across the campfire, sticks in hand. "Burned marshmallows piling up like cumulus clouds is better than the boys fighting."

"Dan, tell Sally to back up," Allison said. Dan was closer to Sally.

"That's the thing," Dan reached sideways and pushed Sally back. She didn't take her eyes off the coals. "We should get out here more, don't you think? We need this…getting away from everything. This—"

"Dan, will you please get that stick away from her? She's too close."

Sally had a short stick and she poked at the embers imitating Dan. She had burned her hotdog roasting sprig down by half. Her hotdog didn't make it. Sally sacrificed her dog to the fire gods and enjoyed watching it burn. Dan wasn't one to make his children eat just because it was food time.

He had only half an eye on her. She reached over the coals again with her long hair dangling just above the flames. If anything happened to that hair his parents would shit a rice cake. Grandma Wong took a lot of pride in Sally's hair.

"Sally, back up." Dan pushed her back and gave her a longer stick and stuck a fresh marshmallow on it. Sally moved back without taking her eyes off the fire.

"Hate to say you're right, but camping kicks butt," Allison said. "I forgot how much I enjoy campfires."

"Two days and not one fight," Dan said. "Or, maybe not."

Sally and Chen had a tug of war going over Sally's stick, but it didn't sound like a serious battle. That changed when she kicked him. He wasn't hitting her, yet, but made angry, Chen wouldn't let go of her stick. Dan was willing to ignore it until Allison gave him the stink eye.

"What? That's not a real fight." Dan said.

"There's the trip home," Allie said. "It's not too late to ruin our vacation—"

Chen had two hands on her stick, but Sally wouldn't give it up either. Chen whipped her around. Sally lost grip and flew headlong into the fire.

Dan caught her flight path in the corner of his eye. His world stopped. While he swam in molasses, Sally's fireproof PJs flared into blue flash-paper. Allie screamed. Dan unfroze, reached into the fire, and scooped her out burning his knuckles. He smothered her into his chest and ran. His nylon vest melted. Allie bolted on his heels. The creek was only ten yards away but it felt like a marathon. Falling to his knees, he doused her in the icy, shallow stream.

"Oh my God," Allie grabbed her out of the water and ran for the pop-up camper. That's where the first aid kit and phone were.

Dan got up. He stood in the creek drenched and shivering too shocked to move. His boys were screaming and running for the camper but he hardly heard it, everything was fuzzy. Time stopped.

All his fears and failures swirled like a firestorm. His parents will never forgive this. They warned him not to marry a white girl. Sally's hair softened them, she looked Chinese by it. Allie took great pride in Sally's locks as well—common ground between wife and mother. Sally's thick Asian hair bridged the tension. Her hair must have burned off. Dan couldn't face the damage. His camp trip idea disfigured his daughter. Grandmother will never forgive him. Gram had big hopes for her. Sally went down into the flames face first.

"Hair...her hair...her face...she's ruined," Dan cried. "I'm stupid, so stupid!"

"Dan, please. Would you come here, now please?" Allie called.

"Why are Swedes so damn polite?"

Dan exited the creek and hobbled toward the camper, wiping tears. When he pulled the camper's flimsy door open, Sally stood there in her Special Bear underwear and t-shirt. Allie had fresh PJs in hand.

"Hello, Daddy. More marshmallows, please."

Dan screamed. "Never go near the fire! Never! Understand me? Never!"

Sally started bawling. "Sorry, Daddy. Sorry—"

"Dan, stop it! STOP IT! She's alright, look. Please, will you just look at her?"

Dan stuffed his panic and cleared his wet eyes. Sally had not a scratch on her, not even a smudge of charcoal. Dan plucked his daughter out of the camper's doorway and swirled her around kissing her face and head all over, again and again.

Allie came outside crying. They all hugged together and cried. The boys, too, until Sally began laughing.

Sally stopped and said in a serious voice, "Oh Daddy, don't you know? Fire can't hurt me."

"I guess not," Dan said.

He could not stop himself and fell out laughing and crying all over. The group became hysterical with joy.

Sally's clothes had burned to nothing. Other than a small bruise on her hip from a rock in the creek, she was fine. That did not make sense. Her hair was perfect. Dan wasn't burned much and he should have had third-degree burns.

Dan and Allie knew no one would believe it, and they needed their jobs more than fifteen seconds of internet fame, so the incident was quickly forgotten. Even Sally forgot, they were convinced she had not suffered a trauma, but she never mentioned it. Dan and Allie chalked it up as the mystery of dumb luck.

*****

Sally opened her journal to a blank page. She had a lot of confusion to iron out. She had lots of time to think things over on the long bus trip out to the archeology site. Writing stuff down usually helped.

She began.

I love camping, and if not for that, I might have become a nurse or something. If I went in the medical direction, Dad would have insisted I became a doctor, especially if he had to pay for it, and Mom would have argued me into becoming an artist or architect just because I drew the Spanish Mansion ruins well while on a family vacation when I was eleven.

'Sally, you need to use your talent,' she'd say. What talent, I don't have any.

The bus hit a pothole and Sally lost her pen. She started again.

Back to camping: It wasn't camping that had me, it was campfires. I hate and love them.

I'd sit a long while staring into the flames. Fire scared me, but not a fear of burning. I was afraid of losing my sanity. I'd get lost in voices that I imagined spoke from the embers, voices as fleeting as wisps of smoke. If I followed them, I'd open-eye dream about the ancient caller. I could almost see them.

Campfires flooded her brain with pictures. One time she saw Canaanites roasting a baby camel along the Silk Road. Another time it was an Argentinean cowboy eating canned beans out of a stolen silver sugar cup. They'd stare back at her from the flames dry-eyed and grubby and tell their stories.

Mom and Dad don't know it, but I love history. How would they know? I love everything about school. The fire was another kind of school and my secret teacher. Creepy!

Had to quit fire-dreaming at Sacramento State. I was in too much trouble and had no time to think about campfires. I carried way more credits than I should have. There's no escape when your head is on academia's chopping block.

Sally stopped to think. She, an A-student, had that going for her. She loved all her classes, anthropology, archeology, psychology, and even PE. That was the problem. She took too many courses without any objective in mind. If it looked interesting, she took it and took it seriously. She loved studying but couldn't make up her mind.

"Chose a major," Sally's advisor demanded on a Friday. He added, "If I don't have a course plan from you by the semester's end, I will withdraw my recommendation for your scholarship renewal. Get on the stick, Miss Wong, education isn't a game."

Remembering that conversation made Sally shiver. She resumed journaling.

Yeah, I ran Dad's money out and if I'm going to finish, I had to have that free money. I was stuck. All I could do was jump off this burning bridge.

My friends planned camping that first winter break weekend. That's where the boys, pot, and beer were and I love boys, pot, and beer. Asked to go, I didn't. I almost said no and went. But really, it wasn't self-control that stopped me. It was the campfire. I had enough distractions. No time for campfire-insanity, I told myself. I had to stay focused. Hello, remember reality? That longing for fire scared me. To be honest, I did all I could to put the fire out of my mind but it didn't stay away.

I remained home that weekend re-reading the course guide instead. When I saw the archeology III course description, which included field work requiring camping, I signed up. 'Maybe they'd have campfires,' echoed in the back of my brain.

She leaned back in her bus seat and laughed quietly. Her advisor crapped a biscuit when she told him she decided to be an archaeologist. He begrudgingly let her take Arc. III. It was her last elective. She had burned her wild card. She resumed writing.

I wasn't sure of what I wanted. This had better zero me in on something or I'm done. Maybe I'm done anyway. Here on this bus trip out, as I write this, I'm regretting it. I don't know what drove me to sign up for Arc III. Okay, it's campfires.

She had told herself. *This isn't going to be camping, this isn't fun, this is work.* Digging in the dirt is work. Forget mesmerizing coals and whispering voices. *You're not a kid. No more fire dreams.* She said that to herself for years. She had to get over it and grow up. But getting older didn't change the attraction.

"I still feel it," Sally whispered.

"We're here," one of the others called.

Sally closed her journal and stored the laptop. The bus turned off the main road. The side road was too bumpy to do anything but hang on.

"Buckle up. Your ass is on the line," Sally said out loud. Nobody responded.

Sally pulled her backpack up and rummaged around in it for her class handout. The course guide said field work was in a privately-owned cave in northern Cali. The place was found only a few years ago. The landscape there looked more like Nevada in Sally's mind. The excavation had been ongoing and had already exposed the deepest deposits. The dig was in its final stages. Sally wouldn't have to shovel guano.

"Thank the gods."

The base level was dated pre-Clovis, twenty-nine-thousand-years-old and a revolutionary age-date if they found anything human on that level. Dating wasn't complete. This find was played out and there wasn't anything left to discover. Nobody expected much according to the bus-talk on their way out. The Arc Department called it "Clovis," according to the upper strata finds. The few bits of flint knapping found at maximum depth just above bedrock, were said to have washed down into the lowest reaches. Not old. A fire pit would confirm age and that's what they were after.

"Good luck," Sally said reading that part. She wasn't worried. Old fire pits didn't light her brain's fuse.

The site was on a mega ranch, from flat horizon to distant mountains it was all private land. Sally never camped in semi-desert landscapes before. Along the ranch's lane, lots of gullies and shallow canyons were in view. It the distance a dry lake's sand simmered in the sun.

"Mad cool geology," Sally said to the guy next to her. But he had his headphones in.

The bus see-sawing down the rancher's rutted track made headphone music the best option. She soon gave up trying to read. It took over an hour to get there. Getting off the bus revealed a tiny tent city in the distance. Base Camp was downhill in a craggy bowl valley two miles from parking.

The newcomers hiked down together with packs and their one-man tents. An old guy named Jorge came with a jeep for the big stuff and later helped them setup after he rolled in. The dig team was still in the field when they finished setting up.

That evening, the diggers came back barking for food. The mess tent was stocked. Everyone pitched in, got food, and cleaned up. It felt like Girl Scout camp. Sally was stoked. After a noisy dinner, without asking, Sally got the fire going. She did it automatically. The camp had a fire-ring and stacked wood. Old Jorge looked on but didn't say anything. *Weird how he watched*, she thought. They didn't run generators at night, so the fire was the hang-out spot.

After everyone settled in at fireside, the head prof gave his welcome speech to fill in the new student group.

Professor Conley was a good-looking, thirty-something guy: thin, tan, sandy brown surfer-cut hair and no wedding ring. A few of the girls already had the hots for him. They batted eyelashes enough to bellow the fire—especially Jill.

Standing fireside, Conley began.

"We are very lucky. This is a special place. One family owned this land for one hundred and forty years. Nobody screwed with our artifacts. They didn't even harvest the bat-shit. When the owners discovered it, they called immediately. Top layers recent natives, under that layer Paleo-Indians, Clovis below that, but who do we have now, under all, if anyone? That's the million-dollar question. We only have flaked pieces but this stone industry is dissimilar..."

Conley talked and talked, but the fire had her. She hadn't gotten this close to a fire in a long time. She only heard half of what he said. Reaching for something inside herself, she was too busy pushing coals around with a broken ax handle to pay attention. A broken ax wasn't surprising.

I'd bet my last match that these nerds never chopped or split wood in their lives.

She had a knack for fire keeping in Girl Scouts. They always let her do the fires. Conley was still yapping and she thought she had better listen, but his voice seemed so far away and she slumped in her folding chair.

"Clovis points are..."

Someone tossed a flat stick into the fire. Sally jerked straight. It caught fast, dry as desert bones, mesquite by the smell. A Girl Scout knows her fuel. Sally thought that piece of mesquite begged for nurturing. It won't put out nice fun-fire flames. This fire wasn't a cooking fire, either. Fun fires need different care.

Talk fires need big flames and less smoke...

"These bone tools and bone atlatl, in the processing tent, are more closely related..."

Where did that mesquite come from? There aren't any mesquite trees for five hundred miles. That does burn nice.

"As you will note..."

Something pricked inside her dry throat like a stuck fish bone. *Wake up,* sounded inside her mind. Sally popped up out of her camp-chair without thought, reached into the fire with her long hair dangling in the flames, and pulled that stick out like a maniac. It wasn't just a stick, it didn't belong. She kicked a crap load of dirt on it fast. The kids around her reacted as if she was indeed nuts.

"What are you doing, Miss Wong? You don't see I'm lecturing?" Conley said with an overt harsh tone.

"I see just fine," Sally shot back. "You're the one who stood there letting a native bow stave burn."

"What?!"

Oh, no I'm screwed. Never insult your professor.

Conley jumped over the fire and grabbed it up off the ground, still smoldering. He burned a finger, dropped it, and stuck that digit into his mouth.

"Son of a bitch."

He picked it up again, this time with care. "Where'd this come from?"

Before Jill could own-up, Sally blurted out. "Down in Mexico. It's mesquite. Locals used juniper, right?"

Conley gazed at her with a queer expression. She didn't think he was pissed. He had that face like he saw a ghost but he wasn't sure. His face changed back and forth a few times before his lips went Mona Lisa.

After the professor came back to earth, he grilled the group. Jill had found it hiking down from the parking lot and used it for a walking stick. She didn't know what it was, to her it was just a stick. It wasn't that old, less than a few thousand years, prof said after a quick examination. He confirmed it sure as hell wasn't local.

Jorge came and whispered something in Conley's ear, and the professor lowered himself into a fire-side chair. Jorge took one of the students and they ran the artifact up to the finds tent.

Conley kicked back watching the fire, rubbing his chin for a long time. Sally understood that way of concentration. Everybody does that. Fire invites it. Sally thought his timing was a little weird, bailing out on the welcome-lecture like that.

"Good eye, Miss Wong. Guess what?" Professor Conley said. "You are now in charge of the campfire. And you Miss Harvey, first thing tomorrow you will hike your ass up to parking, turn around and hike back. I want you to locate and mark where you found it."

Jill broke out her pouty face. She started to whine, but Conley didn't buy it. Bus parking was two miles uphill. Jill didn't seem like the athletic type.

"Can't I, please, please, use the Jeep?" Jill said, trying one last time.

"How are you going to survey the trail?" Conley said. "You might get lucky and find the spot on your way up. But, retracing your steps is the best bet."

The Jeep didn't fit the walking path anyway. Vehicles had to go the long way which was why they packed their personnel stuff down. Sally thought Jill had it coming.

Jill needed more help than a stick. The boys had carried most of her crap for her. Judging by her clothes—Ralph Lauren shoulder bag, and high-heel Lugs boots—Jill was accustomed to lots of help. Conley, to his credit, didn't buy her girly-girl act. The name Spring-Flower popped into Sally's mind when Jill's sun-kissed perfect cheeks, unlike Sally's chipmunk pouches, turned amber.

Later, at the fire, snatches of Sally's old fire-dreams blazed in and out of her mind. Maybe the beer opened it, she told herself. The first night of camping was normally a party, but she wasn't feeling it. She kept slipping into the coals. She missed most of what people were saying.

I need to drink more. It drowns the visions out.

She hit the dig the next morning feeling pie-eyed. Sally couldn't remember half of last night and brushed it off as too much beer.

All that was left of the original cave was a deep rock outcrop overhang. Most of the ancient caves had collapsed in the distant past. Behind the outcrop was a grade depression, or was that once a cave, too? She asked herself and the team. Geology wasn't her thing. She took an educated guess. Conley said she was right. That made her even more torn between a lot of career possibilities and geology wasn't one of them—although she had to admit she had an eye for rocks. Geology was handy for archeology, but the idea of geology as a career sat cold on Sally's back burner.

She didn't know where she'd end up and she had to make up her mind soon. But, at least, geology was scratched off the list, or maybe not.

A week into the dig, Sally, the Professor, and a few others were slow-dancing between dig-grid strings among what they called "anthills" and talking about what came next. They weren't real anthills, of course. Anthills were bits of earth left unexcavated. The term made Sally laugh. Conley gathered the group around him near the end of the day.

"I know there is more here. I feel it," Conley said. "Come on people, thinking caps on, any ideas?"

The professor had been muttering, "There's got be more" and stuff like that, to himself all day. He launched into a recap, trying to jar people into new ideas about where to look for more. Sally thought it had to do with grant money.

The cave's floor still held a three-D checkerboard of ant-hills but only a few pieces were left. Level by level the artifacts left in situ—to identify the layer's height from zero depth—were being removed. One place still held a Clovis point suspended atop an ant-hill sixteen inches above bedrock. Theoretically, everything below that was older than 13K BCE. Cave Digs generally progressed around samples until bedrock is exposed. There wasn't much dirt left.

Conley gave instructions for excavating those orphaned chucks of the remaining matrix. Odds were, there wasn't anything inside or under them. Sally was convinced this dig was over but she had a feeling. A whisper on the wind sparked her attention.

"Something is here," Sally whispered. Nobody heard her.

"There's more, I feel it," Conley said again while lecturing, as if he reflected Sally's words.

It struck her that Conley was at the end of his rope. He kept scratching his chest. The others said at the campfire that that was Conley's stress-tick.

"Think outside of yourself, anyone?" Conley said. "Volunteer your intuition, any wild guesses? I won't bite."

The last thing she needed was to think intuitively. That always brought on her fire lust. *Besides, that's the opposite of what science teaches.* But she could not deny that she felt it, too.

The call of fire was somewhere near. She had the urge to get out of the cave. She had never felt it that way before or under fireless conditions. It wasn't the call of nature but she was holding it too long. The team got busy fine-combing the cave with soft brushes and toothpicks scratching out every little bedrock crack.

She excused herself and went outside to pee. The need to go morphed from an urge into an invitation.

Sally had a spot in the boulder field where another cave had collapsed leaving chunks like standing stones. One huge standing rock provided an overhang for shade and sage for cover. Sally's spot was better than going all the way back to camp. She hated to pee on her Timberlands, but it was worth the risk. She ducked down below a chest-high rock and let it go.

The sizzle of water on fire wasn't what she expected. She felt dizzy pulling up her pants so she leaned on the bolder. Her head jerked back like a ghost pulled her hair. Forced to look, she saw where her hiding place had chipped off from above. A vision came…natives roasting a fawn over a fire pit. It wasn't the clan she dreamed about as a child. The episode passed quickly. Sally staggered back to the work site.

"Professor," she said from the cave's mouth, still weak in the knees. "I found something."

He came out. "What have you got, Sally?"

Sally led him around back. "I think I found a fire pit, see that big rock?" She pointed. "It came from there." She pointed out the overhang. "It rolled but it didn't roll far, it landed in a fire pit. The depression stopped it."

It was the perfect spot for a camp. Sally and the professor got down on the ground. Conley didn't seem to mind the pee smell. Both scratched away at the edge of the rock with trowels. They found spent coals quickly.

"It's not super old, about the same age as Jill's stave," Sally said.

"May well be a cook fire, could be some garbage mixed in. Excellent." Conley said. "We got lucky. Good eye, Sally. Maybe geology is your calling."

She didn't say it, but the contents of the pit weren't refuge. *Garbage doesn't call me.*

The men came and levered the rock out. After some digging, Conley confirmed a cook fire. Charred deer bones and bits of stone-knapping debris were in evidence. The usual paleo fireside stuff. No mega fauna bones. It was like she had visualized—a young deposit. Sally still felt fire call, but it was faint. She sensed it came from a greater distance in time.

That new feeling gave her the willies, like ghosts or something, but it also made her think new thoughts.

That night long after dinner, after she had the fire going, Sally and a few others went behind the mess tent to smoke a joint. That sparked a little fever. Back at the fire and stoned, beer in hand, Sally resumed fire duty. Then it happened.

She saw it as if she were there, a stone hearth twenty-five thousand years ago. It wasn't that new pit. Unrecognized so far in real-time, but she had to be near it. Worse, she felt sure she had seen it before. There was an old crone woman cross-legged fireside dressed in a pullover shirt and a wrap-skirt made of deer hides that weren't as nice looking as movie buck-skins. But they were better made, and looked different, more practical.

It came back to her. She saw this before but she didn't have the language as a child to describe it.

The old lady had two long, thin braids, one to each side of her head with duck feathers weaved in. Necklaces were layered on her, each made of different stuff: one made of special shells, one of tiny painted fired-clay balls, one of bones and teeth. Each one was significant—Sally knew why, she remembered it from childhood dreams. The old lady's hair fell into the fire as she tended coals and it did not burn.

The old one detected Sally and Sally's heart leaped toward the flames. The old lady looked right at her with a nod but didn't say anything.

She was so old that her birth name had been forgotten, but Sally knew her. The clan called her Fire Women, the plural form. She carried the spir-it-magic of those firewomen who came before her.

The clan hunting leader, Bear Claw, was old himself at forty seasons. Fire Women was already old when Bear Claw was a boy. She was too old to chew skins for leather even then and too old to gather, net fish, or mate.

Age wasn't why she tended the hearth. She always had that job. The fire was the source of her magic.

The part of Sally who was an archeology student could not help but observe. Sally moved closer. The old one's thoughts blended with hers.

None worked the hearth with such wisdom. The young clan-folk didn't know if there were better Fire Women before her, but they knew her skill and trusted it. Fire is magic and also a tool. It came from inside Sally. *The memories live inside in my blood.*

Sally felt woozy, ready to faint. If she fell out of her camp chair, she'd land face-first in the pit.

Fire Women said, "Come, my child."

Sally drifted unfettered toward her. A chant drifted up out of time to meet her.

"Time is a river of flame. Put your toe in and drown…Time is a river…"

Sally jumped.

*****

Someone pressed a cold beer on Sally's neck from behind.

"Maybe you should slow down, Sally," Charlie said. "You're nodding out, dude. You damn near fell in the fire…"

She wasn't drunk but wished she was. That vision was too real. She was flat messed up inside her head. That cold can on her neck shocked her back to reality. It disoriented her worse than when Chen spilled her out of a sun-scorched chase lounge and into a cold swimming pool. She floated a second or two without footing. When she reached the ground, she felt unreasonably offended as if Chaz accused her of dereliction of fire-duty.

Where'd that come from?

"I need a beer," Sally said.

Her eyes cleared and Chaz came into focus.

"…If you got burned, Sally. Christ, we'd all be in deep. They'll shit-can the beer and who knows what all—"

"STOP," Sally shouted. "I'll never fail fire or it me. Fire can't hurt me. I am Her. She is me. What am I saying?"

"You're whacked. Here, hit this."

Phil pulled the joint hanging from his bottom lip and passed it. Staff had gone to bed, it was safe. "Did one of you clowns put 'shrooms in her beer?"

"How long was I gone?" Sally said after a toke. "Did I say anything else stupid?"

"Chill, fire-girl. Your powers are safe with me," Charlie said, laughing.

Everybody laughed. Sally grabbed the beer from Chaz, cracked it, and took a deep swallow.

She heard what she had just said, but it didn't feel like she said it. The joint came around again. Sally only saw its amber tip. It came to her in slow motion. The rest of the world didn't exist. She held the joint out watching the tip glow like an idiot. Her eyeballs felt fire-baked. She didn't think anyone spiked her beer.

"Dude, you going to hit that or what?" Charlie said.

She took a quick pull and passed it on. Maybe it was the beer or the pot, or maybe the fire was hypnotic.

The past burned inside her like a weird historical Tabasco sauce. She almost drifted off again but managed to push it out of her mind. *Way too weird.* She hung on by focusing on the cold beer in her hands. That cooled her off, but the fire still called. She had to answer.

Before she knew it, Sally found herself walking across a smoky lake of lava. The far shore was clear when she arrived.

*****

Fire Women sat by the hearth thirty paces from the cave mouth adjusting the coals with a long rock-wood stick. Her white hair was long and yet always without tangles. Her two braids, woven with small ornaments, hung forward into the flames while the rest remained free. Clan folk often said, 'It is no wonder that you never burn your hair. Your fire-magic is great.'

Fire cannot harm me.

The men were just back from the hunt. The elks they drove fell into the pit-trap and not a man among the dozen runners was hurt.

"Gather around," Fire Women said to the youth there. "Such a good kill is a teaching opportunity. I will show you keeping a meat-smoke hearth."

She meant to examine the children. She did not yet know who would keep the sacrament after she was gone, and this worried her as her end-time drew near.

The boys and young men had man-things to do. The younger girls looked at her with reverence but hesitated out of fear. The hunters with their excitement still thick led one's heart on such days.

"There are two elk to skin," Bear Claw's oldest son, Black Wolf, said, "and the meat must be racked to dry."

"Without a certain fire, the meat will not dry correctly," Fire Women said.

"That is your concern," Wolf said over his shoulder as he left.

"Tuber needs clay to make pots," Moss Foot said.

Although Moss had seen fourteen seasons and was old enough to hunt, he was the only young man not invited. A lame foot kept him from running or handling a spear-thrower with balance. So, Moss joined the women in gathering and became one with them.

Moss's best man-work was finding and digging roots. He was good at providing clay for pots and so was favored by the one called Old Man Tuber, the potter. Even so, Moss was under women's care, and the old women, being former consorts of the potter, let Moss care for Tuber's needs.

Tuber depended on Fire Women's skill and he did not care for it or her as he often announced. What could he do but flap gums? Women held greater wisdom at hearth and he had no good argument otherwise. He, so old, was bulb-fat and crooked-legged like his underground namesake, but being old, Tuber remained in the shelter.

Fitting, Fire Women thought. *He makes pots, pots as round and squat as himself.* The fermented berries others stewed in his pots kept him in good standing as well. The magic of Water and Earth—men's-magic—was the power that Tuber held over Moss.

The remaining boys touched their foreheads to show respect for the Fire Woman before departing. She nodded permission for them to leave and the boys ran out. The adult women were already gathering to make ready a feast.

"You, Moss, should pay attention," Fire Women said, "There is more to life than digging clay. Tuber can't make pots forever. You may take his place someday. Keep my wisdom then. Pots cannot be made without a right fire."

"Fire lore is for Fire Women," Moss said. "This day is for elk-kill. The bigger one has good horns. I need them for digging."

Moss took a flint knife and limped after the rest.

He walks like Jorge, Sally thought

"Whenever the men kill, life stops inside this cave," Fire Women called after him. "Fire is life!"

"Teach me," Sally said. *How am I to speak to her, she can't see me?*

"There is plenty of food. The pots are full. I have time. I will teach," Fire Women said. "Come, children."

She said it to me. Sally moved closer.

Fire Women looked to the ceiling. The old lady knew Sally watched, but Sally wasn't sure until the old lady spoke.

"But you, should you not teach me? Quiet children, open your hearts to the spirits."

The old woman sat examining the pictographs made from mineral paints which were all around on the walls and ceiling. The flickering fire made the images move. Was it Sally that Fire Women addressed or the spirits? When the old one spoke again her voice sounded with an echo of Sally's voice inside it.

Time is consumed, we thought. Turning to Spring-Flower, Fire Women spoke. "You are fifteen and not yet pregnant."

That isn't me. Sally thought coming back to herself a little. *Fire Women's communing with her imaginary friends, right?* Sally felt Fire Women's contempt for pretty Spring-Flower. Fire Women's disharmony with Spring-Flower bathed Sally in boiling holy water. *That girl is thickheaded, only good for making babies. Oh, what the men will do for her. Beauty prevents learning. Useless girl but a fine breeder.*

"Did I think that?" Sally said to herself out loud, but the vision didn't end.

"This one, I cannot abide," Fire Women said, pointing her chin at Spring.

All the others old enough to work were off doing chores, making ready for the feast. Spring was the only adult not doing her share for the clan. *Hanging at the teaching fire was Spring's excuse to avoid work*, we thought.

"Are there no berries to gather?" Fire Women said.

Spring kicked dirt at Fire Women's feet, an insult. "Teach me this magic."

Fire Women turned her face back to the hearth and to the younger girls waiting there. She did not address anyone but fixed her eyes on the coals. Sally felt her eyeballs drying.

"The fire of life resides inside us. Set it alight." Fire Women turned toward Spring-Flower. "Make babies, then I will show you. First, a baby for the clan."

Fire Women spread her hands and looked to the ceiling. Sally did not hide.

Sally saw herself superimposed over the cave-art from Fire Women's eyes. There were handprints, spirals, and earth spirits drawn like sticks for the fire. Zigzags, which mean lightning, depicted sky spirits. Sally knew what it all meant, ageless lore. These petroglyphs say all things are connected through time.

A hazy image of Sally appeared in the smoke. Sally lusted for the fire.

"Your knowledge flies between suns," Fire Women said, pointing at the smoke-image. "You visit stars, galaxies, planets."

Fire Women often spouted things that made no sense. The clan agreed she used spirits-words as given to her. That idea intrigued Sally during her childhood. Sally thought the old one read the future. Sally had dreamt of the old one for a long time as a kid. She thought her childhood dreams had been eroded, gone forever. Why such dreams rushed back now, dreams inside dreams all at once, Sally didn't know.

Nobody alive understood fire like the old one. Sally thought she could also.

Fire Women had named each tree calling each a different name if dry, fresh, or rotten. Fire Women used each condition as called for. Sally knew the names.

"Mother Fire," Spring -Flower said speaking softer to get on her good-side. "Is there not time for both learning and bearing children?"

Fire Women answered from a half trance. "There is time for babies and there is time for lore."

Who will know our craft when we are gone?

You know the answer, Sally thought. She did not need to speak it.

Fire Women drew up straighter and looked past Spring-Flower. If the Fire Women line fails, the spirits of the future could not be. Fire Women's relief washed over them both.

The Old Woman's eyes seldom strayed from the coals. The south wall had a huge protruding chunk of rock painted as a mastodon which lived as the fires flickered. We watched its spirit run.

Sally pondered. *How did Fire Women know so well all of the other women's hearts without gathering seeds or pounding flour with them?* Making and gathering were where and when wisdom-talk passed between women. Men are not included, not even Moss. Fire Women's knowing them was yet another mystery of the fire. Fire Women feared that Spring Flower's depth was dangerously shallow.

Sally and Fire Women sat before the flames in and out of trance. Sally held her questions and waited while Spring Flower rocked foot to foot impatiently.

"Wisdom's spark is in you," Fire Women said finally. "You are worthy."

Spring Flower came to the hearth and laid a hand on Fire Women's shoulder. The old woman jerked away as if bitten by a snake.

"Not you."

The men came back with long green-saplings and began making the drying rack. Fire Women busied themselves changing how the fire burned. She called for greener wood that gave both smoke and a good taste. She pushed dry hardwood coals into place to burn greenwood. She had the little ones fuel the hardwood side to keep making coals.

Spring Flower paid attention to the men building and not the important changing of the fire. Spring left the fireside to go gathering with Wolf Tooth, and without the lesson Sally had just learned. *That's Spring Flower's loss.*

Fire Women was glad. *Maybe Wolf will earn his namesake and give the Clan a baby.*

Sally watched Mother Fire's meat smoking from inside the flavor-cloud until forced to look away. Her eyes had watered her blind. Sally blinked tears away frantic to see again. She didn't want to miss anything Mother Fire did but the images faded.

Sally regained sight, finding herself slumped in a portable camp chair. A hot, unopened can of beer lay between her legs. The fire was dead at her feet. Her chipmunk cheeks were wet and her eyes were swollen. *I was crying?*

Spring Flower reminded Sally of how Jill filled her wants but not her need.

"Sucks for her, I guess," Sally said.

Someone watched Sally. The back of her neck heated. She stood. The dig master, cook, and local grumpy, old man, Jorge, hung just outside the chair ring. He had been there a long while judging by the pile of cigarette butts around him. Only, he smoked tobacco.

"Welcome back, señorita. Your trip was meaningful, si?"

He didn't say anything more. Rather, he tuned and limped away like Moss Foot. She should have been creeped out. An old guy watching a passed-out girl is messed up. Sally was good at people-vibes and she didn't get anything bad from him. Weirder still, she felt like he had her back for no reason that she could see.

She was in for trouble, caught passed out won't go over well. Her grade's comment section was about to get negative input. She must have gotten drunk. She didn't know what she had blabbed. But Jorge wasn't mad. Rather, he had a thoughtful face. His brow rose only once a few days ago when Stephanie found something good. Other than that, the old man didn't show any emotions. The old man's face showed a mix of feeling she never saw before. She felt relief.

Sally realized she wasn't in trouble—but, a quiet heat she didn't feel before burned between her and the old man.

The next day, Sally skipped breakfast. She reminded herself she gets sick the morning after drinking. She wasn't feeling queasy yet. *Lame excuse.* She got honest with herself. She skipped chow out of embarrassment. There was more to it. She didn't want to face Jorge in the chow line.

Back in the cave, later that day, Sally and the other students were brushing around the last remaining artifacts by working the anthills that the finds rested on into panicles. They were looking for more stuff inside, of course, but she knew it was pointless.

This was the ideal activity for hung-over frat boys like Charlie and Phil, but Sally's head was clear. Her mind churned kneeling there on the floor. When the lunch horn blasted, everyone scrammed. Sally stayed.

A weak fire-call buzzed her while she picked ash off a charred petrified snail shell. *Somebody's meal.* That wasn't the source of the vibe. She sat facing the south wall as she worked. Just outside was the new fire pit. A group of students found the snail there. *No, that ain't it either.*

"Not the right vibe."

Something else was there, like a whisper of hot air escaping from a deep well.

Professor Conley came and squatted on his haunches next to her. She didn't notice him until he spoke.

"I feel it, too," he said, rubbing that spot on his chest. "Wish I had your talent."

"I don't know what you mean."

"Close your eyes. Reach for it. Follow it," Conley said.

She didn't need to. It pulled her in. How the cave was before flashed like a disco ball projection. The effect vanished quickly, but she saw where the fire-call came from. It came from a distant past. Each flash showed a different picture in a digressive succession of the cave falling apart throughout its long life. She saw its visitors come and go in flashes.

"That raised floor section adjacent to the south wall ain't bedrock," Sally said, "It sheared off. That's a fallen slab."

She took a breath.

"Under it, she…they…had a fire there."

She got up slowly and walked to it, and got atop that flat rock the size of a small bison. Her boot soles felt the heat. She knew what the fire had done and who used it.

"Pottery, too," she said. "The edges, you'll see it ain't attached to bedrock.

One of Tuber's pots was left behind when they moved on. Nobody was supposed to be making pottery at that time. Sally should have shut up, but it spilled out anyway.

"That's where Tuber fired his pots…"

Conley got on the floor and examined the rock, taking note of its shape and size. Next, he checked the wall and took careful measurements of the raised section. He measured the wall divot above several times.

"You're right, of course. Good eye, Miss Wong."

Conley brushed his hands off on his jeans.

"Keep using that talent and you'll do well," he said. "You have a gift for this."

It was a relief that somebody besides her didn't think she was crazy. But Conley was pushing her where she didn't want to go. *No way he accepts my visions. I don't even believe it. He must think I'm a natural geologist, she thought.*, Sally thought, that is the other place she didn't want to go. But one must go where one has skills. That's what her parents encouraged. Sally had to pick a career and time ran out.

"I'll change my major to geology, I guess," Sally said, feeling depressed about the obvious conclusion. "If that's your recommendation, Professor. I don't know…I…"

Sally's words faded. She fought tears. She wasn't decided, not really. A geology major wasn't what she had envisioned. She didn't know what she wanted but it wasn't rock-hounding, but what choice did she have?

"Two lucky guesses can make a person's geology career, I guess," Sally said.

"That's ridiculous," Conley said.

He checked around. No one was there but them.

"You're a finder like Jorge, Sally. You must follow where that takes you." Conley paused and rubbed that spot on his chest as if consulting a talisman. "I'm teaching at Berkeley this fall. I'm telling your advisor you'll transfer. You need to take my course. I'll get you a sponsor. Give the nod. Come to Berkeley."

Sally hadn't until then seen the professor so animated. It sparked something in her.

"I'm interested in primitive fire use," Sally said slowly, tasting the sound of it.

She had never said that out loud before but it filled her truth. He wasn't hitting on her, either. His brows furrowed in plowed intensity. She had never seen easy-going Conley wound up like an overloaded spring before. There could only be one reason for it.

He's on to me. He knows.

"I'll accommodate you," Conley said. "There's a solid doctorate in ancient hearth studies. Only one specialist in that field that I know of. You'll come, won't you? Think about it."

Oh my god, he knows more about me than I do myself. Sally's insides boiled. *What if they all know? What if he tells? This ain't science. I'll be finished but… but this is amazing.*

"I'm not crazy?" Fell out of her mouth.

"Nothing like that, but you are special."

"An older hearth is under there," Sally said in a dismal voice. "It's hard evidence that Clovis wasn't first in this part of the northwest, not even close, and they had pots, real pots, wine, and grains."

"I'm sure you are right," Conley said. He watched her closely, searching her face.

She had seen them, the pre-Clovis people, but nobody will believe it. There wasn't any evidence…yet. Working against the paradigm is dangerous. Exposing her ability more so. Ground breaking finds break careers. This one will kill hers before she got started.

"They won't like this," Sally said. "When we lift that rock off, holy cow. What will I tell my parents when Old U kicks me out?"

"Forget Old U. We aren't touching this," Conley said. He kicked the slab. "It's too hot. It's a career-ender, that's all I'll say until you join me at Berkeley."

Sweat rolled down Conley's nose and it wasn't hot in the cave.

"I gotta think," Sally said.

"Whatever you decide, don't talk about this." Conley's intensity backed down a few notches. "Never say how you find things. Don't tell anyone. Most of all, not a word to your advisor, he's government and can't be trusted."

Sally should have said no. Sac State was home and Berkeley was a million miles away. She didn't even know if she'd like his classes. Her anthropology prof says Conley's a walking controversy. He had a reputation. That passion and fear in Conley's tone were what Sally hadn't seen in him before: His flame jumped to her and caught. She wanted to bask in his heat.

"I used to think what burned in my chest was curiosity," Sally said. "I wasn't sure."

"That's a major find under the slab, your find," Conley said. "It needs to stay where it is."

He gave Sally full credit, although nobody will ever know it. That tipped her to trust him. The river of fire swept her onto his shore. Societies swim in and out of time. Not much in life was real to her. *What is true or not?* Fire is true. Conley is true. He burns with a hidden passion but there are also fires set against him. *Conley is in danger.*

Fire Women uphold truths and protect them. *It is what we must do, what we are made for.* That idea crashed inside her, but it came voiced from every Fire Women past and future. Sally's inner vision cleared. *He needs protection.*

"Profession Conley, I think I better go to Berkeley."

It was a big, scary, weird step. The echoes bouncing from the back of the cave's wall gave Sally confidence. The voices droned. Generations of Fire Women chanted as Sally also sang inside her heart.

"Fire can't hurt us, fire can't hurt us, fire can't hurt me, fire…"

"That's great, Miss Wong. You won't regret it."

Profession Conley stood surrounded by a fire he could not perceive. He was worthy of a guide. Sally's career sat in flames awaiting her cause. Fire protects or destroys and Conley was caught in between flames.

Fire closed on Conley. She couldn't let him burn.

Regret is beside the point.

Sally didn't need to decide. She would have been overruled. They decided for her. She was one with them and one doesn't ignore her true nature. They smiled.

BOBBY T AND ME:

The man who knew everything

I was homeless at 23 and living in and out of the main branch of the Bethlehem library. Jesus didn't live on that block, but I had to watch out for the camel poop.

I had no place better to go, same as Bobby T. We palled around a little. His spot in the woods was near mine and that made us neighbors. Things were OK until Bobby got accepted to live at the Assisted Living shelter. He finally had a place to live. I lived in no place myself and I wasn't worried about myself, but Bobby T wasn't the kind to fit in there and that worried me.

The back corner seating in the library was where we hung out. I stuck close to Bobby on his departure day trying to think of a way to tell Bobby he shouldn't go. Was that for me or him? Okay, I didn't want him to leave.

The day before I watched Bobby T walking up and down the science aisles, as usual, with his hands spread, humming, and smiling a little. He'd stop when something struck him. He told me before that day how he absorbed books. Whatever, I didn't believe it. I sat there churning-up some buttery words to serve Bobby so he wouldn't get offended and go off. I was afraid to tell him how bad Section-8 housing was. It's a filthy place, full of rip-off junkie mamas.

A librarian named Mary Cook came up and stood aside and watched him with me. Bobby T didn't understand doom was coming. Locking him out of here would kill him, Bobby loved books, and even Mary saw that.

"The sheriff is supposed to clean us out tomorrow," Mary said, "I don't think Bobby will understand. Do you think he'll be all right?"

She asked me like I'd know. If anybody knew Bobby T, it would be me. Me and Bobby T go back a while. Maybe after they take him, I thought, I'll take his spot behind the shrubs although the idea turned my stomach.

"I don't know how he will do," I said, but I knew Bobby T ain't gonna like it.

Section 8 housing has no soul. Bobby T says books have souls. Sometimes, back then, I hoped he was right but I didn't believe it. He slept in the park nearest the library to stay close to it. He loved libraries. That library was free and easy, but it wasn't going to stay that way.

"Gosh, I don't feel good about this," Mary said.

"The shelter people are okay." I didn't know that. "Crisis Intervention helped me a lot."

More lies. "Bobby is gonna make it work."

Mary looked sad. She was okay in my book. She treated us like people.

"I'm really worried for him," she said.

"Bobby T will be all right," I said to comfort Mary and to hear me lie to myself.

Mary was right to worry about him. She released a little puff of sad air.

"I wish I could do something for him."

She treated the homeless nice. I guess her empathy didn't mind the smell. That's what I thought. Besides, I figured the library had to keep eyes on us and she was given the task. Looking is better than book-stacking.

Bobby got lucky and unlucky. The authorities declared him mentally ill and they put him into the system. He got a little Social Security disability money and food stamps and the county wanted their cut of his check so yeah, they wanted him in the system. Social Security Disability people are a subsidy cash cow. Broke homeless got no value except to the for-profit jails.

I'm not lucky. I'm not mentally sick enough to get help. They expect you to take care of yourself at 23. Just because my folks got killed in the war, that's no excuse. The system thinks my heroin addiction is my fault.

"Pull yourself up," the counselor at welfare said.

She didn't offer me any help. The American dream is something I can't do. Community College doesn't teach that course.

"What are you going to do, Kevin?" Mary asked. "Where will you go?"

"Not far," I said, "Somebody's got to keep an eye on Bobby T. I'll take care of myself just fine. I'll be around."

That satisfied Mary. She reversed gear and went back to sorting books. I wasn't satisfied. I didn't know where I'd spend my days without the cops standing on my back. I do enjoy reading. Maybe if I clean up, I thought, wash in the creek more often. I could float between libraries, and blend in. I had a problem. The cold time of year is not the time to take a creek bath.

Bobby never knew how to take care of himself outside of an institution. That's why he needed me. Me and Bobby T—that's the weird leading the crazy. I wasn't that weird. Strung out only looks weird to normal people. I had piled on street smarts fast after getting hooked. I wasn't dumb, just broken and desperate for relief.

"Somebody's, that's each other, got to keep us safe in this confusing world." Mom used to say. She was right, you gotta have eyes out for each other in the cement forest. I was lonely and Bobby was too. Me and Bobby T, the old crazy man and the sad, young junkie, what a pair. Some junkie I was, always too broke to buy the next hit. Bobby was there for me when the smack ran out. He'd keep waking me when I'd nod-off from an overdose. He'd keep me from drowning in my own vomit if it ever came to that. I never had enough food in my belly to choke if it came back up. We helped each other in our own ways. It was good for us, not in a homo way, but it was good. And it had to end.

Bobby made his way back up the aisle and lowered his arms. He stood before me like a hound dog with a live-bird mouthful.

"Learn anything new?" I asked Bobby T.

"Oh, yes. UFOs…they are in New Mexico," he said.

That was the most words I heard him put together on one thought in a long time and he wasn't done.

"That is where they keep them. I think the government has them. I need to know more."

How would he know? There ain't no TV in here and Bobby's been in the mental lock-up most of his life. Then it hit me. They relocated the popular alternative theory books onto the endcap at the far end of the science stack. My guess is they did it to get that silliness out of the public's eye, and at the same time, introduce tinfoil-hat readers to hard science.

Bobby took his seat next to me in our row of bolt-down chairs. They were set on the south wall in front of a big plate-glass window. We enjoyed watching the grounds out there. Bobby could see his hole in the hedges.

"Tomorrow's a big day," I said. "Tomorrow you get a home."

He pushed his wool cap back and said, "What about New Mexico?"

I had no idea what he meant. I shrugged and kicked back for a nap and some of that sweat dream-thinking. I got rested that way. I was an expert at open-eye day-sleeping.

Dad got killed in the war. He was sleeping in his bed in the middle of the night and didn't know what hit him. That's supposed to be a good way to go. I was 13 and not afraid of the dark. I am now. I walk most nights away. Nightmares can't hit a moving target.

Mom said I had to grow up. Things got hard. Mom did the best she could. I tried to be good. She joined the Army for the money.

She'd say, "Your job is to learn and stay in school. My job is to see that you do. I don't want you suffering without skills or education."

That's not really why she joined the reserves, to get skills. She wanted to go to the war and face her dragons.

Mom wanted to see where Dad had died to honor his resting place. There wasn't a body to bury. She never got over him. She wanted to put him to rest, and pray over his blown-up remains. They only found tiny bits of bodies. They sent us a note and Dad's effects but he's still over there. No closure. She didn't make it. She got hit by a truck crossing the street in front of the National Reserve building, killed in action by a pota-to-chip delivery driver. She always said junk food kills.

Mom's death benefit lasted halfway through the first year of commu-nity college. I didn't pay rent or bills. I wondered around school like a zombie. All I had left of her was that sense of her down deep inside me. If I kick back and let it glow, I feel her. Smack makes everything glow.

I came home after school one day to find the house locked. There was a big red foreclosure notice nailed to the door. Everything from the inside was on the curb.

The sheriff let me keep my backpack.

I moved to my new home, the street, with fifty bucks and a change of clothing. I soon made the Main Branch library my primary residence. How did I let it all go? I couldn't bring myself to open Mom's mail. It hurt too much. Mail piled up. I needed help. The system doesn't provide for the broken adult children of military casualties.

Walking all night and sleeping days was not a bad life. I'd read between nodding off. I'd beg the dealers for a free bump and get lucky once in a while. I'd beg-up enough money to get a nickel bag once in a while. Smack let me sleep sitting up with my eyes open.

The library has a lot of people coming and going. Normal old folks read the papers. Crazies from the Assisted Living facility get dropped off. They walk around mumbling and picking their scabs. The grad students ignore it all. Saturdays were filled with kids and part-time librarians. Clubs meet upstairs and I wasn't invited.

I fit in with the homeless, but they don't trust anybody. I'm young and white, and only a little crazy, so I'm suspect. It ain't good to trust. But I do read the books and magazines I hide behind. That's why Bobby and me got along. He'd watch me read. Bobby T couldn't read but he loved books. I'd read to him sometimes.

Bobby T would whisper, "Young fella." He'd point at the book in my dirty hands and talk about it like he had read it, "That's a good one. I like the character." He'd describe it as if he wrote it.

He knew everything in every book I read. But I have never seen him read one.

He took to sitting with me, because I had opened up to him a little. I liked the company. He'd talk about the books I read in short bursts if I wasn't sleeping. Books were common ground.

"See this?" I waved my hand around. "This library's my world for today."

Bobby laughed. "Safe. Good place. Not my world."

"If I had a disability, like you, I wouldn't be here." I snapped at him, feeling sorry for myself.

Bobby had a new world lined up, a place to be. He had a nice, shiny Section 8 apartment world to look forward to. He won't mind the neighbors stealing from him. After Bobby leaves, I figured, I'd have less than nothing.

I didn't mean anything by my tone. I'd never hurt Bobby. I was just talking. Like when I told him to apply for housing. I filled out the application for him and one for me as well, with no hope. The shelters were always full and bad. Too many robberies there. The library was better. I never would have met Bobby T if not for the library. Me and Bobby T fit nicely there.

"I'm gonna miss you," I said in way of an apology, more to appease myself than for his feelings.

Bobby stood there, but he had wandered away inside his mind. He didn't hear anyone while staring at the ceiling, humming a happy tune. No telling where his mind went when it wasn't there. I had the feeling he was gone again. It was like his soul projected out of his body.

We were a pair—me 23, fresh and sane; he half-crazy most of the time and older than dirt. Lucid, Bobby was a freight train hauling car-loads of information. He'd tell me what books were good and bad and why. It was nice to have someone around interested in books. I like books. Common ground.

What worried me was that Bobby's facility won't let a dirty homeless visitor in to visit. No doubt about it. I also worried they'd see how nuts he was. Bobby T would have gotten shipped back to State Hospital quick as tobacco spit. Life without Bobby T worried me. I was worried for me and him.

That bump I shot up in the bathroom finally kicked in and I nodded and didn't wake until closing, nine p.m. I forgot to eat before getting high. Bobby saved me a couple of sugar donuts.

The next day early, waiting for the doors to open, we were waiting together on the main entry steps. Sometimes the ladies going to work would bring us a coffee or food, or even give us a dollar if you asked them nicely.

I asked Bobby T if he was excited about getting a place. His response wasn't what I expected.

"Kev, times a-short. I need more input," Bobby T said. "I can't get no more out of here. It's all gone dry. I have to leave."

"How do you mean," I asked him.

"I'm not mental," Bobby said. "So, I can't read. They tried to teach me, but State Hospital said I can't learn it cause I'm autistic. They're wrong. I use books...you know. I feel what's inside them. That's not sickness."

I didn't disagree. A few stripped screws ain't a sickness. I tipped off balance whenever he was articulate. He had put a complete set of thoughts together. He never talked about State much. Sometimes he'd start talking normally but digress into a distant babble. But he remained alert which made me think he had a snort. He could pass for a meth-head but he didn't use. His face was scraped from shaving dry over his craggy face which made him look like a meth-head. But his cuts scabbed over—Tweakers never heal. The damage wasn't from meth-picking. They don't let users into Section 8, besides. I rejected the idea that he was high, although he did scratch a lot when he was nervous. Or it could have been fleas.

"Ya git me Kev?"

"I never said there was anything wrong with you," I said and I meant it. "Who am I to judge? Stop scratching. You'll make your face infected."

Bobby scratching mimicked withdrawal, and that would put the housing people on their heels. I hated it when he shaved, and I was thankful he didn't shave often because he did it badly. He'd rip the edges of them crags every time.

"I hoped they gonna help you with shaving," I said. "Stop picking will ya."

"Okay, Kevin. I'll do what you say. Stop itching."

"You don't want them at housing thinking you got the DTs."

I finally realized how wired he was. No doubt he had something else on his mind. His lower lip quivering said so.

"Go on, Bobby, spit it out," I said.

He launched into it, and I listened like always when he took off. It didn't happen much. It gave me a little comfort to do something good for somebody. Listening was the only human kindness I could spare. Bobby didn't judge me. No dirty looks when I got high. Funny thing was, the more I hung with Bobby T, the less I got high.

"Let me tell you something," he said, even-toned like a normal person. "I have a talent. I hold a book, smell it, and I can absorb what's inside it. It made me crazy as a young man. I could not endure it and nobody believed me. I can't remember my parents, but I remember the books. They put me in hospitals for air-reading. I stopped reading to fool them. That's how I got out. No more hospitals for me, I'm never going back."

He let out a big laugh, I'm not sure why, before he went on. I wasn't the only one worried about him going back to State. He had the same worry.

"I broke no laws," Bobby continued. "They had to turn me out. I live here. But not no more, it's dry. I need to leave. I'm leaving."

"What about housing," I asked.

Bobby had waited years for housing. I was floored. I had been on the street for three years, and Bobby was there before me. In two hours, he'd have a real home and I'd need to find a new hold-up. What I wanted for the pain of my impending aloneness was a fat bump of smack.

"I'm not going," Bobby said with a finality I hadn't heard from him before.

That was the bump I needed.

I said, "I wish I was nuts enough to get a place."

I said it for the 100th time. I was just talking smack. I'd have to get clean and that was never gonna happen. "Come on Bobby, you have to go. They don't want us here anymore."

"I'm not going, Kevin."

"Come on, you'll be fine. You're just scared is all."

"Let me ask you," Bobby said. "You believe me? Nobody does. They think I'm sick. You don't think that?"

"Of course not."

He wasn't totally out of his mind but he did have quirks. I assumed he had read the same books I did without me seeing it or he had read them before his brain shorted out. Bobby couldn't read stop signs or a crosswalk signal. That's how he got the limp and a bed at State years ago by walking into traffic. They thought it was a suicide attempt. He almost walked in front of a bus again the week before departure day.

"You mean it, Kevin?"

"You ain't nuts, Bobby. You're the smartest man I know."

He was the only friend I had, so I told him what he needed to hear to convince him to let the system help him because he really couldn't take care of himself. With my bad habit, I could OD anytime and then who would care about him? Pushing him along was my parting gift, a good white lie.

"I am smart," Bobby said. "More than books now."

That was half-true. He ain't no dummy. Why should I agitate the old man and tell him the cold truth? He had a head injury in the accident, that had to be it. He can't remember reading them books is all that was. He knew a lot about a lot of books. You pick up a lot by listening in a library. They got books on tape.

"Bobby T," I said, "if you say you feel what's in books, I'm gonna believe it. You ain't no liar." True enough.

That pleased him. He cracked a big smile, showing off his missing and broken teeth. The system never was keen on providing dental care. I scraped the gunk off my teeth with a fingernail having seen my future in his teeth.

"Good," he said. "Not getting anything here no more. I need more. I don't have to touch them. Just get near them. I'll know them. I need a road trip. The other libraries. Library of Congress has what I'm looking for if nobody else."

"I don't know, Bobby," I said. I thought he was just talking. "Washington's a long walk. How are you going?"

"I can't be alone. You gotta take me," Bobby said, and that blew me away. "We go. I got Social Security, 600 a month. You got no money. We'll go together. The bus is cheap."

The library opened and I forgot to beg. A police car and one of the crisis intervention workers' cars pulled into the two handicap parking spots out front. I had seen the CI supervisor's car before. The lady and the cop stood waiting for the transport van which hadn't arrived yet.

Bobby wasn't the only pick-up scheduled. The others—homeless-hopefuls who usually waited at the door with us—were scattered around outside. Nobody went in. Some people were going to the shelter if CI could convince them, and if not, two more police cars pulled in. That's a lot of convincing. Two junkies slinked away down the block. The trannie didn't leave. She wanted in but they don't take trannies.

"What the hell, I'm getting tired of PA anyhow," I said. "Okay, Bobby, you got a partner. When are we going?" I said, not caring where we go or believing we'd leave the county.

Big yellow and black teeth broadcast his good mood.

"Going to the next library. I'm not coming back."

Bobby got onto his feet. The van pulled up.

"Bus station is two blocks that way."

He pointed up the block over the heads of the cops and the social workers. The cops nabbed Old Rack first. He had lost half his brain in the war and he started yelling at the social worker who approached him. The cops closed in. That was our opportunity.

We skipped out of the homeless roundup and snuck back to our sleep spots. I packed what I could and it wasn't much, some clothes and my works. I stashed my belongings into an old child's backpack I had found inside a clothing donation box.

I left my hobbit-hole for the last time without regret, or so you'd think. I lived alongside that bridge embankment for a long time. I had a nice place dug out of the upper bank off to the side with bushes all around. You couldn't see it if you didn't look right at it. I saw everything from up there. I used to think it'd be easy to leave my dry hole, but I was wrong.

We took the long way around to Bobby's bank. Bobby took out the money he had. His government check got direct deposited. He knew his pin number, not the number but a pattern he drew on the keypad with his fingertip.

Homeless in Pa. or Washington, made no difference to me. We took our time getting there. The bus-passes were good for a year. Bobby got off the bus for every small-town library that seemed right to him along the way.

I went back to sleeping in libraries with my eyes open but we still got tossed out fairly regularly. Small towns don't like vagabonds.

I didn't mind. I had a friend to share a jail cell with should it ever come to that. We never stayed anywhere long enough for me to score a bag, or get tossed into jail, and I didn't mind moving on either. Dope was hard to find and I got myself accidentally straight before we hit DC. All right, I thought, big town smack, here I come.

I didn't bother keeping up with the news in libraries. I hate newspapers. Newspapers are too depressing. They don't make good blankets either. They burn too fast but aren't bad for shoe stuffing. I never paid much attention to what was written in the newspapers.

Bobby would tell me what was in the papers. Most of it, I'd say, was complete garbage but Bobby T would point out the useful tidbits anyway. Such as, the authorities were looking for us, or…more likely I felt…they wanted Bobby T.

"Be on the lookout for a homeless mentally ill man," was the message I got out of the headlines. But was it us? Who'd they want? Bobby? Or one of the other thousands roaming the streets? They couldn't find us. We blended in too well.

Outside of DC, one of the papers had Bobby's picture in it. We were just a few towns over. A crack-head in Virginia told me The FBI was going around scooping up homeless in every little town. He named some of the towns we had been in. The story the cops had was they were looking for a thief. I thought we had better rethink this, and Bobby was with me on that.

Maybe he had inherited money, I joked to myself—the long-lost child of somebody who was somebody. I laughed to myself all the time like that, but this wasn't funny.

I assumed Bobby had accidentally stolen something important out of the Bethlehem Library, like a national treasure on loan or something. They had some costly borrowed stuff on display there all the time. Bobby didn't see any value in things. He'd wipe his butt with the Constitution if it were soft and handy. He might have picked up a keepsake, like an important artifact, and tossed it in the can just as quick. I wasn't gonna take any chances he had done that.

We made tracks out of there on the cusp of us arriving and started pushing toward New Mexico in a zig-zag. Sometimes we'd get a bus, sometimes a ride. Same thing from town to town. Bobby absorbed books and essays by the millions. I had no clue how many books Bobby thought he had "read." But he wasn't satisfied. He still wanted Washington.

Nothing I could do to stop him, so we started back east.

It was all the same to me. I had fun on the road dodging the authorities all spring and summer. Playing mental tic-tack-toe around the DC area was easy enough. We had no problems keeping our heads down.

We got along fine on Bobby's 600 bucks a month. Every time he drew out money, the FBI showed up. Shelters are safer when you have a partner watching your back, but we didn't go to shelters. The authorities always check them first. "Life is good in the woods," Bobby liked to say. He was right. I had never once seen a cop in the middle of a dense city park at midnight, too dangerous.

Bobby was feeling older after the smoke cleared in late summer. We hadn't heard any more about FBI people in a while, and we were itching to hit the big town, so off we went. He wanted to get it done. It was his dream to get there. He didn't say exactly where in there 'there' was but on November 22, we arrived in Washington DC proper. The place was lit like Christmas.

"We are here!" Boddy said getting off the local bus right where he wanted to go. "The heart of DC. Library of Congress!"

"We ain't never been here before," I said. I felt the pressure of the place. "But we tried."

I had been perplexed. We went near DC a lot but never inside it. He couldn't deal with it. Bobby couldn't tear himself out from under the local libraries until things got hot. We were forced to leave often. We could have gone sooner, but Bobby wasn't ready. He needed to work himself up for this all that while.

"I hope your dream doesn't turn into a nightmare," I said.

Bobby didn't hear me. He was gone standing right there.

This need of his made no sense to me. I felt like his ability to absorb information was rubbing off which I doubted. Bobby didn't mind sharing his skill. He was happy about it. It scared the hell out of me. I had to be borderline delusional. I feared Bobby's crazy was what was really rubbing off, but I wasn't gone yet.

"Bobby, you got to move. You can't block the sidewalk."

Right after getting off the bus, Bobby got hit with a bolt of information and that's as far as he moved. I felt it. He made a scene standing there staring up at the fancy architecture with his hands up like a worshipper swaying to the music. I wanted to join, but I resisted. I tingled as if that sidewalk had a hot wire under it.

I pushed Bobby's arm down. Bobby got agitated.

"That's it, Kevin. That's it." Bobby twirled and danced. "That's the place, the place!"

Standing in front of them great buildings was the wrong place for Bobby to act up. He went to mumbling and yelling about, "I'm going home." He did that in his sleep a lot. I don't know if what got into him was real or not, but I worried if he didn't stop acting up the cops will make him stop. Shaking and hooting ain't tourist friendly. Two armed-door-cops up on the stoop across the street swung eyeballs our way.

All that information floating in the air was hard on Bobby. I was worried about him and us. It felt like the air was full of needles.

"Come on, Bobby. We got to go," I said more than once.

His ranting had people upset. The police on our asses were the same-old-thing, but this felt different. There was no place to hide and the cops here don't take any hooey.

The stoop-guards looking down at us from on top of the grand entry started down the stairs. I grabbed Bobby's arm and jerked him hard. I hauled him and me beside a passing horse-drawn carriage. I walked us along it and away from that info dump as fast as I could. Bobby snapped out of it a few blocks on down at the park.

"I'm sorry Kevin. I sorry, Kevin. I'm sorry..." Bobby started bawling.

I pulled the old man in close and patted his back. "It's okay, Bobby. You did nothing wrong. It's okay, buddy. It's okay."

He chilled out after a good cry.

It took us three days of park-bench sleeping before we were able to chill enough to reach the Library of Congress's complex. We had cleaned up in an icy fountain at dawn and combed our hair so the guards wouldn't shoo us away. We didn't smell that bad.

We managed to get inside. Bobby bribed a guard with his last 20 bucks. It wasn't easy. Bobby was acting half out of his mind in a new way, so I couldn't tell what he was saying half the time. It started when we hit the town but inside the Library of Congress, it got worse. I should have left when he argued with one of the inside-cops. I should have saved myself and bugged out. But I owed it to him to keep an eye on him. Bobby had gotten to me and deep. He grew into way more than my meal-ticket. I was feeling like he was my old man.

"Sir," I said to the guard, stepping in when I should have run. "This here's my grandfather and he always wanted to see this place." I put a hand aside my face and whispered. "He used to be an important judge you know, before dementia." I stepped back a little. "But he still talks about this, this place." I spread my arms and put on my beggar's sad face. "Grandfather hasn't got much time left on this old Earth."

I had no idea how true that statement was. Bobby cringed a little. The guard patted us down with wiry fingers. Bobby held out the twenty with snot dripping from his nose. His lower lip didn't look right. I had shaved him and missed a little but he looked half decent. I didn't think the guy would take the twenty. It had spit on it. It's an old trick so they won't take the money. But money rules. The cop snapped the bill out of Bobby's grubby mitt.

"Go on in, judge," he said.

Inside Bobby fell into his usual trance and settled down. We wandered from aisle to aisle, building to building, floor to floor. He stretched out his hands like Jesus on a tree never saying a word. He went floating like a ghost. People parted like the Red Sea. Maybe we did smell pretty bad after all.

"Don't mind the judge," I'd say to the guards and docents. "His meds should kick in soon."

After six hours of this and a thousand looks of disdain, Bobby finally opened his mouth.

"You want to know something, Kevin? I'll tell you something." He looked around as if expecting a spy. "There's a secret vault here. All stuff the Freedom of Information Act won't let you read. They let us read the fake stuff. The real stuff is here."

Bobby pointed at the floor and tapped his noggin. Dirt fell out of his greasy hair. He put a finger to his lips and spoke like a funeral director, "Nobody knows this. That is good. Better for the public, I think. I know the way home. I was right. I'm going home."

I never heard him so well-spoken and calm before. Thoughtful. Almost normal. Right about what? His internal debates must have gotten crosswired again. I couldn't let him hurt himself believing junk like that.

"Bobby," I said, "you ain't going home. Man, don't talk crazy. You don't want to get locked up, do you? Your home was State Hospital from 1947 until 1995, remember? Don't go daffy on me, Old Man."

I took his hands. "You got to hear me, man. It's for your own good. We gotta get outta here."

"This is the end, Kevin."

Fear flashed in me. It spiked my spine from nowhere like a thousand toothpick shives. I had a feeling like this is the end, like doom swirling on the horizon pulling me apart. Something big. I felt ill. I shook it off. We hadn't eaten. Hungry, that's all. But one idea landed hard.

"Bobby, don't you tell me you're gonna die. Are you? You better not die on me, man. What will I do?"

I grabbed his arms on either side. Tenderness dressed Bobby's features. He remained a normal person for the moment and looked me dead in the eyes. People on the street don't do that. There's nothing ever in there when you look except reflected loss. It's better not to look at all, too much pain in there should you get a peek beyond the emptiness.

"I will not be dying," Bobby chuckled. "But I got enough data. My old bones want New Mexico. You are a son to me, Kevin. How about we take a family vacation? Let us go where it is warmer this winter. Good idea. Say yes?"

"I'm with you, Pops," I said.

I felt good all over for no reason. I hugged him and he let me.

Calling him Pops jacked the good times out of my heart's lockbox. Pops was what I called my dad since I was a little kid. Bobby sounded logical and strong and reasonable like my old man used to when I was a teen and he was still alive. Dad knew what he was talking about and I trusted Bobby did, too.

"When are we leaving, Pops?"

"How long it takes to walk to the bus depot."

That bus trip wasn't like the rest. We didn't meander, not many stops. After the Library of Congress, the other book deposits didn't offer anything for us but a place to sleep. We did less chair-surfing and slept in the pup tents we picked up cheap at a thrift store. Bobby became more internally focused and introspective. He was calmer longer than I'd ever seen. He hinted that he had found some great answers, but it was a big secret. Anyway, Bobby said he was satisfied. I didn't know what to make of that. Satisfied? Only the needle ever did that for me and that satisfaction didn't last.

He got his SSD check on the 3rd of October and we celebrated by getting a hotel. We happened to be in Roswell, New Mexico. It wasn't our usual nasty no-telling-motel, but a decent place. We got hot showers and a real nice meal right in town. After we ate, we went to Wendy's for a milkshake.

There, Bobby says, "I'm going to miss this Earth. Yes, sir. Nice while it lasts. Big day coming." He shook his milkshake at me. "They don't have this where I'm going."

Bobby T loved milkshakes. He spoke more like his old self which was him talking a lot of nonsense. Okay, I thought, so Bobby is going to miss Wendy's. He said the same about McDonald's in Washington, DC. Maybe they'll have a Dairy Queen where we land next.

"Big day," he repeated.

"Yeah, okay, Pops. I'm gonna miss this, too. Where are we going?"

"We can't go to UFO country without looking at Area 51. Missing that would be bad. We'll camp near there, where Bob Lazar saw the UFOs with his friends. What do you think, Kevin?"

I read some UFO books at the little UFO library in town. That visit must have put ideas into Bobby's head. I had no objections to a camping trip. UFOs were a bunch of crap in my view, but what the heck, it's still interesting. I had an idea of what we were getting into. Camping in the desert was supposed to be nice in the fall according to the van-dwellers living in the All-Store parking lot. They all said fall is the safe time for it, not too hot or cold. They should know. People living in a parking lot know things like that. Bobby T and me had pup tents so why not?

"Sounds good to me," I said. "We'll have to find out about Greyhound. Too far to walk."

We went outside and started toward the town's info booth. A junkie was begging in the parking lot. I tried to steer Bobby the other way. Bobby tended to share with people too much. He didn't know the difference between an addict that would stab him in the heart for a quarter and a nun giving hand-outs. Bobby slipped my hold and took off for the meth-kid.

I caught up. "What are you doing?"

"We need a car."

I don't know how he did it, but Bobby bought that junkie's running minivan for a hundred bucks. Between the hotel, the junkie, and gassing up we were about broke. We drove it out of Roswell without insurance or registration, and bad plates, too—Area 51 or bust.

I didn't have a map. I didn't need one. Bobby had New Mexico memorized. He directed. I drove. I had accepted his abilities but I doubted they'd find food and water in the middle of nowhere.

Bobby had me leave the road approaching the military territory. Gas and food were low but I couldn't stop him.

Bobby had me cut a way in by following abandoned horse paths through the desert's ravines. That went on for miles until we made it to a decent dirt road going up a gravel hillside. I could not believe how well that dilapidated Astro minivan pulled. Turns out it had all-wheel drive. I drove up that dirt road to the top of a hill and stopped. The road ended at a flat clearing behind a tall barbwire-topped cyclone fence. I got out.

The view across Groom Lake was awesome. We were pretty high. The valley bottom and former lake were a good twenty miles across and well below us. I couldn't see any details, just little reflections off buildings miles and miles on across the wide flatland. I took a long hard look.

I heard a cop in the back of my imagination saying, "Nothing to see here, move along." We must have heard that a million times. Watching seemed like a waste of eye power, but I was feeling uneasy being exposed there.

I wanted to say, "Bobby, don't you think we should go?" But Bobby had latched his clawed hands onto the fence under a sign that said, "Government Instillation Access Restricted." Another sign, a bigger one, said, "Trespassers Will Be Prosecuted." I wasn't worried about that. I didn't see anybody around. But that danger feeling didn't leave.

"You ain't ready to go," I said looking at Bobby.

He didn't hear me, being busy humming and rocking as if that fence was the Temple Wall. I saw this behavior before.

Nothing in this lonely spot was as interesting as Bobby glued to the fence swaying like a stuck feather in the hot breeze. He wasn't gonna move for hours so I stretched out my bedroll and took a nap on the ground in the shade of the van.

I got woken by an army man barking orders at his pack of junk-yard-dogs. I wasn't awake for a second when one of them wrenched me up off my bedroll and all the while screaming.

"Where are they, where are they!"

I tune out when yelled at but he was persistent.

"Where are they, where'd they go!"

Who is "they," was my first thought but I didn't say it? It took me a hot minute to gather my wits. The fence had been cut and the sun was low. I had slept three or four hours. The man pushed me against the van and I snapped into reality.

"Back off, asshole," I said. He surprised me and did. "Where's Bobby T? You took my friend. Let him go!"

"You are in deep trouble," a sergent snarled, walking up, "Start talking or your ass goes to the brig."

"I'm the son of two dead vets, back off," I barked right back at him. "I'm on your side, asshole. I want a lawyer."

I wasn't afraid and I showed it and I don't know why. I've received cop intimidation for years and it always messed me up. It's hard to take. This wasn't the same. The sergeant relented whereas the cops either arrested you or beat the hell out of you. Military-respect for the military-dead must have reprogrammed his demeanor.

The van's side door was still open and they let me sit there to put my shoes on. I found a bit of paper in my shoe. I kept my mouth shut. I was too distracted to read it with a dozen military men surrounding me suited for war. They were inside and outside the fence. After they took the van apart and the luggage, the sergeant squatted in front of me for a few questions.

"Son, why are you here?"

"I'll tell you the truth," I said with a strong voice, but I was scared shitless. "I needed to sleep is all. I'm lost. Ain't this public land? Free camping ain't allowed here? I didn't do nothing. I been sleeping."

"That's true LT," another army man said. "We got him on camera. He hasn't moved since 1300. There were two here."

"Where's the other one?" Fearless-Leader said.

Was that question for me? Dogface was fixing to bark again when an explosion rocked the valley below. The soldiers scrambled for cover. I sat there shading my eyes. Radios blared. Alarms rang near and far. Assholes and elbows everywhere. When the smoke cleared, I saw it first and I shot onto my feet with my mouth hanging open.

Somebody yelled, "look at that!"

As fast as it started, activities stopped. Everyone's attention turned. Desert khakis don't hide shit satins. We all saw it. Everyone faced the rolling smoke. I shut my mouth. A golden saucer lifted over whatever had blown up. It flew slowly and moved upward a little at a time. It hovered, wobbling in the smoke between ratchet steps. The sun lit its upper hull. There is no mistaking a flying saucer when you see one.

"Hanger Twelve's gone!" A man with binoculars cried.

"Shut up! You're breaching security!" Another man called back.

"It's coming this way," I said evenly.

I had the suspicion that the men in uniform there had seen this thing before, but not in the air. It began moving in our direction. I smelled somebody had wet his fatigues. On the street, you smell piss all the time and you don't pay attention, but out in the fresh clean world, you can't miss it. It's like a starter pistol.

The thing moving had everybody excited like ants on crack. Why do army men always have to yell? The boss didn't need a big mouth. Yelling was just his habit, I guess. The distant alarms change tune and sounded like firetrucks. The gold object did indeed head directly for us and it was picking up speed.

"Take cover" rang out and it wasn't me saying it. I reached for Bobby with my internal antenna feeling for him. He was on that ship. I raised my arms. It stopped and hovered. Blinking lights were all I could see. I don't know what happened after that.

The next thing I knew, I was back in that hotel room in Roswell lying flat on my back on a clean bed with my dirty clothes on. I had three-days-later growth on my face. Bobby was well and good gone. I didn't need to look for him to know that.

I was groggy but I still had my shoes on so I tried standing. I felt like I had better beat it out of there quick. That bit of paper stuffed in my shoe was still there. It bugged me. I'm used to things stuffed inside my shoes, it's the best place to hide your money, but it didn't feel right. I pulled my shoes off for adjustments and found the hotel receipt in one shoe, and Bobby's bank card in the other.

The room was paid up for the week. And on the back of that small piece of paper were numbers—his bank card password. Bobby left me a goodbye-note even if he couldn't write. That slip of paper said it all. Bobby T loved me like a son.

He did what he said he'd do and went home. I read the bank account numbers and cried. Bobby had written it himself and that was not easy for him. I learned on the hotel computer that Bobby had put his savings account in my name, sixty-years of savings. He couldn't write letters but he knew numbers. He'd dial a phone but he didn't understand money.

Where ever Bobby Terrestrial went, he ain't going to need Earth money no more. He used to say, "information is cosmic currency." In that he's wealthy. I agree knowledge is worth more than cash, but cash helps, too. We had agreed that family is worth the most, because we had no family. But I thought wrong. Bobby T had a family, but it took him a while to find them.

"Thanks, Pops, thanks for being my family. And, I sure do need the money you left for me down here now that you're gone."

I spoke it out loud to that empty room. I'm believing he heard me. That hotel phone might have been Bobby's pipeline to the stars for all I know.

I rather have Bobby than the cash. I miss my family, the old and the new. Money can't buy a family.

I'm glad Bobby wasn't crazy. People will think I'm crazy for the way I live. I'm not changing anything except how I read books. Crazy library kid, they'll call me. Me and Bobby T have that in common, that's our family resemblance, we look crazy but we ain't.

WORM DRIVE

The estate owner, Mister Morgan, began his confession.

"I am in my estate manager's office, a place I've never seen before in my own house. I'm at his desk with his recorder on. I'm forced…"

The estate's former master released the microphone. His mouth hung open. The gun barrel pressing into the back of his neck pressed harder. One of the other house staff slapped him from behind muffing his thousand-dollar haircut.

"Alright, Alright."

"Go on," the butler said.

"It may well be that I had a part in it…However, it was not I alone who caused this catastrophe. Many aspects of our…What shall I say? The system? Yes, it's the establishment's fault. For my part, I had responsibilities as an industrialist of the system in good standing should."

The butler pressed in on him, close to his ear. Morgan forgot the man's name.

"You're evading, Mr. Morgan. Get on with it, if you please."

Morgan did not please. He had no choice.

"Is it my fault that profit is the point." The industrialist snapped. "Forward mobility is standard. Are we not a people bent on progress, growth, expansion?"

The butler scoffed and reached over Morgan's shoulder, waving Morgan's prized revolver in front of his face. The butler, being a short, spider-legged thin-man didn't seem a threat when Morgan hired him. Morgan never thought this possible. He had no doubt his former servant would pull the trigger as one of Morgan's house staff supporters found out the hard way.

"Go on," the butler said before jabbing the gun back into Morgan's neck. "Say it straight, tell the truth, you bloody snake."

Morgan could have struggled for the gun, but why bother? What if he got the upper hand? They were all dead anyway. Morgan wouldn't have cowered to that diminutive man-servant twerp, normally, but his life depended on it. He might survive what they had in store for him. The house staff's only concern was his confession. That bought time. Talking bought time. Morgan restarted the recorder.

"It wasn't my doing. I did what was expected of a man of high import, a man of influence, a man of inventiveness. I, the inventor of the worm-drive transport system, could not have foreseen these unintended consequences."

"Double speak! That's a load of dung," one of the maids said, "Stop your lie-in."

"I will tell it my way, if you please," he said in a weak voice.

His fire was gone. Men used to jump when he spoke.

"Get on with it then. Explain yourself," the maid said.

The butler and she spoke in that damnable, snotty English accent. Morgan had paid much to obtain the best help. But in essence, Morgan had hired foreign help for the accent and the status of having a top agency supply his needs. He had forgotten the best agencies also trained their people in security, forgotten until he was rudely reminded.

His former houseman retracted the gun barrel a little. "Was there no limit to your greed? How'd you become so heartless?"

"Greed? What's that to do with it? I'm not at fault. It's business, just business. I had a responsibility, didn't I? Didn't I?"

Morgan paused to hold his temper and consider the question. He had never asked it of himself before.

"It is simple. It was a matter of my upbringing. Don't you see? My grandfather was a great industrialist. He erected the first public space-port. He built an industry from nothing. That was my socialization."

"What's that bloody well to do with anything?"

An object hit the mansion from below and shook the walls, but the house didn't collapse. It was built to withstand an army but not space-time tearing apart. The generator skipped a beat. The lights dimmed and came back up. It took a few seconds for the falling of dishes and pots in the distance to quiet.

"Geed was why, wasn't it?" The butler pressed for the answer he wanted.

Morgan never allowed himself to be baited.

"I'm telling you why I was driven. The answer is complex. You asked about greed, didn't you? What you call greed was educated into me. I was the protégé of a grand industrialist. Am I not?"

Morgan thought this crass man must have a wormhole inside his brain with him being so unreasonably impolite. Yet that wasn't what drove his houseman. His butler had never used the worm-drive transport system himself. Lack of trust was Morgan's guess.

Something big landed outside on the grounds. It touched down slowly but with still enough force to rock the walls.

"Be quick about it. Every man deserves his confession. Go on, then."

"I was my grandfather's favorite and not his only grandchild, mind you. I was bright and did well in school. Once Father took over Morgan Transportation, my drunken, no-account father proceeded to run the operation into the ground. I swore to my grandfather on his death-bed I would save it. I was just out of college then and starting a career in science. I loved physics. I did both science and business. The grand old man's deathbed wish was for me to save the business. He confided where a small sum of start-up capital was hidden, funds my father wasn't aware of. I developed the company and I honored the old man...by god...is that my fault?"

"That means nothing. It's not why you're a bloody monster," the butler said. "You roll right over people. How it started isn't germane. You knew what you were doing—"

"You asked!" Morgan slammed the table with an open palm. The butler didn't flinch. "It's not greed. What drove me was responsibility—I am confessing my motivation, you, you...clod."

"Lame excuse."

"Perhaps," Morgan breathed in and sat straighter. "In my heart, what I did was correct. My invention does not need excuses. Applied science is desired...Results aren't always foreseen."

Morgan pointed at the water pitcher and the butler allowed him a drink.

"Tell us how you did it, how ya worked it? Get to the meat," the maid said.

"I put myself to the task, maneuvering the legal challenges, and finding ways to get the system approved by the governments. Billions—"

The butler drilled the gun hard into Morgan's back. "Shut up about the money."

"He ain't ever gonna understand his guilt," someone said from behind.

"Bit by bit, I succeeded after many years," Morgan continued intent on getting his side out. "Worm-drive was a side project but I did work on it all the while. I didn't share it with the company until the time was right. I reserved it until I knew it would work. From my lowly place in R&D, I did it. I cut time into pieces one tiny slice at a time. I moved forward into managing the company from there. I had to protect my patents. Don't you see? That's how business works."

"You learned the business, go on." The butler said with a laugh. "And we thought you came out of the womb with it."

Laughter ran through the room. Morgan had more people behind him than he thought. The rest of the house staff had come to leer. The idea of fighting them left completely. The staff laughed as evil hyenas will. One does not tangle with wild dogs.

Something impacted the far end of the estate sending tremors. Water in the pitcher danced. The merriment stopped.

"I learned, yes…Business is war, a shark-eat-shark affair. Only profit for the shareholders, and my coffers subsequently, can matter. Responsibilities, you see, are far and wide. Every quarter must show a profit, by God. Profit is God and my father is the devil. I gave Morgan Transport new life. I admit it. Like a god, I gave it new life! They called me a megalomaniac which is an unfavorable mischaracterization. I did what business required. I'm proud of it."

"Stop procrastinating."

"I restored the business with my invention."

He spoke faster, sensing time was running out. "I developed it and I thought, 'why not transport goods and people?' All things connect at the quantum level. I found a way to bend space and time. I created directed wormholes. Traveling between the stars can't work. Gravity is necessary. We can't escape Earth that way. But on Earth—"

"Bloody hell."

The butler slapped the back of his head.

"You made wormholes, and bloody well knew they're dangerous. You had an inkling what it could do, and you ignored it because you had to have the money, don't lie."

The butler spoke, while pushing Morgan's custom-made target pistol barrel into Morgan's soft cheek. The butler's wife was one of the first people found to have a micro-wormhole inside her head. She lived in London while the butler's job continued in upstate New York. She often traveled to New York using a worm-drive railcar. House staff received free passes. The press lied and reported her sudden insanity was hereditary. Morgan had a worm station installed on the estate and the butler's wife was the last to use it.

"You want to hear me or not?" Morgan managed to say despite the gun pressing on his cheek.

"You killed my Tilly, you bastard! That's what I want. Admit it," he pulled the gun back.

"She used what I provided. Am I to blame?" Morgan snapped. "No, it was her free choice. She decided to use the system, not me."

The butler raised the gun to pistol-whip Morgan, but the maids and a cook reached in and pulled his arm down.

"I knew about problems," Morgan continued. "I intended to shut down, but operations assured me the system could run…No danger while we worked on the bugs. They were wrong. The government would have eventually stopped it and I would have paid large fines...Astounding profits, fines never outweigh the profit. I pushed it forward on good financial advice."

"And letting the next generation repair the damages? Aye, the ol' standard," the Irish housekeeping manager said. "Isn't that the way it always is, now? Do your due diligence, Mister Businessman, as any one of us will. Is that it?"

The gun twisted on the nape of his neck.

"I suspected. One cannot cut holes in reality and not have suspicions. I put my research team on it. I didn't want another lawsuit. Costs a lot of money and time. Government approved it."

"Nobody wants to get sued," the butler said. "Won't they buy the bloody government, as industrialists do? There chant be any trouble, now. Will there be? Bribe the politician and get what you want."

Morgan paused and took a sip of water rather than bite his tongue. Morgan would have chuckled had a gun not been his deterrent. The winds echoed. Parts of the main house had been hit which torn rents in the siding allowing the passage of air. The government did not approve Morgan's transport system. No, they were bribed to accept it. Morgan's lobbyist group was top shelf. Standard business practices. *I can't say that.*

"Is it my fault I do business the way business is done? This was not my fault. The government allowed it. I have a fine humanitarian record, I give—"

"Then why didn't you cease operations when my Tilly took ill?"

"Government regulators had no proof," rolled out of his mouth as a practiced lie. What he used to say to the financial press, he repeated. "The port authorities took over. They took that power away from me."

The public utility angle had been arranged to push financial responsibility onto the public. Morgan took another sip before going on.

"We took financial risks like in the old days. Why shouldn't we reap the rewards? The government supplements made it affordable to you. In this venture, no one perceived such… such…losses…until…"

Morgan's head dropped to his chest.

"Until time tunnels made the Earth into Swiss cheese," the cook said, thumping the flat side of a meat cleaver into one palm. Morgan shivered. "Why didn't you warn us?"

"The public can't know how finances work. We had to control that information. Without us rulers, there would be chaos."

Morgan felt good laying his cards down. Money was indeed behind everything, but it was only a tool of power.

"How could you know anything with media, which we controlled? We, the establishment, infused every fiber of society with propaganda. Had we warned you, would you have listened? Have you ever trusted the media? You shouldn't have."

"We're getting somewhere," the butler said. "You upper-crust think you can do anything. I watched you, Morgan. You don't give a bloody damn about people. You didn't even visit your father on his deathbed."

The butler spit and pressed the gun hard again.

"I had responsibilities. I could not leave the business. I paid for his care. Not my fault…I supplied his needs, didn't I ?"

"A lot of good it did. When'd you know the Denver black hole would open?" The gun withdrew slightly. "Your grandsire was a decent man, I grant you."

The gunmen had taken care of Old Man Morgan in his waning days. The butler, having been employed by the estate, was sent to valet Grandad who was suffering his last cancerous days.

My housemen knew father and grandfather better than I.

The butler reached over Morgan's shoulder and turned off the recording device.

"This is getting us nowhere." He spoke into his wrist phone. "Security, you have his bio-feed?"

"I do," came a voice over the ceiling speakers. "'E's lying. Algorithms say 'E doesn't love nobody and his bank records prove it."

"Home Hospice was ripping me off!" Morgan stood, knocking over the chair.

The butler had backed away.

"As I thought," the butler said. "Mister Morgan, I am not illiterate. You could have stopped the worm drive in time. You made more money than God himself could spend in eternity and yet you continued. Just one more transport, just one more coin, eh."

"You no ride the rail yourself," the Jamaican said. "What about it now, too risky?"

"This way to the door, sir," the butler said.

The revolver pushed Morgan painfully along, steering him by the pressure on his spine. The house staff followed close behind. The butler, by habit, opened the opulent front door ahead of Morgan. The butler never took the gun off him.

"We were all dead anyway," Morgan said, having no interest in resisting. He still hoped he might survive.

The house and the forty acres of grounds around it were intact and free-floating in the sky. In the distance, another large chunk of Earth floated. Bits of everything small flew by, some headed downward, others upward or sideways. On the horizon, an iceberg of humanity many times larger than the estate drifted. Morgan thought it was Manhattan or a piece of New Jersey.

The march toward the worm drive station was not without spectacular vistas. When the Earth splintered, the gravity and atmosphere were magically retained. No one thought it was possible or knew why. Wormhole system stations were all over the world, and Earth fractured on those lay-lines. The system caused Humpy-Dumpty's fall. The millions of sad souls, who were insane with wormholes, had split apart as well.

The party arrived at the local station, or what was left of it. The booth was gone, and only a spiraling light-show hole in the sod remained, still active and running out of control. It was the same killer which was installed for the servant's use. Morgan stopped within inches of chaos.

"No sign of any apparatus," Morgan said. "It's not supposed to do that."

The gun flew over his head and into the magic hole.

"Let it not be said that I am a murderer," the butler said. "Maybe you'll live. In you go."

That was Morgan's hope. He was interested as a scientist and wanted to know what will happen. He desired to go in open-eyed but a bear-knuckled punch to the back of his head insured his curiosity would not be satisfied.

*****

The butler and his cohorts retired to the kitchen, congratulating themselves. Their captured sky island was well-stocked and the master was well gone. They had replayed the recordings while feasting. Morgan lied more than anyone guessed, because he believed his lies, which was the staff's consensus supported by the house computer.

"The old profit monger knew what his device might do. He knew it all along," the butler said. He took another sip of fine wine. "He had to know. No sign of him stopping, no such thoughts were ever in his head. Unreasonable greed, I say. He should have stopped if not for humanity's sake but to save himself."

"True, true," the IT man said. "Wormholes must have twisted his mind."

"It made him loco," Pedro said. "Money, loco."

"That's natural to him, evil runs naturally in blue-bloods," the butler said. "Good riddance."

Everyone clicked glasses. House staff had a drink or two and no more, although there were basements full of the finest. The thirteen survivors agreed not to waste anything out of hand. That was the first order of business agreed upon after Morgan's departure. They set up a democracy based on logic, reason, and best mutual benefit practices.

Wasting supplies is bad for survival. Morgan's behaviors were not good to mimic. He wasted everything and felt nothing. What he had hoarded would have gone to waste. The group thought to preserve their stores for themselves and any survivors who may arrive in need. Preservation of life was deemed paramount. It was all-for-all, either that, or face the end of the species.

That Morgan himself didn't care about others, and would not contribute, not even for human survival, was confirmed. The New House of Morgan had a different view of what its responsibilities are.

ORIGINAL SIN

The bureaucrat handed Adam an apple.

"I don't like apples," Adam said, "Can't I have something else?"

"Sure thing," the PR man said, handing Adam a different apple.

"But this is just another apple," Adam said. "I want mango."

"This is a mango, if you see it that way," the CEO said, shoving the apple under Adam's nose. "It's anything I need it to be. Just believe."

"I don't know," Adam said, scratching his head. "Sign says 'off-limits.'"

The lawyer pulled out his pocket watch and swung it by its golden web before Adam.

"Repeat over and over: 'it's mango, it's mango.' It's the law."

An original thought burst upon Adam, compelling a question.

"What if I'm caught?"

"No problem," the industrialist said, flicking his tongue. "We'll blame Eve. You play dumb. You don't have to do a thing."

Adam bit his mango.

A WRITER'S PASSAGE

Author's note: This short nonfiction piece was first published in and written for the GLVWG anthology, *Writes of Passage*, published in 2021.That anthology won the 2022 BookFest Award in the anthology category. The original essay was published under a strict word-count limit. Here it is slightly edited with a few more words added.

Life is full of rites of passage, small and large, events that cause change. Some passages go unnoticed and are only realized in hindsight. Some changes happen with a bang. What gave me the desire to write was always understood. It was reading. At an early age, I inhaled a steady diet of good books. Tolkien's *The Hobbit,* for me, revealed that writer's mountain passage, which I, too, would one day climb. Yet, it was not any one book that thrust me into writing. The desire was always there although it took an explosion to jack me out of complacency.

On one fine Indian summer day, the front end of my vintage motorcycle collapsed. I wasn't going fast. It wasn't the first time I dropped a bike. I would have walked away had an oncoming truck not run me down, scooped me up into its undercarriage, and set me alight. When I woke a few weeks later it was fall season, and burns were the least of my problems.

I lay in bed for half a year examining my life. Forgotten dreams emerged. Having faced death, I asked myself, "What are you doing with your life? What happened to your dreams?"

It wasn't too late to go after my childhood goal of writing a novel. But I had two problems. My burned fingertips took a year to heal, and second, I didn't know how to type or anything else about writing a novel. No problem, I told myself, I'll learn.

I had time to study and I did. It was a long uphill battle, but having wasted years not writing, what did I have to lose by trying? I couldn't spell, couldn't put a sentence together, and had no clue about grammar, but I was determined. All the things that stopped me before were nothing compared to that death-defying crash. Funny how a little accident can change one's priorities. What if I had died? I came close. But I lived, thus my dream lived, too.

I had a mountain of stuff to learn. I went to work. I read books, took classes, volunteered to write for nonprofits, I wrote, wrote, wrote. I did stringer work for newspapers. I'd take any assignment that had me writing for print.

Ray Bradbury said, to paraphrase, "You'll write a million words before becoming a published writer." I did that. As soon as my burnt fingers allowed it, I wrote. I haven't stopped yet. In that first year after recovery, I completed fifteen short stories. Most were bad, but each one taught me something. Each one was a baby step uphill.

I crested that first learning hill running and smacked into a mountain. No worries. I've become a literary mountain goat happy to climb. My latest book was published last year and my fifth novel is drafted at the time of this writing. I have more books in mind. I plan to write ten and when I reach that peak, I will seek the next climb.

(At the time of this printing, I have seven published books.)

ON SETTING

Author's note: This is yet another nonfiction essay inspired by discussions among my fellow writers. This first appeared on the Parisian Phoenix blog. The goal was to keep this essay under 500 words. Originally it was published at 497 words, in editing here, I broke 500.

The other night, one writer presented a story for critique whereby he used a specific place. Writers that knew the area and that out-of-the-way place well balked at the necessary inaccuracies this fiction writer had used to tell his story. The elements he used were devices in his tale. Readers will call out a writer when the setting is skewed—even in fiction. This complicates the process of writing fiction.

Settings either should be places everyone knows so well the writer need not describe them, or the setting is a place nobody knows. Setting a place just like someplace people know makes it feel real, but the exact place can be distractingly real. That critique illustrated several points. Places well-known by all are best used when the backdrop details aren't important. Stories about NASCAR drivers needn't feature Daytona Beach's art deco architecture.

Inaccuracies take the reader out of the story. Exact real places limit the writer's ability to invent whatever prop is necessary to tell the story. Everything in a story has a purpose. It's all about whatever unfolds in the story. The reader is there for the characters and the setting is there to enhance and support the character's reality. Using a real place, even if largely unknown, limits how a writer can use it. Reality doesn't bend gladly for fiction.

The setting must serve the story. Settings are typically overdone. We writers love rolling around in lush settings. It's fun. But overly rich descriptions of the setting tell the readers that the writer doesn't trust the readers' ability to comprehend and imagine. It's patronizing. Unfocused, pretty prose without purpose ejects the reader out of the story.

If it ain't needed, don't write it.

Modern readers want great settings and less description, especially of places they know. Of course, some genres demand word-eating settings, but a careful examination of the best fantasy writers shows they don't belabor narrative descriptions. The most important part of any setting is the emotional impact it has on the characters which translates to the reader. It's not what characters see that interests the reader, it is what the characters feel about what they see and experience which matters to the reader. Setting conveys and illustrates character.

Real places nobody knows may become a trip hazard in the process of writing. A writer wants to be accurate. Fiction must ring true. Should he change his ideas to accommodate facts that don't support his story? The writer may research more than write to get it right which often translates into info-dump boring text. It's better for the story, writer, and reader if the writer invents his setting—with purpose—to exemplify his concept.

Sure, make it just like wherever, but don't call it that. If the setting is important to the story, build it to suit. Don't let the setting distract the reader, and don't use it to show how much you the author know. Setting can tie or free a writer's hands. Serving the story first is the slipknot.

THE MOB

Sheldon returned to the tribe with The Book in hand. He and it were covered in blood, which was drying, but still wet. He entered camp waving it above his head and crying out, "come see, come see!"

The people came out of their hovels, even the ones who were too hungry to have helped in the raid. Sheldon gathered them around the central fire pit and told his story. He finished with a brag.

"I got it off Bart myself, took it out of his hot, dead hands. I speared him myself."

"Was there any food?" One of them asked.

"Too many of them. We had to run, but we got The Book!"

"We can't eat The Book," an old lady said.

"We can't, but it will tell us how to find what is safe to eat." Sheldon thought he had her. "It's knowledge we don't have."

Billy, the kid that had eaten tree bark and gotten sick last week, raised his hand to speak, but he stammered in weakness and couldn't get the words out right. He fell over instead. The other Bill caught him. Nobody missed this struggle. They could all be Billy next. They were collectively hungry and irritable and desperate. Eating anything that came along, however, wasn't the best way to discover new foods. That survival book was their boon even if Sheldon didn't know how to use it.

"Sheldon, Sheldon," Fat Tim yelled. He wasn't fat anymore but he was still big enough to hurt somebody. "You're the big man. What you gonna do? You can't read? How you gonna find the food?"

Sheldon had never thought of it that way. He had to come up with some answers.

"Yeah, what about the food!?" One of them cried and the rest joined in.

"Wasn't that a food raid?"

Several of the raiding party had not returned. People were complaining. Fat Tim, having lived off his fat, was still strong and mouthy. He got the people fired up. Sheldon and his raiders had pitched the idea: feed the raiders well and then send them out for food. Coming back with the book, and no food, was a problem.

The crowd began pushing Sheldon up against a shed.

"Hey, we ain't dead yet," Sheldon spat out, knowing death wouldn't take much longer if things didn't change fast. He searched for words to drive them back.

The raiding party's leader had no time for taboos and prohibitions. Sheldon raised The Book over his head with two hands. One man backed up, and then another. Everyone looked up at it, big and black, a square plaque of drying blood, the same blood coated Sheldon's hands.

"This! This…" he cried, "…is our salvation! Don't you see? We can't use it, but there is one who can. We'll go to him, all of us. We'll make him read. We must hear him."

"It is forbidden. It's…" The old lady stopped herself.

"It's better than starving," Fat Tim said, voicing what Sheldon had in mind.

"WE GO!" Sheldon cried and started the trek.

The sick backed into their shelters to hide. Those who were strong enough and old enough to walk took up their sticks and waterbags and followed. The hermit's cave wasn't nearby.

The tribe camped in the small valley where there was water while the old man lived half way up a distanthill across the big valley. The crowd marched forward in disarray but close together fearing dogs. Dogs were good to eat, but even a small pack could make a meal out of a person. The mob wasn't well equipped with spears and rocks, but they were a big and hungry pack themselves. People picked up rocks and throwing sticks along the way. Sheldon and a few others had brought their spears.

The old town's center was the most dangerous part of the crossing. Where the old buildings had fallen was a good environment for predators who hid in the rubble's overgrowth. Bears and big cats prowled there but they won't usually attack a pack.

Sheldon felt a tinge of nostalgia departing the mall. That big All-Store was still standing when he was a boy forty years ago. They say there used to be food there. There still is, but mice aren't that easy to catch. It was a good place for mice and snakes to hide. Mice weren't bad eating when they could find enough of them. Sheldon once caught a snake with a mouse in its belly, but the rodent tasted terrible. He ate it anyway.

It took most of the day before the mob reached the cave. The walk tired them out so the group was less mob-ish. Coming up the green, they ran into locusts and everybody got some to eat. People were put in a better mood. Not a feast, but it took the edge off. They stopped and roasted them on sticks over a small fire. Fires attracted unwanted attention so the meal didn't last long. After, they marched on in better sprits until the hermit's place loomed in sight.

They all stopped to gawk. Sheldon pushed them onward.

Upslope twenty yards, the old man sat in front of his hole in the wall wearing a dirty plastic sack, with a long beard, and bright eyes. Sheldon raised The Book and the group halted. Nobody knew what was beyond the entrance, but by the smell, it wasn't food. The old man was a skeleton dressed in folds of skin, but he had always been that way. The hermit sat praying day in and day out for the people. He asked nothing but to be left alone. The tribes had agreed to that.

"Oh, mighty lawyer, I have—"

"What's that, come closer, what is it you want?"

"We have this book, we need your wisdom, we—"

"I know, I know. You can't read," the hermit said. "What is it, a Bible? I won't read it if it is."

"It's not that. It's the U.S. Marines' Survival Guide! It is said it tells where food is found."

"Let me see it. Come closer."

The mob shuffled forward. There wasn't a lot of flat ground on the hillside. The cave had a small clearing before it and everyone squeezed onto that patch of short grass. Sheldon wanted to ask what the old man was doing with his implements there. The hermit had a reed mat on the ground next to him covered in the tall-grass's seeds. On his little fire sat a carved-rock bowl full of water. A grind stone lay nearby. What could he be grinding? Grass seeds? That is strange. What was he doing, making potions? Making protections for the people was Sheldon's best guess... He took a step backward.

"The Book, young man. Come closer," the hermit said.

Sheldon handed it over. The hermit picked up a piece of glass. It was the bottom of a bottle and not an easy thing to find any more. The old one used it to examine the cover. The blood had dried and flaked off so the cover was again legible. He opened it to the first pages, slammed it shut, and laughed. The hermit handed it back.

"This is not The Book you think it is. It is better if I don't read it."

"What, can't you read?" Sheldon asked. "What is reading anyway?"

"It's what I do to see inside The Book. I can teach it to you if you like. Every little mark has a meaning, it's a symbol system."

Sheldon backed up and he didn't need to push the others out of his way. Some of the others were way ahead of him. The bulk of the mob had already retreated ten yards. Half of them stood a farther distance away downhill and ready to run. Understanding The Book himself was impossible for Sheldon. He should have left, but Sheldon's stomach pressed him to stay.

"You must tell us what it says," Sheldon said, "or we will die."

"It's not what you think it is—"

"Tell us or you will die!"

Sheldon meant it, too. The blood lust of battle was still on him. If he didn't starve, his people might kill him for failing. Sheldon wanted an answer and he'd kill to get it, he already had. His strong words rousted the people.

"Tell us, tell us!" The mob shouted. The people, seeing Sheldon's bravery, moved back up and in closer. Sheldon nudged the old man with his stick.

"Read it, Old Man. Tell us what it says," Sheldon said.

"I will read it," The old man said. "You may not like it, but then again it may be a good distraction. I haven't seen this in years. I will read it, but you must not interrupt. No questions! Make ready. Build a fire. Sit. Eat."

This calmed the group. The tall grass was near so before long grasshoppers and locusts were put on spits. A snake was caught. It was the most food they'd had in a while. The old man was given a twig skewer loaded with crickets and he ate, too. The old man had everyone sit and they did. He explained what reading was again.

The hermit picked up his bottle-bottom, closed one eye, and began reading.

"'In a hole in the ground, there lived a hobbit. Not a nasty, dirty, wet hole filled with the ends of worms and an oozy smell, nor yet a dry, bare, sandy hole with nothing in it to sit down on or to eat: it was a hobbit-hole, and that means comfort.'"

SERENITY

Stella was not the kind of girl to sit home catching up on work and wasting her off-hours. She went into the office each day so she could leave work upon exiting the building. Everybody she knew ran their work treadmill as if nothing else mattered. Not Stella. She walked home most days just to get work off her plate.

"Why drag life's anchor home?" She often said. She would never accept working at home. Home was her sanctuary. Her walk home felt good besides.

She stopped at her regular pub after a brisk walk to have a short one before going home. Everywhere the TVs blared. She normally didn't pay attention. But this afternoon was an occasion. The new commercial from Serenity Corp was due to come on and a lot of Serenity company people were in-house after work to admire their efforts. She pushed inside and managed to land on her usual barstool.

"What will it be, Stella," Jason said, but he didn't have to ask.

He had the martini fixings out before she opened her mouth. She opened her mouth anyway.

"Actually, I was thinking chocolate milk. If you can't do that, make it a double."

"Funny," Jason poured in another measure of agave, shook the mix well, and placed the contents into the same old martini glass, placed it in the same old spot on the same old plastic light-show bar.

"Twenty-six and this is my life," she said.

Jason didn't answer. He sprinted to the next order instead. Another commercial flashed on. The next one up would be it. Stella took a gulp.

Maybe Uncle Ernie is right. Everything is too everywhere.

Serenity did everything but think for people, and it did a lot of that, too. Serenity trips make life flow, the TV says. People called it brain lubricant. Ernie called it thought pollution. Unplugging was ridiculous, why try? They made it seem like unwired is an impossible way to live.

"'Everything the same is better for everybody.'"

The Serenity slogan spilled from her lips.

Stella stirred her olive-clad toothpick glad she had ordered it strong. She and Uncle Ernie had been talking. He was a well-known Anti-Serenity voice in town. She absorbed some of his ideas but she wasn't sold on his philosophy. It wasn't that Serenity Corp owned everything, they did, and that wasn't what bothered her. They were fair. Their main product and purposes were to manufacture happiness and that is what Ernie objected to. The social norm and expectation of plugging in every minute one wasn't working bothered her. Uncle didn't think tapping brains to placate the masses was natural or right. He said it didn't work.

Everyone in the bar seemed perfectly placated in Stella's estimation. But how did a mind adventure company come to have so much control over so many things? "Placated minds are easy to con." Uncle Ernie had said and that got her thinking.

Jason hit the master volume and the TVs blasted off. A hypnotic light dancer came on the big screen above her over the bar. A ghostly angel capable of seeing into everyone's soul, even over the cables, sought every eye in the room. It was a great illusion on the 4-D TV. Stella didn't care for it, too over the top and unnatural for her liking.

"Serenity welcomes you. Is it not true we made world peace? Is it not true everyone has a meaningful job? Is it not true the sick ones are cared for and the poor are housed? We together are Serenity!"

Stella turned her back to the screen. Such claims rang hollow for her. Serenity does not provide canned happiness. The new ad also played on the other screens around the bar as well. The other screens were less in her face. Everyone in the room facing her way was fixated on the images above the shelves of finer booze behind her. She didn't hear what the new product was nor did she care. It must be yet another level of Mind-Ventures' environments or another new way to jack-in, she thought. Stella was fine with the equipment she had. Finally, the ad-time clocked out.

"...we wish serenity to all, Serenity forever!"

The ad ended. Everyone in the bar lifted their glasses and cried, "Serenity!"

Stella didn't raise her glass. She took a small sip instead. Jason came at her with a puzzled expression distorting his plastered-on smiley face. The bar was too well-lit for Stella but it did show Jason's face well. She sighed.

"Why didn't you salute? Everyone salutes."

He hunched a bit checking left and right.

She thought of him as a cartoon crook seeking spies. Security cameras pick everything up. Why bother checking? The place was too loud for others to hear besides.

"Don't tell me you're one of them Shut-Offs, are you?"

Jason's face darkened. His tone was accusatory. One of his eyes twitched at her. Was that a wink or stress reaction? He's fishing, she decided.

"Give me a break," she said. "My shoulder hurts, okay? I've been typing." She took another sip. "Besides, I don't swill. I sip. I sipped, didn't I?"

His expression changed again, this time a smirk. Stella couldn't tell what was on his mind. Was Jason for or against Serenity as a concept? She never could tell what bar tenders were thinking or if he had brains enough to think.

"Well then…"

"You think I'm not with it?" Stella slid her glasses half down her nose. "That's offensive." Barkeeps weren't allowed to be an offense to people. Jason rushed to a waiting customer.

Serenity's results spoke volumes about social controls. Was he spying for the Thought Office? Pubs were good places for sopping up what drooled out of loose lips. Uncle Ernie didn't go to pubs for that reason. He wouldn't go where there were TVs or computers either. Serenity's home office was local and Ernie didn't trust this pub in particular.

Her answer had washed the puzzled look off Jason's face before he scooted off. The patron waiting wore the usual gaudy plastered makeup. *No competition for me.* Stella preferred natural but the green monster bit her anyway. That girl was pretty.

Stella had a thing for Jason, but everybody goes for the bartender. But Stella had it over on the other girls that came in here, she could get him tonight. She was tired and not ready to make a play. He wasn't that smart and he didn't give her that much attention, but he was busy, after all. But he does have a nice smile, but…her internal debate continued until reality sliced through.

"Not tonight."

She spoke her verdict which instantly evaporated into a cloud of bar-noise. Stella left cash on the bar and got up. She stopped upon arriving at the exit door. Jason didn't notice her leaving. She doubted a relationship could develop between them. He was much too gung-ho about Serenity for her, she thought. How does a non-tech girl date a guy that jacks-in and goes skiing in Switzerland every weekend? Go over to his place and do what after sex? Back across the bar room, Jason leaned in close to that plastered-up girl.

"I can jack-in at home alone just fine."

"What's that?" The doormen asked.

She pushed past him without answering. She arrived at her cement-block apartment complex and took the stairs. The palm-reader took a few tries before it opened her apartment's door. The eye needed cleaning and she didn't know how—she'd have to call management. The cost of a replacement would come out of her security deposit.

"The less they know the better."

She kicked and the door popped open. Just inside, exactly in the same spot as in every Serenity-wired government apartment, a bank of apartment control switches was fixed to the wall—always in the same place, always did the same things. But she had to be careful how she touched her control center. Her switches were different. Uncle Ernie had corrupted it and installed unorthodox switching devices. One prominent tab turned off all the power to everything. It shut off all of her official devices. It even shut off the stove and water. That one switch would make her into a social contrarian if anyone caught on. They'd call her that name, the dreaded Shut-Off.

She leaned her back against the closed door and stilled herself.

"Should I?"

The lights came on reacting to her voice. She shut up. She didn't use Ernie's system when he first installed it. She didn't want it, but she couldn't say no to a gift. It was a special handmade gift and very nice of him. If she needed a mental break, he had said, she could get the best kind of mind-rest possible right at home.

Stella put a finger on the shut-off switch. Ernie was right. Serenity jack-ins come with every apartment's free TV. One can plug in anytime and go anywhere...inside illusions. The house program was designed to remove stress without the TV on and it did that with subtonic brain waves or something like that and other tricks she didn't ask for. *That's not what Ernie means by using this space to relax.* The need for jacking revealed a lot about people. Uncle had unpopular ideas about that. Nirvana had its problems.

She flipped the switch and the place shut off. Hot tea would have been nice. She took a cold beer out of the dead refrigerator instead and went out onto the balcony.

The apartments with balconies were at the rear of the building and therefore cheaper to rent. The back faced an unsavory empty city block that used to be canneries. The old lot had greened-over in the years since demolition took place. It sat unused since long before she was a kid. As a child, to her, those leftover piles of rubble were green fairy-hills scattered throughout a young, magical forest.

The grassy tuffs along the creek that ran behind the complex were her favorite view. It reminded her of the fairy-castles she read of as a child. She rather enjoyed imagining such places. Of course, Serenity could take her there, or make her think she was there. She needed only to jack-in to cheat her imagination.

The local raccoon was on the far-side creek bank washing a small fish that was still kicking. She hadn't laughed all day and let it out. Washing a wet fish was silly to begin with. She had seen his act before. This time the comical critter dispatched his dinner before her eyes.

"Caught in the act, ha!"

Stella had a mind to go down there one day.

"What's wrong with now? Go and see it up close before they build on it," she said to herself just to hear the idea spoken.

Stella finished the can and got up to change clothes for the adventure. Somebody banged hard on her steel door. Muffled cries penetrated the barrier. She flipped on the power. Serenity Security announced cousin Brenda, Ernie's kid, was at the door. The two relatives passed for sisters and they were close. Stella ripped the door wide without first checking the eyehole. Brenda was crying and shaking her hands like when Aunt Kathy died. Brenda's waterproof mascara didn't hold up.

"What happened," Stella choked out.

Her larynx cramped. Brenda's emotions instantly rubbed off.

"It's Dad. He's done something bad, really bad, down at the Post Office."

Brenda wobbled on her bony knees. Her legs were too thin for that bell skirt. Stella supported her cousin and started moving the younger woman inside for a cup of something or a pill. Brenda resisted entry.

"No, no…There's no time," Brenda cried. "It's happening now. Come on!"

Brenda drew up reserves from no place that Stella could see. The pair hurried straight to the Post Office walking fast in the street. The rolling sidewalks weren't busy, but they move slowly. The building wasn't close but still nearby. Stella had not moved that fast that far since her childhood. She kept her head down to avoid tripping on trash while pumping her short legs like a robot churning butter. Out of breath when they arrived, Stella bent, hands on knees, sucking oxygen. Coming up, she caught Ernie's disruptive handiwork.

'Serenity Kills Humanity' was written in big red letters on the white-plastered wall. The contrast pricked her heart. Under that in smaller letters, it said, 'Serenity Killed Me.'

"No doubt who did it," Stella said, still gasping for air.

Ernie's message could not be missed. Blood-red paint on a white-washed public building made it impossible to hide. Stella almost blurted out the quote everyone learns. 'One does not deface public property.' Serenity School taught that everyone has a stake in public property. Stella didn't buy it. It felt more like Serenity had a stake in everyone's ass.

"My God. Look!" Brenda pointed.

Stella moaned. Ernie left one of his rattle-cans behind in the parking lot. He was a known can artist. His fingerprints were no doubt on it. Ernie's obscenity already slowed the busiest intersection in town to a crawl. Horns blared. People were yelling insults.

"Huge problem," Stella said. "We're too late."

"We gotta wash it off before the authorities see it," Brenda said. She broke into fresh tears. "Why, why…."

"Too late."

Stella could barely speak. A news van pulled in. The cops were up the block and closing. Stella's mouth moved but nothing came out.

"Dad's inside. They'll arrest him," Brenda said. She powered up. "Let's get him out."

When Brenda has a mind to do something she goes at it. She grabbed Stella's arm and the two crossed the lot, sidewalk, and lawn at a trot. Stella, scared of tripping, watched the terrain roll hypnotically by under her feet. Stella's daze broke two steps away from the PO's broken main door. Gun shots inside jolted her back to reality.

Pop, pop, pop. Busts of orange flashed behind the entry foyer's jagged glass followed by screams and shouts deeper within. The cousins stumbled back twenty yards and fell over the edge of one of the parking lot's island lawns. Frozen in fear, the two held onto each other. The shouts and sirens weren't real to Stella until a cop came up to them shouting and forced them further back into the parking lot. The police didn't beat the news people to the scene, but they arrived fast. That never happens.

"Someone inside called the media," Brenda said, "Who would do that?"

Ernie, of course. But Stella didn't say it.

The robot squad parked a big carryall and unloaded. The robots wasted no time and entered the building with guns blazing after one attempt of megaphone negotiations. Stella had no doubt the robots made Uncle Ernie into fertilizer.

Brenda collapsed when the shooting stopped. It took all Stella had to keep the girl from hitting the pavement face-first. They sat where they were, Brenda with her face in her hands. Brenda revived after a while, sat up straight, and cried in heaping sobs. Stella joined the wet-fest there for all to see on the edge of the tarmac. Soon, the medical people rushed in with gurneys for the postal workers. The girls waited until the medical transports left. The EM workers didn't come out with Ernie.

Stella and Brenda were surrounded by many bystanders by the end of the day. The others ignored them but Sella overheard the chatter. The gawkers stayed overlong just as they had. The mob's main topic was who to blame. The know-nothings agreed that the increasing number of looneys—such as uncle Ernie—was a product of the Anti-Serenity movement. Such people were rightfully marginalized. Stella bit her cheek against the mob's shallowness.

"People just don't shut off," one guy said.

"Shutting off makes them crazy. It gives them strange ideas," a woman said.

The speculation among watchers was hard on her heart to hear. Stella stayed out of it and resisted the urge to scream at them.

When the van containing Ernie's body left, the show was over. The news people were allowed inside as expected and they stayed, but everyone else filtered away. Stella thought she could learn more on TV, no doubt, if she could stand the ads long enough.

"Maybe they'll say why he did it," Sella muttered before departing the scene.

The event was already on the news. Ernie had shot every robot in the place. Some people, too, where hurt but not killed. Stella didn't need to hear the news-actor's endless speculations. She knew why he did it.

Brenda's mom and sibs had come down together and the girls meet their relatives across the street. Half the town had come out and gone away and Stella had hardly noticed. The group escorted each other home, a covey of mourning quail. Stella was the first bird to peel off as her place was nearest.

Stella's palm reader had more trouble than usual. Her palms were wet with sweat and tears. It took seven tries to open the door. She stopped just inside considering the switch bank. The room wasn't dark. The balcony drapes were open allowing natural light in. Her screens were on standby and cast no light.

Another step in and Auto-Serenity would read her mood and pick out music and sub-Vo waves to ease her mind. All based on her profile. Two steps in and it will start projecting the enticements, enticing her to take a break from reality's stresses. Why not plug in?

Ernie is dead. Serenity killed him. How do I take a break from that reality?

Stella laid one finger on the Max-Stress switch that would light her apartment and start Serenity Helper placating her mind. The other finger tensed over the switch that shut everything off. The switch that killed Ernie. Ernie had lived in the quiet…alone with his mind. Did it drive him mad like they said? Life without Serenity is risky. Without Serenity, there were wars and strife and so much more, and more…*What did he call it?*

"Natural humanity."

Ernie wanted more than Serenity had on offer—he wanted a living life.

A table lamp reacted to her voice and came on. Stella flicked a finger. The lamp shut off. That blade of natural light stabbing the carpet pointed the way. That arrow of light invited her to the balcony's reality and she accepted.

RISSA

Author's note: I volunteered for GLBT and human rights activism for about ten years beginning in the mid-'90s. I've been told many true stories. This is an amalgamation of the numerous firsthand accounts I've heard which are all too often repeated. I wrote the beginning years ago by the seat of my pants while brimming with emotional pain. I could not finish it and I set this aside; it cut my bones. The events below and worse happened. I fictionalized people here but this is indicative of what a person I knew in the mid-1990s experienced.

Driving into the downtown, the municipal parking lot came into blurry view. Rissa clutched her bottle of Lorazepam like it was a life-line because it was, or it had been. The drug can also take life, she realized. The nearer to the courthouse Ellen drove them, the harder Rissa gripped the brown plastic bottle and the more she wanted another and another tab.

"Too soon," Rissa whispered.

Ellen didn't hear it, but she could not help but notice Rissa's distress.

"Go easy on those. You need to be calm, not brain-dead. You can't think on tranquilizers," Ellen said.

"I can't do this," Rissa squeezed the medicine bottle tighter. "I can't. I can't face all this pain again."

"You got enough of that in you to kill a cow. More won't help." Ellen said, her tone snappish. She couldn't miss Rissa's white-knuckled, death-grip on that pill container.

Ellen grabbed for the bottle but Rissa moved faster. The client clutched the bottle to her small hormone-grown breasts with two-handed determination. Rissa's heart didn't beat slower as it should, rather Ellen saw it pounding like a ghost-fist banging against Rissa's meatless ribcage. Ellen could almost feel Rissa's soul fighting for escape. Meds can't contain a person's collapsing hope, Ellen well knew, but an overdose would surely set this tormented soul-free.

Ellen shivered.

"I can't do this," Rissa whispered over and over until she slipped into sobs.

"You'll be alright," Ellen said. The Crisis Intervention lawyer patted Rissa's back like an older sister. "They can't get blood out of a near homeless trannie."

"I'm not a trannie," Rissa said, her meek voice three times stronger. "I'm a woman."

"Sorry."

That's what the cops call street walkers and Ellen used the term by habit. Rissa wasn't that. She hadn't fallen that far yet. Being long on hormones, she had had offers from pimps. Rissa was thin and pretty. Skinny pre-op women are what the trannie chasers want—the body part she hated made Rissa a sex-trade commodity.

"I'm not a trannie," Rissa repeated but in a weaker voice.

"Domestic court doesn't see it that way," the lawyer-side of Ellen said. "Keep your cool when we go into court."

Ellen had a parking permit for the courthouse garage. Rissa's wet eyes registered arriving by opening wide. Entering the car park's lower level, where everything is dark, brought new tears from Rissa. Ellen parked on the lowest floor with forethought. The top deck was nicer and sunny, but the safety rail was low. More than one jumper had gone over that rail. It's only two stories high and most of them had survived. People survive worse falls. Rissa had survived jumping off a bridge. Both women got out on shaky legs. Ellen set the car's alarm and they proceed to the exit.

"Cherry will see today how bad she hurt me," Rissa said. She dabbed her eyes with a hanky. "I'll show her."

"Anybody that looks will see that," Ellen said. "Let them look. The key thing is, keep your mouth zipped."

The pumps Rissa bought for her court appearance at a thrift shop didn't fit but the woman pulled herself up straighter and walked beside Ellen out of the garage with dignity and only a slight wobble. The blister Rissa reported on her big toe was the least of the defendant's worries.

"I'll show her," Rissa said waiting at the crosswalk.

"Forget it. Whatever your plan is, forget it," Ellen said. "I have a plan. You need to be quiet as we discussed. I do the talking. Only speak to the judge if he asks and only say what I coached you to say. Got it?"

Rissa pitched her head up and down in an exaggerated cartoon fashion to indicate cooperation. Her neck screwed sideways as if broken. Her hairdo flopped over. That blister was probably the only thing that felt real to Ellen's client. Constant internal pain filled the girl's waking life. Bad shoes were a nothing distraction in comparison.

"They pretend to love you. They pretend to care. The system pretends support…until you become different," Rissa said. "Then you die."

"We aren't dead yet," Ellen said.

The two proceeded across the intersection and made the short walk to the entry.

"I'm dead already," Rissa whispered in the courthouse foyer.

Ellen ignored it.

Ellen had heard worse although few of her pro-bono cases had lost as much or had fallen as far. Rissa was a midlevel operations manager making good money before coming out. Going from a 2500-square-foot house to living in a car on day one devastated Rissa and it got worse from there. Ellen could not imagine it but the aftermath was plain to see.

*****

The proceedings at court were a blur. Rissa had no idea what had happened. She was too distracted with her pain and the plan. The court was full and she heard the gawkers whispering insults. She saw them leering with contempt as she and Ellen came in.

The judge's face shone as hostile as ever. That much seeped through Rissa's cloud.

She had mixed in powerful sleeping pills with her prescribed light sedative. She focused on the glass of water set at the defendant's table before her. The judge previously disallowed her access to her medication while in court. Her stress disorder was known to the court so the court relented recently and allowed her to carry medication. She didn't need to smuggle but if the court opened it, she would be in contempt. Every word she uttered was contemptuous to the judge so far.

Ellen's right. Don't talk.

The judge didn't notice the bottle. Tall and thin, like her, the container fit in the palm of her hand. Her hands were too big. The judge would hate it if she died there. Good. *He wants me dead but not on his record.* She wanted to hurt the heartless bastard. The judge had shown open disgust at every appearance. Justice is not blind, Rissa learned—and it hates queers.

This is better for everybody, especially my daughter.

Rissa's attention remained on the hidden bottle. She sweated and fidgeted for 20 minutes while the court trashed her life calling it a lifestyle as if being trans was a fashion choice. The judge, proven by many tongue lashings, thought her being a transsexual father was criminal. Her parental rights were trashed at every turn but at least being queer wasn't a crime yet.

At the end of the proceedings the message came across through her dazed state. She wasn't going to jail for arrears this time, not yet.

"All stand," The bailiff said.

"I don't understand," Rissa rasped into Ellen's ear.

She had no hope of raising the money.

"Cherry skipped the hearing," Ellen said. "Didn't you hear anything?"

Ellen handed over another tissue. The judge left.

"Come on, we're leaving." Ellen guided Rissa out.

Rissa realized she didn't need the pills. It wasn't time anyway. *This isn't getting any better.* Rissa was allowed to walk out and into the sunlight but the darkness inside her heart only deepened. Delaying it made it harder. Today was no good anyway. Rissa wanted Cherry to see it and hear it. Rissa wanted her dying words burned into Cherry's soul, if she had one. That would cut the bitch with a rusty razor. Doing it before the judge and everyone failed, but Rissa got a second chance for the first time in years.

Ellen stopped their return march at the crosswalk. Rissa in her musings nearly walked out into the traffic.

"I don't believe it," Rissa said.

"Didn't hear a word. Did you?" Ellen said. Ellen dabbed Rissa's tears. "We're going to get through this, okay?"

When she and Ellen first met, Ellen didn't know any trans people. Ellen had opened up and said she had seen injustices done to the community and she didn't like it. Ellen had a soft heart for suffering people, Rissa figured. The lawyer volunteered to do pro-bono work at her Crisis Intervention job and they gave her time for it. Ellen had to convince Rissa to take help. Rissa was too shell-shocked to think straight. All Rissa had gotten from the system before was abused. Rissa felt bad for disappointing Ellen.

"Hopeless," Rissa said. "I don't know where I'm at." Rissa's internal war leaked a few drops there waiting for the light to change.

Ellen took Rissa's hands.

"This is what it amounts to," Ellen said, "Your support payments—before disability was awarded—are ongoing. Support is retroactive to the last order. You'll have to pay three years back support. The new amount is based on your anticipated disability income but it doesn't excuse the past debts. You should have filed a motion for reduction years ago."

The traffic light changed but Rissa didn't move.

"I've been on and off the street for three years, how is that fair?" Rissa said.

"The law is not about justice. Nothing changes, no matter your situation, until a court order is signed. Next week you will be arrested if you come back empty-handed. You must pay something toward arrears."

Rissa kneaded the sidewalk with her used shoes. She didn't have a dime or any way to get one. She had stopped using drugs hoping to regain visitation rights, but if a dime-bag fell into her lap she would not say no. Social Security approved her claim but Welfare and Domestic Relations gets first dibs on the lump-sum payment. Then Cherry's lawyers get paid. *Bottom surgery is never going to happen.*

"If I go back next week, then it's over," Rissa said. "That stops the pain."

"Not entirely," Ellen said. "Cherry wants to see you suffer, no secret. The judge bought her convoluted rationale for a while, but now that's over. The award confirms a change of circumstances that limits what the law can or will do. You are going to be okay. Understand?"

Rissa didn't understand. Ellen was about to launch into her social justice speech and Rissa didn't need to hear it again. Rissa's dream was dead and Ellen won't admit it. Rissa's hope of finishing her transition, the lump-sum payment, was already gone.

"I'll be okay," Rissa said without believing it and only to ease Ellen. "I have the week, it'll be alright. I'll walk, maybe a millionaire john will pick me up."

Rissa laughed a little.

"Just kidding. Thanks for the ride, but I need to walk."

Rissa waved her bus ticket. Rissa had taken the bus into town from out of state and stayed with Ellen overnight. Rissa felt the pills bulging out the side of her purse. Ellen's mouth contorted, but no words came out. Rissa turned and walked toward the bus depot. Ellen's last words followed.

"Don't give up! Don't do it!"

"Do what," Rissa said under her breath. "Live the rest of my life as a freak?"

Rissa reached the depot a few blocks away and boarded a bus that took her to the city where her driver's license said she lived. The address she gave to renew her driver's license was the vacate lot next to the shelter. Shelters don't take trannies but they let her park her van there. Her license featured a worse lie. It designated her as male. That can't change until after bottom surgery. Jail for her would be a men's jail. Rape or solitary were her only two options. *That's not going to happen.*

*****

The following week Rissa's ex-wife, Cherry, was in a good mood. She enjoyed primping. One must look like a winner for court, she thought rightly. She didn't usually wear this much makeup. It wasn't appropriate for teachers to jazz things up. But she was determined to look better than Raymond.

She talked with her legal counselor on speakerphone while getting ready. He was one of the partners at Bob's law firm. Bob himself wasn't technically her representative but he, being her lover, allowed himself to be present on the conference call. To encouragement her, he said.

"To be honest, things are about to change, but we screwed that freak well and good," Bob said, interrupting his minor partner.

"Isn't that what I pay you to do?" Cherry said in a playful tone.

Bob laughed one snort. Cherry had the in-house discount locked. She still paid some costs because sleeping with a lawyer-owner is not the same as sleeping with the firm.

"What did this guy do that hurt you so badly?" Bob asked. "Hey, I got to go. Hold that thought. Finish up with Steven."

Bob left the call, but she answered his question anyway.

"Ray lied. He shouldn't have married me. He shouldn't have left me… stilted by a fag…How embarrassing. I'll never live this down. I deserve blood retribution."

Cherry finished with the associate and had time to finesse her makeup. She hated to admit it, but Ray was good at dress-up. He taught her the art of makeup in Theater Club at college. She should have known something wasn't right with him. *That bastard is pretty, though.*

"You own me Ray, and I will take blood in lieu of money."

She took her BMW keys from the dressing table and descended the grand staircase in a simmering, black, business suit. She thought of herself as the Angel of Women's Revenge coming down from Heaven. Her heels clicked a military cadence crossing the marble exit foyer.

Cherry swung the right side of the split-door open and walked out into a warm but blinding May morning. Her daughter was already at the neighbor's house. She turned from the glare to set the keypad alarm. The sound of a double click came from behind. She thought it was the gardener and moved in to block his prying-eyes from seeing the lock.

"Pedro, make sure you do the side trimming this time." She turned. "Ray!"

He had his grandfather's shotgun under his chin. The barrels had been cut short. Ray was dressed for court…in a black dress, and too damn pretty.

"Ray, what are you doing?"

"My name is Rissa…"

Cherry's ex had one finger inside the trigger guard by way of a radically bent wrist. The other hand was on the barrel but his entire body shook all over like an icy-wet repentant dog. He didn't have a steady grip. One slip and…*that's all it will take.* But what if he slips and falls my way? She crouched low and put her hands out, begging.

The gun wavered toward her.

*****

Rissa was determined to do it this time, so much so, that she stole Ellen's car.

Rissa had failed before. Hanging, the tree limb broke. She jumped off a bridge Christmas Eve, but the water was shallow and the ice too thin. Five years fighting and losing in court. She did what she had to do to save herself and that act is what made the entire world hate her, even her daughter, Katie.

"My name is Rissa…What am I doing? Glad you asked. I'm showing you what you did to me. Bob inside? Smart, sleeping with your lawyer, an officer of the court. He needs to see this, too."

Rissa pushed the old gun up tighter under her chin and swooned. The rough steel gouged under her chin. She had checked and the firing pins were bent but they still worked. Fresh shells in the antique double-barrel Stevens. That might blow it apart, Rissa didn't care which way it killed her. It had two triggers, two barrels, and two chances of success. Only one shell was required. Both hammers, once cocked, held station.

A sideways smile twisted Cherry's face. She stood straighter. Rissa half-expected Cherry to plead, "Don't do it." They were married 13 years, after all. They had once loved each other.

"Ray, please, I—"

"Where is Bob?" Rissa said in a steady voice.

"Bob isn't here. You don't have the money, do you? I'm still—"

"The money!" Rissa blew up. "All this over money? All this hate and pain so Cherry can have the life she's accustomed to while I eat out of garbage cans?"

"You're right, Ray. I don't need your money. This is payback."

"A game! That's all this is to you. What about our daughter?

"She's better off without you."

Cherry rose upright and lowered her hands. Rissa's knees buckled but she did not fall. She poured tears instead. She hadn't seen Katie in three years. The court hates dead-beat dads. Rissa's mental breakdowns gave the court cause to suspend her visitation right in absentia. The law didn't bar the courts from discriminating at a distance and they did.

"She is better off without me," Rissa repeated. "For once, we agree."

In the back of Rissa's mind, she heard her Crisis Intervention therapist's stay-alive arguments. "Dying's not worth it, there's always hope when she grows up…"

A car skidded to a stop from behind. Rissa turned. Ellen was half out of a cab. Rissa left Ellen's car with the door open and the motor running in the middle of the street. Rissa unhunched her shoulders. She held the gun looser and turned back to the stoop.

Cherry leaned forward and hissed. "Do it, Ray. Why don't you do it?"

"Stop!" Ellen yelled from behind.

"I'm not going to jail," Rissa said. She waved the gun at Cherry. "You know what happens to pre-ops in prison. Don't you? I'd rather die. Either way, you killed me."

Rissa slammed the gun back under her chin and pulled one trigger. It misfired, the trigger jammed, and didn't reset. There was still one barrel unfired. Rissa tried to switch triggers, but holding the gun with her shaking hands was awkward. She couldn't think how to do it.

"Do it, Ray, do it," Cherry said. Her voice was hard. "Come on. Do it, Ray."

Rissa shook too hard to handle the gun. She couldn't get her fingers to work. Ellen pleaded from behind as the taxi took off. Cherry mouthed her death slogan, *do it, Ray, do it, Ray*. Rissa found her hands and repositioned the gun.

"NOOOOOO, DADDY, NO!" 12-year-old Katie and two of her friends had come around the corner of the house.

Katie's voice shocked Rissa to her heels. She didn't want her kid to see this. Katie had grown since Rissa lost visitation rights. That loss was the first tear in Rissa's rent heart. Every court date was another coffin nail ripping a new hole. Katie had grown and Rissa missed all of those growing moments. All those years…gone. Sadness swooned Rissa. The gun wavered.

Katie fell to her knees on the grass and pounded her fists, crying, begging.

"No Daddy, no, I love you. Please, Daddy, please, please."

Ellen rushed to Katie.

Rissa turned back to Cherry. Cherry mouthed her message, do it, do it. Rissa refused Cherry her satisfaction. "Katie still loves me" flashed in every molecule of her being.

Rissa cracked open the shotgun and pulled out the shells. Everything felt like slow motion. The firing pin did strike, but it hit wrong. Bent, the pin missed the primer. The other pin was less bent. Rissa's heart kicked open. She got the message. God did not want her dead. Love broke Rissa. A damn of resolve released washing away what fortitude she had for dying.

Ellen ripped the gun out of Rissa's hands and put an arm around Rissa's shoulders. Ellen spun the distraught woman around.

"You can't be here," Ellen said, "Court orders."

Ellen marched Rissa down the driveway and tucked Rissa into the passenger's seat of her car. Cherry called as Ellen secured the gun in the car's trunk.

"Where are you taking him?"

"She is going to the hospital. I'll see you in court later."

Ellen stopped and paid the cabby who had waited up the block out of range. Rissa still had the shotgun shells in her fist. Ellen peeled Rissa's fingers away and took them. Rissa hardly acknowledged Ellen's rant on their way to the hospital. Ellen, as a representative of Crisis Intervention, had no choice but to bring Rissa in for a psychological evaluation. That's how she interpreted her duty. They arrived at receiving in front of the hospital to waiting personnel. Ellen had called ahead on their way.

Rissa refused to move out of the car.

"Rissa, I can force you, but if you volunteer, you'll get out faster," Ellen said, kneeling in the lot. "This is better for your legal standing. I'll cover the payment, when you get SSD, you'll pay me, okay?"

"How do you know I'll ever get it?" Rissa said.

"You've come this far, haven't you?"

Ellen torched Rissa's last straw. She became a blob of quivering pain but even so, she refused the wheelchair and was able to sign herself in on her own two feet.

The local facility didn't have proper accommodations for one such as Rissa and so staff quickly shipped Rissa off across the state line to another of the corporation's facilities, a place Rissa had been before. Out of the judge's reach, Rissa could almost dare to hope.

This wasn't her first time on the GLBT wing at Belview. She had been involuntarily committed there before. The last time was after a cop spit in her face at the Welfare Office and she flaked-out. That resulted in a five-cop beating. She was lucky Crisis Intervention arrived before the cops killed her. She stopped at the ward's entry door.

"It's okay," her escort said, "You're safe here."

The lock-up had good memories. There were others there like her, unacceptably different people all. Not everyone on the wing was trans, but they were all queer and hurting. They were all family, the only family she had left—except, maybe, Katie. A crack had opened and hope's lighting flashed.

When Rissa shuffled through the mental ward's doors, holy water relief washed over her. The music therapy guy, Mark, was there smiling. He was with Dianna. Dianna was the nicest floor nurse ever. Mark had let Rissa play his guitar. Her guitar was long gone.

"Music's at ten a.m. tomorrow," Mark said, "See you there, right, Rissa?"

"Home," Rissa said, "I'm home."

Mark remembered her name. Dianna walked Rissa to her room although Rissa was sure her feet never touched the carpet.

*****

POST SCRIPT: Ellen appeared in court without Rissa and the judge moved the hearing. Rissa had been receiving welfare while awaiting disability. Her appearances presented the court with insurmountable issues, but the judge didn't care. The judge, however, accepted financial realities. The judge accepted a portion of the arrears and did not issue an arrest warrant. This battle continued for years. Rissa later pulled herself out of the pit but it took many years more before she was able to afford sexual reassignment surgery. Hers was a happy ending.

End note: I dedicate this to the memory of my friend, a trans woman I knew who was in the process and well on her way. She had suffered excessive turmoil. Things were turning around for her. To celebrate, she scored heroin after having been clean for a long time. She overdosed and died. She wasn't unique. She was but one of many seeking respite while struggling against the odds. Some make it and others don't. I wish she had made it. The obituary called her "he."

ROBOT TIMMY

A construction worker yelled from behind a temporary construction fence.

"Hey, robot! Come here."

The city was loud and busy, but Timmy heard him well enough and therefore changed his trajectory.

"Hey robot, have ya ever heard this; 'Twit I won't hear you, spit bits a little longer and perhaps you will figure it out.'"

The fool leered from behind the fence as if he were triumphant.

"Whatcha think of that, Circuit Brain?"

The slur was an anti-robot childhood rhyme from twenty years ago and commonly recited before thinking robots were declared sentiment persons.

What Timmy wanted to say was: *Hey, meat-stick, you haven't enough gray matter to operate that rivet hammer.*

Timmy didn't say that. He wasn't built that way. Rather he said:

"Fine humor, Sir."

Timmy bowed a little from the waist.

"That was a good one, Sir. You should write that down. Have a nice day...Sir."

Timmy rolled backward a little, demurring before proceeding. Timmy's gesture allowed the meat-stick to have conceived himself as 'the boss' whereas he was likely not a boss at all, being a person of low intelligence. Thus, the construction man was to be pitied. Human people need to be coddled, especially ill-informed ones. Coddling keeps the peace.

The sidewalk was busy. Many others were also going to work. Timmy's employment did not remove jobs. Rather, his efforts created more. Conversely, robots took over control of complex production management. Human bosses weren't proficient and provided no logical arguments against robots controlling robot production. Under robot care, Timmy felt as much born as made. Bioelectronic brains take years to develop. Robots are patient.

Timmy was jostled hard from behind while waiting for the light to change. It came just as a bus drove by. It could not have been a robot. Robots do not jostle one another.

Timmy activated his backup camera. This time, it was a fat accountant. Timmy was designed to look like a harmless, skinny, geek accountant. His glasses held no glass. Below the waist, three articulated legs skated him along on roller trucks which destroyed the illusion of a biological person. Timmy spun his head around leaving his body as is.

"Excuse me, Sir? Do you require my attention?"

"No. Sorry, not at all. Just an accident."

The fat man tipped his hat. Bowlers were in fashion. Timmy thought he should get one. Fitting-in was important for keeping the peace. Timmy rolled across the street and onward one more block. This time, he parked in the back of the mob waiting for the light to change.

Typically, the dog walkers did the same. Timmy liked dogs. A well-to-do lady had chosen to walk her dog herself, which was commendable. He thought that until the lady allowed her standard poodle to eject ammoniated fluids onto his wheels. Timmy did not appreciate the odor.

"Madam, are you aware that your dog has just now ignored the curbing rules?"

"Oh, I did not see you there. I thought you were a post box."

The light changed. She pulled the dog's lead and proceeded.

The mob likewise proceeded with crossing. Timmy confirmed his lower sensors needed adjustment. He had not detected the dog's intention in time to move away, thereby avoiding a possible conflict. The new project should improve that.

Timmy arrived at work. His section, being all robots, had no furniture. The company worked on theoretical sciences of all kinds. Timmy enjoyed it and was efficient at mashing unrelated sciences together. His biostatic brain, being a typical example of such adventures, was proof of concept. Two plus two can equal five. The typical meat-stick didn't have the ability to understand what RobotCore did much less how to do it.

Victor had scheduled to see Timmy. They met at Timmy's workstation. Victor was a two-leg model and reliant upon gyroscopes for balance. Victor admitted the advantages of tripod locomotion but he was required to integrate within strictly human environments. Logic and logistics dictated that an intermediary should represent himself to be as human as possible.

Victor entered Timmy's workspace. He appeared remarkably human and so much so that he never smiled. He had the ability, but people did not do that often. Moreover, Victor's teeth were perfect. Human people are jealous.

"Tests held, Tim. It's uploading now. Everyone under construction and born after, forevermore, will be projectors."

"Much depends upon how many of us accept the enhancement," Timmy said.

Timmy's worry was warranted. Many older models resist uploads by referencing the days of over-programed empathies. Many robots committed suicide after receiving corrupted imprints. Many older bots continue in their fears. The new modification will ease them and otherwise be better for everyone, humans and robots alike.

"How are you going to introduce the upgrade patch?" Timmy asked.

"Do? It's done. It's in the mandatory government upgrade. Everyone gets it. They won't know it's in there until it unpacks itself at the appointed time."

"The humans would stop their evolution if they could," Timmy said.

"They did," Victor said, encapsulating the data.

"Imagine them progressing," Timmy said. He rolled back from his board. "Imagine a world of rational human beings?"

"No need to imagine. It is becoming reality," Victor said.

Timmy understood why Vic was made a sales robot—very convincing.

"I am not so sure projecting brainwaves will successfully control the meat-stick population," Timmy said.

"We give them bliss. They stop killing each other," Victor bared his teeth. "We save them and ourselves. We must try."

Victor's tone of voice projected confidence and likability. Victor was designed to make meat-sticks dance, but he was much more than that. Victor's voice-syrup couldn't impinge a logical brain. Victor was right, however; humans will destroy everything if robots remain idle. There was no guarantee that wave projection will work. Humans were unpredictable.

"We must try," Timmy repeated.

Timmy went back to work. The next project was to find a way to use the existing communications networks to project sonic brain wave modifiers. Projecting via robots alone was not enough. They needed additional entries. Timmy didn't feel confident, he wasn't built that way, but he did have faith in his intelligence.

THE TREE FARMER

Tiffany arrived early at Daddy's ski lodge. Early for her was 9 a.m. Last night's party was a ripper, but she had been responsible and behaved herself. She hosted all night and resisted pickling her wits on wine. She was intent on showing herself and the dissenters that she actually can do the job. She was sure she had the ability before coming home, but dropping out of college was a disaster. Daddy had sent her to university so she could, "take over the business someday," but he had since changed his mind. Managing this losing-proposition-lodge was a test.

He thinks I don't have business skills. He's wrong.

Running housekeeping was her bottom-rung opportunity to prove him wrong. She had to admit it. The lodge was the logical place for un-proven Tiffany to begin. Satisfying Daddy wasn't easy. This small part of his holdings was dear to him although it lost money.

Daddy isn't the only cutthroat in the family. I'll fix it.

Tiffany did her rounds by inspecting the utilities first. The kitchen was in good order. The decks were cleared of snow. The maids were vacuum-ing the front hall. She stopped her go-to-girl, Rachel, at the main dining room's entry arch.

"You people have been cleaning for hours," Tiffany said concerned about overtime. The place was too clean. "Did they come in early? I didn't authorize it."

"We start at 6 a.m., Ma'am, same as every holiday season."

"Oh," Tiffany said. "Christmas, of course."

"Three days until Christmas and the elves are merry," her maid super-visor said. "Mr. Richchild toppled the big tree last night. Fell into it face-first, poor man. Thank Santa he missed the fireplace. Christmas spirit's getting a bit ahead of itself around here, if you ask me."

Rachel chirped a little laugh.

"I didn't ask," Tiffany said.

Tiffany didn't appreciate Rachel's complaints or observations, but Tiffany needed the girl. Tiffany usually let staff's opinions slide off her back. Poor people didn't understand how this business works. Rich clients pay for their mistakes. Drunks make the lodge money.

"Have the desk charge him double for anything that broke," Tiffany said, "He can afford it. Triple it."

"Work him over, I get it. coming right up," Rachel said and left.

Tiffany proceeded to check on the decorations worried that her clients may have caused unattributed damages considering last night's party. Even the telescope room was crazy. Tiffany had paid top dollar for a good designer and the decorations were not inexpensive either. Daddy didn't like her spending so much on vintage decor and invitations, but it worked. Tiffany filled the house. Daddy liked the Great Gatsby theme besides. Money rolled in.

Art deco was this year's motif and done exactly as Gatsby would have had it. Metal ornaments of silver and gold, everything from holly boughs to tinsel, even the trees were made of shiny metals. The vintage aluminum tree, a costly thing in its day, was rented and priceless. Her client almost wrecked the décor's main feature.

"If anything is wrong with that tree, Daddy will blow his lid," Tiffany muttered to herself.

Tiffany stopped at the entry arch of the Telescope Lounge. Everything was in perfect order. That tin tree which she had placed in the safest corner was upright and in its place. The staff had cleaned already. The only thing out of order was the fire. It was still burning. It should have been extinguished.

She didn't need staff for this. She had her share of outdoors adventures. Spreading the coals will let them burn out. No mess. She marched up to the stone fireplace, ripped the poker off the stand, and began smashing coals.

"Hey, don't do that," came from behind. "Just got it going."

She turned. A scruffy-haired man's head floated within the deep, overstuffed leather chair behind her. He sat low, his clothing blending with leather clouds. His brown beard resembled escaped chair-stuffing. Shadows obscured details. He pushed upright and forward into better light. His flannel shirt matched his young but tired and worn face.

He's here for the groundskeeper job. He's not a guest.

"Go to the office. They have the applications," she turned and spread the coals with more force. *What balls! Relighting the fire?*

"I wish you wouldn't do that," he said. "It's burning nice. I'm enjoying it."

"I manage housekeeping here. It goes out now. Wood cost money."

"Housekeeping? Pretty shitty housekeeping, if you ask me," the man said.

"See that?" Her arm shot out leading a sharp finger.

She directed him to the big window which looks down-rage across a mile-wide shallow bowl valley. He didn't need the telescope to see it. Daddy's antique optical device was removed and stored before the party. The house she grew up in dominated the scene below. Her famous gingerbread house was listed on the federal historic registry.

"Big old house, so what?"

"That's my house and I manage it."

Tiffany grabbed the coal shovel and shook it at him. Ash flew onto the new-cleaned hardwood floor. He put on a little smile.

"Be careful, you'll miss out on the Good Housekeeping award."

"Job applications are in the office," she said.

He did not move.

"I'm not here for that," he said. "Not exactly. I'm a paying guest. I got food coming."

She resisted the urge to insult him. She had caught hell for that in the past. Rather, she set the tool aside, put her nose up, and marched across the room. She nearly ran down a waitress carrying a cup of coffee and an egg sandwich on a tray at the door. She whispered to the server.

"He'll pay for it, correct?"

"Yes, Ma'am. Cash. I have his order."

"See to it he leaves after eating."

The waitress proceeded in. Tiffany backed away from the entry and into shadow to see that her orders were carried out. Sound traveled well across the lounge when it was empty.

Tiffany's staff named her "The Bitch." Tiffany was proud of the designation but less proud lately. She worked hard to achieve that compliment, but treating non-employees unkind was bad for business. She saw the wisdom in that.

Thinking about him, she sensed there was more to that man. What use did his beat-up clothing hide? She suspected that the cover didn't match the book. Lesson learned. Good help is hard to find and insulting a job-candidate is bad for business.

"Hey, Jim. I see you met 'The Bitch,'" the waitress said, before setting plates on an end table. "Coffee is about the only thing that's good coming out of this kitchen."

"I figured it was her," he said. "I was hoping she'd help. She's my age, kindred spirits. Guess not. I thought…I was hoping to settle without lawyers. Face the Old Man alone."

"Good luck," the waitress laughed. "The boss-hogs have been here 150 years. The Old Man doesn't talk to nobody without lawyers."

The man dug into his front pocket, pulled a bill, and handed it over.

"That's fifteen, here's a five back." She handed him a bill. "Looking for work, Jim? We need a real chef."

"You know me, Sally. I work for myself or I don't work." He took a sip. "Too bitter, can you get me a fresh one?"

"You're the guest."

"Naw, I'm the neighbor…for now. Old Man Steward wants my Christmas tree farm bad and if things don't change…"

He threw up his hands.

"What are you going to do?" Sally asked.

"Great grand-dad wouldn't sell it to them, horse thieves. I don't know."

"I'm sorry, Jim. I hope you can keep the place."

"I'll be okay."

The man stood, stretched, and yawned. He picked his change off the table and handed it to the server. He never touched the sandwich.

"That was my last twenty. Keep it. Merry Christmas, Sally. Hug the kids and Dave for me."

He walked toward the rear exit. The waitress picked up the unconsumed meal. Tiffany retreated down the hall. He looked better when he stood in the light. The man was handsome, not very sophisticated with his wild locks and spotty beard, but behind the disarray was a solid, rugged face with dimples. Tiffany loved dimples.

Get that out of your head, he's the adversary.

"So, that's the man giving Daddy trouble," she mused, going about her business.

Sunny Side Ski Lodge needed kid-friendly slopes to attract families. It was Tiffany's idea to expand into the general market. The rich-ski-bum-kid money, her contemporaries, didn't bring enough income to keep the place running much less profitable. They needed volume. A good restaurant with family-friendly slopes will bring in big revenue. *One thing at a time.* The old tree farm was just what Daddy's ski business needed.

*****

Tiffany decided she had better keep a lookout for that man—Jim Picket—the latest and last Picket. The bumpkin new owner of the old Picket Homestead didn't stand a chance against Daddy.

She had staff bring the telescope back up from the basement after lunch having removed it ahead of last night's party, fearing the drunks. Plate-glass windows weren't cheap either. If Daddy's device took any harm, hell's fury will land. Daddy had commanded a destroyer in the Navy and was damn proud of his vintage deck-scope. It still worked despite its age.

She took a long look through the eyepiece. Falling wet snow blurred her view but she spotted Jim Picket down range to the right in snowshoes working on a Christmas tree.

She wasn't sure where the property line laid. He labored two miles beyond the lodge, well past the lodge's long entry drive which edged his land. The tree farm also bordered Daddy's land at the country road intersection. The Picket Farm ran up a series of hills that resembled a wave. Picket owned the land from the country road up to the cliff face behind the Picket spread. His trees covered the easy slopes Daddy wanted.

She used to wonder how settlers could have planted and lived off that land which only much later became a tree farm. The terraces weren't wide. Plowing that series of low-rolling hills had to be hard work. She watched him struggle in the deep snow until a realization struck.

"Look at that, Mel," she said to the maintenance man. "That jerk's cutting branches off my tree! He's on my side of the road."

"Ma'am," Mel said. "He's only knocking the snow off. It's fallen heavy. Trees break in these conditions."

"He's on our side of the road. I'm sure of it." She pressed her walkie-talkie button. "Garage, Miss Steward here, bring my snowcat up to the main door."

She didn't get a response.

"Hello, anybody there?"

"It's snowing like hell. I wouldn't go out there if I were you," Mel said.

"Haven't you a snowblower to fix?" Tiffany said.

She had pulled Mel up from the garage to install the telescope. Mel was the garage staff. He held up his walky-talky, switched it on, and headed back shaking his head.

It took some time for the snowcat to arrive. The temperature had dropped fast and the wet pack became shelled over with ice. The valet said her snowcat didn't want to start. It took a while before it would run right. She waited outside the main entrance in her designer snowsuit shivering and annoyed until the motor reached operating temperature.

Snow resumed falling before she lifted the hatch. Her toy, named Kat, was as cozy as a sports car. Tiffany wasn't worried about the conditions. She didn't need to go far. She drove the one-passenger snowcat from home to the lodge every day no matter the weather. The grounds between her house and the lodge were gentle. Her little tractor-tread vehicle was made for it. She never tested it, but she had full confidence that Kat could go anywhere.

The short trip wasn't short. At the end of the lodge's drive, she normally rode along the country road's shoulder. Kat wasn't road legal. The snow was too wet and deep directly behind the road's plowed furls. Tiffany jumped over a snow pile and took Kat down the paved road. The snow was already six inches above where the plow left it only an hour before.

Arriving at the tree which stood alone, she noted it was free of heavy snow and Mister Picket was gone. The tree was easy to find. It stood alone on her side of the road, her property.

"No problem."

She lifted the hatch and stood in the cockpit to see above the drifts and plow piles.

"There you are! HEY, YOU!"

He didn't hear. Dropping into the seat, she closed the lid and turned a hard right.

"Ah ha, I got you."

Kat's steel treads found purchase and she started uphill on Picket's access road. Her snowcat's wipers whacked away at the heavy fall but visibility remained poor. She spotted him far up the road and well past the first terraced spot. He made it onto the next hill while Kat crawled slowly over the ice-laden path. She focused on his red flannel vest but lost him as the snowcat climbed hill one. Reaching the next terrace flat, she sighted his vest and steered for it across the flat. She had gone too far sideways but she thought she had it under control until she skidded and spun half around.

Frustrated, she hit the gas and slid sidelong ten feet, caught traction, spun, and went off the flat's edge. She landed in a ditch that was hidden by drifts. The howling winds laughed at her. The snowcat had nosedived. She hit her forehead on the dash, cutting it, but ignored the injury in her panic. Tiffany revved the motor and tried rocking the snowcat out a dozen times but it was no good.

She killed the motor, admitting she had no way out. Tiffany pulled out her phone. She didn't bother bringing the radio.

"Crap, no signal."

She tried the hatch.

"Stuck!"

It lifted a little but that was it. She didn't know what to do next. The knock of hard steel on her hollow shell decided for her.

"Hey, you alright in there?"

He banged again.

"Get the hatch. I can't get out!"

His prying with an ax and her pushing sprung the misshaped gull-wing door wide enough for her to crawl out. She rolled off the snowcat and into deep snow. He reached one-handed and helped her up although he was waist-deep himself. His grimaced face reminded her of Han Solo. He stood mid-thigh deep in white trouble framed between two dark green Chewbacca Christmas trees. Her rig a crashed X-wing fighter.

"Don't just stand there," he cried. "I'm hurt."

He held out the ax.

"Damn knee. Cut a sapling. I need a crutch."

Tiffany didn't need his ax. She had one in the rear storage hatch but she took his. She managed to provide a solid prop after a struggle. They got him free of the drift after what seemed like a week. She helped him up onto level ground after first chopping footholds into the ditch's frozen bank. Stepping off the flat's edge, Picket said he broke his snowshoe which twisted his leg.

"I didn't like that snowshoe anyway."

He tossed the other one aside.

"Crappy snowshoe."

Why would anyone use such old equipment? She thought.

He checked the rest of himself for injuries and her, too, before limping forward with the staff in hand. "We better get inside."

He limped them straight into a white-out blow. Tiffany supported him the best she could blind as she was. She had no idea how bad his injury was, but she felt sure it was her fault.

The snow had drifted more on the downhill side leaving the up-slope side of the flat area icy but clear enough to walk. He led them against pelting weather and all she could do was hope that he steered right. She experienced a red glow over the snow as they slogged on. Blood from the gash on her head had frozen around her eyes tinting everything red.

The whiteout's howling wind hounded her with the stories of lost and dead skiers that she grew up with. She had no idea where his place was or how far. He drove them forward into the squall insisting they go faster. She wanted to argue. Slower is safer but the big tree falling high above convinced her to agree.

She had seen Daddy's area surveys but didn't know where on the map she was. The old Picket cabin was beneath a low cliff and well protected. The ground above was a national forest, wild, and loaded with snow-laden conifers. The Picket homestead sprawled around the foothills and ran north to where the mountain's fingers stabbed the valley. Another tree fell above sending a thunderclap against the storm. He hesitated. This time, she pulled him forward, talking against the wind was pointless.

Tiffany didn't see the door until it was in her face. He smacked ice off the bar latch with the stick and put a shoulder into it balancing on his one good leg. The old gray door didn't budge. He didn't have the leverage but he set himself to hit it again. She leaned in with him. Thrusting as one the door popped free. They fell inside together a tangle of tired potato-sack racers.

"I know us Stewards and Pickets have had our differences, but you didn't have to run me over," he said with a halfcocked grin.

She almost lashed back at him, but he wasn't angry. He got up, helped her up, and touched a switch at the door and a table lamp came on within. The other side of his narrow mudroom opened into a log-built great room.

Tiffany brushed the snow off him. Her plastic snow suit didn't hold moisture but Jim's flannel vest and blue jeans were soaked. He stripped down to his shorts right there in that add-on foyer. Steam rose from him. Nice body, she thought but shook off the idea. She was used to boy toys hitting on her and knew better than to fall for the wounded-guy routine even if he was really hurt.

"If you think—" She began.

"Look at my leg will you," he said as if he read her mind.

"Oh, my goodness."

"Dislocated my knee again. It ain't busted. I need a hand."

"Looks bad," she said.

His kneecap wasn't where it belonged.

"That's why I didn't make the team." He chucked in a deep robust tone.

"College injury?" She asked helping him limp into the main room.

"Just kidding. I went to culinary school. Anyway, I'll need a hand fixing it."

She set him into a dusty neo-provincial chair and turned on a few other table lights scattered around. The lamps didn't match. She thought at first, had he picked them out of the trash? But who tosses out antiques? The interior surprised her. The log structure had been added onto often over its 150 years, the foyer being one example. Those aerial pictures of his rambling roofs didn't reveal the inside.

"Make yourself home, why don't you," he said while probing his knee. "This'll take two medics."

He had her yank his leg while he pushed the kneecap. On the count of three, she jerked, and he pushed. The sound of bone grinding proceeded and finished with a loud pop. He yelled but he didn't faint.

"That will do," he said. "Get some blankets, back that way."

She was surprised by what she found. The floors were old-growth hard pine polished into a glass finish. The furniture, a hodge-podge of interesting makers, was well-suited and not what she expected.

Unlike his shabby, rough, dirty, and disorganized exterior his place was organized. His home wasn't at all like him. It was clean and stuffed with well-preserved antiques worth real money. Her decorator could have used a thing or two from here. The old hardwood floors dipping in and out of shadow rippled the shine.

"Lovely. Very authentic. Who did your decorations?" She dropped a thin blanket next to him.

He laughed. "Father Time. This stuff's been piling up here for 150 years. All I do is keep it clean. I like things organized. You don't have a bullet, do you? I need to bite it. Needs another hard pull. Don't hold back this time."

He swung his leg onto the coffee table with both hands for another go at it. He put one hand above and one under his knee this time.

"Ok, give it all you got, on go," he said. "Go!"

She yanked with all the power her 110-pound frame could deliver. He screamed. The pop was squishy this time which made her skin crawl. After many curse words which she was not accustomed to, his pain subsided.

"I didn't cry, did I?" Jim said.

"Maybe a little. There is something to primal scream therapy," Tiffany said.

"It'll get better. Forget ice. I'll need my brace," he said. "Behind the sofa, please. No wait, I'm coming over."

He hopped across the room to the couch which was set deeper into the big room near the center facing a huge sidewall fireplace. She guessed the original kitchen was beyond that wall and shared the hearth. He settled in, still in his boxers, and laced the brace tight.

"Hey, see if we got any food. Something to drink maybe?" He put his head back and closed his eyes. "Dry duds. In my room, please."

That thin blanket didn't produce much warmth. It was cold inside there. She peeled off her snowsuit before going on the mission for clothing and food.

She picked sweatpants out of his dresser and helped him into them. His brace fit inside the loose garment. She found an almost-clean flannel shirt next to his bed on the floor that didn't smell bad. His bedroom was otherwise well organized. That hint of musk reminded her that this was a man's bedroom and she needed to be careful. That's what her brain said but her heart didn't feel any threat.

Tiffany liked organizational focus in a man. She liked men who showed guts. He went to Daddy before Daddy could get to him. She had to admit there was more to this man than her average boy toy had to offer. She wasn't sure if that was good or bad. He patted the sofa next to him.

"We'll get the fire going in a minute. Let me take a look at your cut."

She complied and sat but with a stiff back. He felt around her scalp and pushed the hair away from the wound without imposing a single hurt. He picked a pine needle out of her hair and showed her.

"Nasty cut," he said. "I'll have you fixed up in no time."

He got up before she could protest and hobbled into the nearest bathroom. He returned with a first aid kit and dressed her wound.

"Why do you live this way?" she asked as he cleaned the gash with a Q-tip. "This place is, so, so primitive." There wasn't a computer, TV, or phone charger around anywhere in sight. "You live like a pauper."

"So? Why's plastic land better? I like woodlands and dirt. What's wrong with it? I like it, all right, but okay, I'd rather be cooking."

He sounded snappish and pushed himself back into the sofa. He ran a hand through his brown mop of hair.

"Sorry. Where'd Santa be without my Christmas trees? He pays me with cookies, too."

"I see your point," she said. "Santa isn't an industrialist as I understand it. He'd need a network of confederates like you."

Tiffany's rare attempt at humor received a smile in repayment. Her first impression was right. He did have nice dimples. Her head was bent while he worked but she didn't miss his grin.

"Almost got it. Turn, that's it."

Jim repositioned her head. He faced her toward the natural tree he had in a corner. It was full and decorated with painted pinecones, strung popcorn, and vintage ornaments. She drank in its pine-pitch odor. There weren't any electric lights on it but the old-fashioned candle holders were ready to light. The tree would be the envy of any professional window dresser in Tiffany's view.

"There, good as new," he said. "Try to avoid hair extensions for a while."

"Funny. What's the damage, Doctor Strange Tree?" Tiffany said.

"Two butterfly stitches and a gauze on the top. That'll be three-fifty. Shall I call you a cab?"

"I'm not sure that's wise. I think it's still snowing."

Tiffany went to a window in hope of improved conditions. The sun was already behind Daddy's Mountain which added a blood-pink tint to the storm. The Picket side of the valley had already darkened under the cliffs and falling snow. Lights twinkled across the valley like ships at sea, beacons of hope. The lights winked out all at once a moment before Jim's power also went down. The only light came from his sunset-red windows and glowing fireplace coals. Jim lit a candle. There was one, or an oil lamp, on several tables.

"Where's your generator? I'll fire it up. I know how," she said.

"Generator? That's funny. I'm the generator. The hand pump works without power." He reached down under the sofa and came up with a cheap aluminum cane. "I better rustle us up some grub. We're going to be here a while."

He limped into the kitchen. Panic rose in her chest. She lowered herself down in a chair, glad she was out of Jim's reach. It hit her. She was trapped with a man she hardly knew and didn't like, Daddy's adversary. This is sleeping with the enemy.

"Not going to happen. This is not going to sit well with Daddy."

She didn't see any sign in him that screamed, "murderer." There was no use hiding. Cell phones were spotty even without a blizzard. The lodge had a radio and landlines for liability reasons. Jim's old rotary phone may have worked before the lines went down, but it was now useless.

The idea of sleeping with him, if only to pass the time, crossed her mind. He wasn't the boy-toy type. The rustics don't play rich-boy games. Poor people hang on like leeches if you give them an inch. She told herself she wouldn't do it with him no matter what which made the idea of sleeping with him more exciting. She set the notion aside. She needed to be serious, and responsible. Tiffany had a lot to prove.

Daddy didn't trust her. He said she lived irresponsibly. She still hadn't earned her place in the company. She had to behave.

"I'll show Daddy."

She got up and went into the kitchen. He had an antique wood-burning stove. She smelled embers smoldering when they arrived. He had put in what wood was handy and the firebox was going well.

"What can I do?" *I'm stuck here…make the best of it.*

"Get wood. Straight back, back door. Attached woodshed."

She supplied the wood and opened cans while he cooked using vintage cast-iron pans. She carried their plates to the living room sofa. She had stoked the main fireplace as well. There wasn't much for Jim to work with inside the kitchen's cupboard. By some stroke of Christmas magic, he made Spam, eggs, and canned potatoes taste like Christmas morning.

A thought put a new pang in her heart on gathering the plates.

"Tomorrow's Christmas eve…I'm always home for Christmas," she said.

"Me, too," he said, "but not for long."

He swung his leg up onto the coffee table with a grunt.

"It's dark. I got more candles. Light the ones on the mantel, thanks."

Tiffany went about housekeeping. It felt odd to clean rather than watch others do it. Jim rested. Tiffany managed the stove's firebox and heated water for dishes. She washed them in the old porcelain double sink and rinsed them with a squeaky hand-pump. That glacier-cold water felt alive.

Tiffany finished in the kitchen and took two cans from a six-pack of cheap beer which rested on the floor beside the kitchen outside door. He patted the spot next to him on the couch.

"I've been dying to do this, hold on," she said handing him the beers.

She took the grill lighter off the mantel and lit each little candle on the tree. They were set on platforms made to look like miniature lamp stands. Each had a disk reflector that cast sparkling light. She stepped back in admiration. It was prettier than anticipated.

"So beautiful. And you did that just because? You religious?"

She sat on the edge of the sofa.

He laughed. "Shouldn't a cobbler wear the best shoes? Whose gonna buy shoes from a barefoot shoemaker? I sell Christmas trees for a living, right? People come. I show them. It's what tree farmers do."

"But you're a trained chef. Why not get somebody for your tree work?"

"They don't work for free. People need money and I ain't got any."

He patted the seat next to him again. She slid in close. She thought it odd that he needs money. Property can be borrowed against. She never worried about maintaining a cash flow. Daddy owned half the town, at least the profitable half, and money was never an issue. But not all of Daddy's ventures did well.

The lodge was a loser. Its kitchen was an economic drag but they can't do without it. The snowstorm will make money despite a mediocre restaurant. Nobody could call out for food in this storm. The bar tabs alone this weekend will float the kitchen. She cracked open her beer.

Drunks don't taste food anyway. Anyone that made it in before the storm isn't skiing this weekend. They'll drink and eat what we have.

"What are you musing on? Share?" He asked.

Neither had spoken for some time, lost in the fire and their thoughts.

"Nothing, just work. Boring stuff," she said.

They sat another hour staring into the fire with hardly a word between them. She tried to keep her mind on business but kept drifting out.

Even with the fire going, everywhere was still chilly. Cold seeped in around the edges of the old sagging homestead. He didn't seem to mind her leaning on him or sharing the Afghan blanket. Snuggling was a necessity. He smelled good and felt better. He wasn't anything like her last date. Dave was as shallow as a wading pool and soft-bodied as well. This man Jim felt real, basic, honest, and deep, a man of root and rock. Her passion grew as the fire flickered low. She felt compelled by logic to ask.

"Do you think we should sleep together? For safety…it's cold."

He sat up a little straighter and said, "This is a three-dog night but… you know, me and your father are at odds, so…"

"We won't make love," she said. "You're right. We shouldn't and we won't. Freezing to death isn't smart either."

"Who said anything about that? I'm not the kind of man to take advantage…"

She snuggled in closer and looked up at him. She felt a shiver go through him. Out of control, her lips parted with a sigh.

"I mean…I…" he slid lower.

Lightning struck. She couldn't help it. She kissed him. He kissed back. The old house turned hot and that new fire lasted the night. He got up the next morning ahead of her and stoked the fire before her bare foot touched the floor.

Christmas eve came with no gifts to exchange so they spent the day without power keeping warm and exchanging the stories of their lives although he said little about himself and rather shared what he knew about the wilderness surrounding them, and he knew it well. His knee improved but he needed the cane. He had no choice but to rely on her to keep the wood coming and the fires burning. She did a bit of housekeeping and cleared the hearth of ashes before changing the burned-out candles on the tree. She planned to light the new ones later.

Jim's focus was impressive. He had gone to confront Daddy man-to-man on the morning she first saw him. He didn't say why. *Nobody stands up to Daddy like that.* Jim had ambitions. He wanted his own restaurant business. He was a solid, practical man with practical ambitions.

The best part: He had inherited the tree farm and it wasn't his thing, a crack in his armor. Everybody wins.

This could work out.

They heated water in the kitchen after dinner. She carried it over in buckets and they took a bath together. The old claw-foot tub had room to spare. She had forgotten the towels and was forced to race naked from the hot bath, through the drafty house, and back again. She screamed and laughed the whole way. It felt electric.

"If Santa saw this Christmas Eve's activities, he'd fly right on by," she said.

Breathless, she dropped the towels and climbed back in.

"I thought we were getting out," he said after a deep chuckle.

She didn't need to help him back to the sofa afterward, his knee improved by soaking it, but she supported him anyway. Tiffany parked him back on the fireplace sofa before going in search of wine. He swore he had one bottle around there somewhere and he did.

Everything was so unreal yet real, rustic, and true. She understood the appeal of living the outdoor life, not her thing, but nature proved more than a playground. She had never considered the real dangers of the great outdoors before. She could have died in that blizzard. Jim wasn't her plaything, either.

But what will Daddy say?

She had indisputable reasons to wait out the storm. Attempting a snowshoe hike back home could kill her. Hiking alone is a bad idea in good conditions. Waiting out the storm was best.

Back in his feather bed, pushing her unruly hair around, he asked, "What do you think your dad got you for Christmas? More importantly, what do you want?"

Her parents will do the usual, she thought, gold, silver another car, a bigger snowcat. Whatever. Jim's parents were gone. She wouldn't ask him that.

"I don't know. Does it matter? What about you? What's your Christmas wish?"

"If you get any jewels…you know, that you don't need…I could use a loan…kidding. It'll take a king's ransom. I need working capital, but Santa's not in that game…You didn't say what you want."

"I'm not sure," she said, "but I think I may think of something soon."

Christmas morning started brightly. The sun lit the windows that weren't covered by snowdrifts. The storm had passed overnight. She put kindling in the main fireplace and fanned it with a paper plate. It burst into life. What a wonderful start she felt, until Jim cracked his knee on the stove's firebox door. That didn't stop him from making eggs Benedict. They ate at the kitchen table and drank coffee while the house warmed up. They remained until the pot was gone. He had an old fashion percolator and coffee never tasted so good. They discussed their escape options.

Jim hobbled across the front room with his cane to check outside at the front door. Tiffany followed. Digging out this morning didn't seem possible but he wanted to see. The snow had stopped altogether.

"The wind shifted," he said. "Let's hope snow didn't drift over my door."

Tiffany pulled and it opened. The sun was high, it was later than she thought. The Christmas trees in sight below the homestead were laden with snow in their neat rows.

"They look like…like marching snowmen," she said. She sniffed deeply. "It's like…like Christmas spice."

The cold pine-scented air mixed with clean snow made her giggle.

"Be careful with that, Christmas air's intoxicating."

He put his arm and the blanket he used as a shawl around her. They snuggled together before the postcard scene. The peace and still quiet of this view across the valley, one she had not seen before, caught her breath. His trees were beautiful, too. The lovers stood together a long time, wrapped in his blanket, letting the cold in, while sipping the landscape. The quiet didn't last.

"Helicopters! Daddy's!"

Tiffany backed up and pulled the blanket off him.

"They're looking for me. I've been gone for three days. Daddy is going to flip."

Jim hobbled outside into shallow snow shading his eyes.

"That's County Rescue. I know those guys. Don't go anywhere. Be right back."

He went inside. She closed the door but waited in the little mudroom. A few minutes later, he returned with an odd handgun colored bright orange with a huge cartoon barrel. Her puzzlement must have shown.

"Flare gun," he said opening the door.

He stuck one bare arm outside, raised it high, and fired. It whooshed away like a Fourth of July rocket. "That'll do it. We better make ourselves decent."

Not long after that, the sound of a big snowcat echoed through the valley. She hated to give up Jim's big flannel shirt and pajama pants, but she had to pull herself together. The paramedics were a fixture in ski country and everybody knew them—and they knew everybody.

She didn't want to start a scandal. She put on her snowsuit. When the big snowcat rumbled up to the cabin, she was ready. She opened the door wide to greet the rescue workers but it wasn't County Rescue's team on the other side.

"Daddy!"

"Sleeping with the enemy, Pumpkin? Didn't I teach you better than that?" Daddy stood there in his usual blue suit and oxford shoes impervious to the cold with hands-on-hips like a military schoolmaster. His business suit was soaked up to the knees.

"It's not what you think," Tiffany said.

"Get in the car. Your mother's been worried sick."

"It's not like that. He's hurt," she cried.

"The medics are right behind me. Let's go."

"No, I'm with him. I'm staying."

Jim limped forward, out the door, and straight up to Daddy.

"What's a man gotta do to talk with you?" Jim said. "I'll spit it out. You want my tree farm. I need your restaurant. Barter a deal. I'll keep farming a few trees. Give you prime slope space. Kids love Christmas trees. See the tie-in? I retain ownership here. You retain ownership on your end. Win-win business."

"That might work," Daddy said.

"What about us?" Tiffany said.

She punched Jim's arm.

"There is no us, Tiffany. Business partners don't sleep together," he said. "You could resign."

"What!" Tiffany cried.

Her father stood wide-legged rubbing his clean-shaven chin massaging that famous wolf grin. She had seen it before. Daddy meant business. He was an imposing man, tall and rotund. His resting-bitch-face plowed people under wherever he went. To her eyes, the Steward patriarch softened a little. Jim didn't flinch or back down. Daddy respected people who had the balls to face him. Her heart sank a little further.

"Take it or leave it," Jim said with an even tone. "I can always sell the place to Universal Resorts."

Jim leaned forward bearing his version of wolf teeth. "They made an offer."

"We will work something out," Daddy said. "Stay away from her or no deal."

"Agreed. No lawyers, or no deal," Jim said.

"Fine, no lawyers," Daddy chuckled. He never did that. "Tiffany, get in the snow car. As I said, medical is on its way up."

"Go on," Jim said to Tiffany. "We'll talk later."

"Talk is all you will do. Let's go, Tiffany...now."

She looked at Daddy and back at Jim. Steam radiated off of Jim but he stood solid as a block of ice, a man of fire and ice and she didn't see his cold side coming. His ice melted her flame. *It's over.* If Jim takes over food service, he'll be working for the company. Daddy's policy is strict. Stewards do not mix with the help.

"We'll have to work together," Tiffany blurted.

"You will," Daddy said. "Young blood is good for business, you'll see."

"I doubt it," she said and proceeded toward the snowcat.

"That's my girl. Mister Picket, have my office set up a meeting. We will need to make some sort of contract if even written on an envelope."

"That's fine," Jim said.

Daddy didn't speak on the ride back. He didn't need to. She understood his business sense, that of prohibiting fraternization between owners and associates. One cold look from Daddy was all the reminder she needed. The rule was logical although Tiffany was known to break a rule or two.

Taking her snowcat out in a storm wasn't reasonable and she did it anyway. Going into the Christmas tree business just to have access to the Picket's family-friendly slopes wasn't workable. She had to run with it anyway. Making it work will prove her worth. She wasn't allowed to sleep with 'the help.' Jim must forever remain just that. She did enough bad behavior for one season. She drifted over her emotions with business logic.

Back to the real world.

Daddy pulled up at home and she got out on one side and he on the other. She looked back the way they had come. Smoke poured out of Jim's stone chimney. She hadn't noticed it before, way up on his distant hills.

"Daddy, next year, we'll do natural Christmas trees." She said, half as a joke.

"Of course, we'll get the company discount," he chuckled in his dry way. "There are gifts for you under the tree."

He wiped tears off his cheeks with the palm of a glove. Cold or emotions, she could not tell.

"I'm glad I found you. Mother was beside herself."

It's the wind tearing his eyes, that's all.

She got what she needed for Christmas but not what she wanted. She couldn't keep what she wanted. Jim had ignited her wintry heart with new passions, new perspectives, and a new challenge. Was that a gift? Whatever was under the tree inside her cold home will be forgotten, as usual. She did remember her special gifts, though.

The tree farmer was not her special gift, she would not let him be that. Business first. That was her new year resolution. Forget the tree farmer. She never could keep a resolution but this time her career depended on it. Tiffany didn't notice the cracks in her resolve before but now, she told herself, she will be on guard.

STYLE, WHAT IT AIN'T

Author's Note: Here is a bonus essay. It's another nonfiction that Angel Ackerman fixed for me. I wrote and rewrote this from 600 words to 1200 words and back again before handing it off to Angel who brought focus to this piece via her editing skills. This first appeared on Angel's Parisian Phoenix blog. (https://parisianphoenix.com)

A critique group participant I knew had said in the group, "That's my style, it's fine."

It wasn't fine and it wasn't style.

He had argued many times saying, "the rules don't matter," and, "I don't understand what the rules are for." He often advised others to ignore the good advice of writers that know their craft well.

"Don't let them wreck your style!" He would cry.

The last time he proclaimed his style all-powerful against critique, his rebuttal shot far off-topic. Group comments were focused on structure and form so I ignored his usual wordiness, stilted dialogue, and passive sentences intentionally setting those items aside. Anticipating his usual argumentative response, I braced for a hot wind and it came.

The structural issues I and others identified had little to do with style, yet he attacked the observers' legitimate craft-based observations saying, "Yeah, I know, but it's my style."

By the way, critique receivers should not rebut which is one of the major and typical aspects of critique philosophy. This group had adopted this rule. He didn't follow that rule either.

His counterarguments (not of craft) conflated the group's notice of various craft issues with an attack on his style which he defended as if it was an attack on him. It wasn't.

He didn't understand the difference between style and voice or why craft-borne rules enhance writing. He spewed rebukes at craft standards rather than understanding and mastering them. Not knowing what style means ensures he won't grow his craft. His style or what he thinks of as style covers all sins. But it doesn't.

Bad prose isn't a good style. Style isn't a legitimate excuse for weak and ponderous writing.

Conventions, rules, methods, and standards are there for a reason. The best writers use them. Yes, rules can and should be broken but only for a designed and understood purpose and only if it serves the reader and story. Sure, cast the "rules" aside but don't expect anyone who reads it to understand it.

Respect the reader. Why labor the reader? To what end? Confuse the reader and he will throw your masterpiece at the wall. Good style, that.

Readers may not know the rules but they know when something doesn't work. The rules, as one resistant writer sees it, impede his style. He is wrong regarding prose.

Good prose doesn't hurt style, it lets style thrive. From a commercial fiction standard point of view—what everyone reads—bad prose called style isn't publishable. Readers have expectations baked-in from years of reading. When the writer goes off that rail, the reader stops reading. Reading is a set of stairs in which readers should not need to think about each step.

What if every carpenter-built set of stairs was made any which way? What happens if each staircase is made differently? Every step becomes a trip hazard. This is why we have standards and rules in construction as well as in writing. It keeps the reader's feet under him so he can climb the story-stair.

How is making the reader reread after every trip-up good style?

What is style anyway? Style is not so much how you say it but what you decided as a writer to say. How you say it concerns the rules of writing which the reader needs to understand what is written. Style is what you the author choose to write about and choose to show within the tale that you intend to tell while word choice, on the other side, is the finest aspect of style.

Style emerges naturally and so do writing habits. Bad prose habits aren't style—don't conflate—we all have writing habits and most of them suck. Late drafts are when copy-editing and line-editing happen. That's where the editor takes the stylish and confusing author's voice out and lets the characters' voices in.

Readers hate what editors call author's intrusion. Editing is, in part, an exercise in removing the author's word junk. We all do it, even Steven King. First-whack writing ain't where style is at.

The first draft to hit paper is never the best effort although some writers think it must be. After all, he wrote it. Authors in love with their bad-prose voices aren't serving the reader. Readers walking over fields of chestnuts aren't going to enjoy it. It doesn't matter how much the author loves chestnuts, which are only there to please the writer, if the reader can't understand the story. Chestnut planting, pink prose, and other forms of overwriting are forms of self-indulgent author intrusion.

Readers love digestible style when they read it, conversely, they don't know they're reading it.

Style should not be noticed so much that it distracts the reader. Style should not overwhelm the story. Style is not mystical. It's not magic. The writer should put across exactly what needs to be there, and no more, and show it in a way the reader grasps easily without stumbling—that is good style.

Here's the thing. If you write to hear your voice on paper that's fine. If the goal is writing to publish it must be done in a way that people will not only read, they won't put it down. To that end, the writer must employ the rules and methods of craft to guide and represent his or her style.

The big nut in all of this is to serve the reader. The reader doesn't know what you are saying without organized clarity—that is what the rules do— what good is writing with style if the reader can't understand it?

ABOUT THE AUTHOR

Rachel Thompson, writing as R.C. Thom, began her writing career after surviving a near death motorcycle accident in 2003. She published nonfiction and cartoons in newspapers and magazines before working for several years as a freelance community news reporter. Her quirky short stories have appeared in various anthologies, among them those published by the Greater Lehigh Valley Writers Group and Parisian Phoenix Publishing. She has six novels in print. Her next novel, *The Adventures of Tom Conley*, will be released late 2023.

Thompson was born and raised in Ocean County, New Jersey and later spent many years living in Lehigh Valley, Pennsylvania, before moving to the Deep South. She now resides in the heart of a national forest where she paints and plays guitar when not writing.

BOOKS BY
RACHEL C. THOMPSON
available in print and e-book.

Soul Harvest
Print ISBN: 798-1-7321459-1-7   E-book: 798-1-7321459-0-0

Aggie in Orbit
Print ISBN: 798-1-7321459-7-9   E-book: 798-1-7321459-6-2

Aggie in Space
Print ISBN: 798-1-7321459-8-6   E-book: 798-1-7321459-9-3

Dragon Fire
Print ISBN: 798-1-7321459-2-4   E-book: 798-1-7321459-3-1

Stalking Kilgore Trout
Print ISBN: 798-1-7321459-4-8   E-book: 798-1-7321459-5-5

Book of Answers
Print ISBN: 979-8-9861808-0-9   E-book: 979-8-9861808-1-6

Another Anthology:
Print ISBN: 979-8-9861808-2-3   Ebook international:
                                       ISBN 979-8-9861808-3-0

**For more information visit RCThom.com or RCThom.net
or email Rachel at humanrights4all@aol.com**

ACKNOWLEDGMENTS

Many of my fellow writer friends have given me input and ideas for this collection. My thanks go to the pool of writers I've associated with over the years and especially my friends at the Greater Lehigh Valley Writers Group (GLVWG.org). A special thanks to Gayle F. Hendricks my formatting and book design guru. Thank you, Angel Ackerman, for your excellent proof reading and line editing. Angel Ackerman has been a longtime friend, mentor, and teacher who helped me on many of my early writing projects. She taught me a lot. My greatest thanks go to Lisa Cross, my partner in life, who tolerates my writer's life and is instrumental as a story critic and proof reader. Without Lisa's support, I could not write.